The Goodfellow

Chronicles

THE GOODFELLOW CHRONICLES

BOOK ONE

THE SACRED SEAL

J. C. MILLS

KEY PORTER BOOKS

National Library of Canadian Cataloguing in Publication Data

Mills, Judith
  A sacred seal / J.C. Mills

(The Goodfellow chronicles ; bk. 1)
ISBN 1-55263-328-4

I. Title. II. Series: Mills, Judith. Goodfellows chronicles ; bk. 1.

PS8576.1571S32 2001   jC813'.54   C2001-900856-2
PZ7.M639775Sa 2001

THE CANADA COUNCIL | LE CONSEIL DES ARTS
FOR THE ARTS | DU CANADA
SINCE 1957 | DEPUIS 1957

ONTARIO ARTS COUNCIL
CONSEIL DES ARTS DE L'ONTARIO

The publisher gratefully acknowledges the support of the Canada Council for the Arts and the Ontario Arts Council for its publishing program.

We acknowledge the financial support of the Government of Canada through the Book Publishing Industry Development Program (BPIDP) for our publishing activities.

Key Porter Books Limited
70 The Esplanade
Toronto, Ontario
Canada M5E 1R2

www.keyporter.com

Design: Peter Maher
Electronic formatting: Jean Lightfoot Peters

Printed and bound in Canada

03 04 05 06 07 7 6 5 4 3

"Search all things, hold fast that which is true,
Take heed of many, the advice of few,
And always paddle your own canoe."

FROM "Favorite Proverbs"
AS COLLECTED AND COMPILED BY J. GOODFELLOW
LONDON, 1949

CONTENTS

For Sam (of course)
and his beloved cousins,
Kate and Rachel

1

FROM SMALL BEGINNINGS
COME GREAT THINGS

S am popped the last candy into his mouth and gently rolled it around with his tongue. This one just *had* to be red, he thought. It was too dark in his room to distinguish which color was which as he picked away at the thin layers of silver waxy paper that surrounded the four candies. While unpacking, he had discovered the half-eaten roll at the bottom of his duffel bag—a lost souvenir, he surmised, from this past summer's camping trip to Yosemite. Thankfully, it was a salvageable treasure, being only slightly lint-covered at the edges.

Sam had tolerated the first, orange-flavored candy, and even the pale yellow pineappley one that followed. The third candy, though (the lime green one that he would normally pass to his less discriminating father), had been launched across the room in a fit of frustration. Sam had held the last candy in his hand for some time before proceeding with the final taste test. Surely, there ought to be *something* redeemable about this day, he thought, as he lifted it to his lips.

It only took a few seconds. Then, the rich, deep flavor of cherry cascaded along Sam's taste buds. There would be no crunching of this candy; Sam was determined to linger over every swallow.

It was almost midnight before the clouds finally began to clear from the night sky. Sam was still awake. From the sleeping bag on the floor of his new room, he could now see the eerie glow of the full moon. It was, of course, the same moon as always, but somehow this moon's face looked cold and sour, not friendly like the one that had smiled down on him through the window in his old room. In fact, from where Sam lay tonight, the whole world seemed unfamiliar. It had only been a few weeks since the real estate lady had called about the old colonial house that was for sale in New England. Spacious and rambling and full of character, it was everything Sam's parents had been looking for. She had neglected to mention, however, the dusty, musty and creepy part. Sam did not like this house one bit.

Sam's dad had said that all the old house needed was a bit of cleaning and fixing up. His mother assured him that once their furniture arrived it would start to look more like home. But Sam wasn't so easily convinced. He had tried to understand how excited his parents were about opening up their own art gallery specializing in early American folk art. After all, they had talked of nothing else for as long as he could remember. Being something of an artist himself, Sam genuinely appreciated the bold and colorful (and highly regarded) collection of paintings and sculptures that had been accumulating around their house over the years. He also had to admit that it was perfectly reasonable for his parents to relocate to New England. This house made an ideal setting for their new art gallery. New England was also close to the auction houses of New York, Boston, and Europe. Though Sam couldn't argue with any of these facts, he had still stubbornly refused to believe that they were really going until the moving van had pulled into their driveway. He resented dragging his stuff from his house in the Pacific Northwest (that he had known for his entire life) to this town, and this house, that he didn't know at all.

The trip had been five whole hours by plane (not including the stopover) and then another hour and a half by car. It was a long time to expect a ten-year-old boy to sit still, so Sam's mother had packed an extensive survival kit. First she'd cleared the local art store of enough supplies to last weeks and then she'd assembled a collection that even Picasso, the great painter, would have envied. There were three sets of multi-colored markers (regular, neon, and scented); a half dozen pencils with two-tone leads; pens of gold, silver, and bronze; white paper, black paper, foil paper, and even a pencil sharpener in the shape of an Egyptian pyramid. These treats presented a temptation that was almost too much to withstand, so Sam had to try very hard to ignore them. This was not the first time his parents had attempted some form of bribery, but Sam had figured that by sacrificing the multi-colored markers and foil paper, his parents would realize what a huge mistake they were making. But they never noticed. They had spent the entire plane trip sitting across the aisle—chattering, laughing, and making plans.

Trevor and Peggy Middleton were finally realizing a marriage-long dream. Their excitement transformed them (in Sam's eyes, at least) into two large and giddy children. From time to time, though, they did glance over at their son with expressions of concern, and whenever Sam noticed these looks, he would sigh loudly and drop his gaze to the floor.

Sam had sat stone-faced, his arms tightly folded, for as much of the trip as possible (not exactly an easy feat). Except for the arrival of the molded food trays (especially the one with the butterscotch pudding and blob of whipped cream), he had remained stoic in refusing all overtures, including the art supplies. Though Sam's misery wasn't able to stop the move, it did manage to divert his attention from his more immediate worry—and that was flying. Whenever he'd turned to look out the window to the carpet of clouds below, he'd felt distinctly dizzy and a bit nauseated too (of course, it could have been the third helping of butterscotch pudding).

Looking back now, as he lay in his sleeping bag on the hard wooden floor, Sam decided that the saddest part about leaving had been the final view of his home as the taxi pulled away from the curb and turned around the corner.

Sam had lived in that house ever since he'd been just two years old. He had toddled through the rooms, tumbled down the staircase, careened through the hallways, scraped most of the skin off his knees learning to ride his two-wheeler in the driveway, and scribbled his most notable abstract (at age four) across the living room wall in indelible laundry marker.

He would miss his old room, too, especially the ancient maple tree that stood outside his window. Never again would he hear its branches tapping against the glass, or smell spring in its leaves after a thunderstorm. Never again would he smile at the moon face (the friendly one) that peeped out from behind the big, weathered trunk when the wind blew, or wonder about the hundreds of twinkling stars framed behind its branches, or the vast and mysterious world beyond that.

And that was only the half of it. It was his "best friend"— his beloved backyard—that he would miss most of all. Sam knew every square inch of that yard—every anthill and wasp nest, every hiding place. It had taken him a long time to design it, too. At the swampy spot that ran along the back fence, a whole summer's worth of Popsicle sticks (and a substantial portion of Sam's allowance) had been invested in his

Riverlet Diversion Project and the creation of Insect Island. He had used almost ten boxes of toothpicks to build the suspension bridge. Then, after weeks of path-making, Sam had finally managed to get troops of ants to scurry like tiny, crazed commuters back and forth across the bridge. Along the banks at either side of the river, whisper-thin butterflies flitted between rows of colorful flags and whirligigs that had been designed and painted with painstaking care. Sam had spent endless, glorious days observing and cataloguing the butterflies and beetles, sow bugs and centipedes that had appeared throughout the seasons. To say that he had an extraordinary ability to immerse himself in whatever he was doing would have been a great understatement. Whenever something captured his attention, no amount of driving rain, gale force wind, or frantic calls from his mother could lure him away. The yard had been Sam's own little piece of bug heaven—and now it would belong to someone else. The thought of this was almost too much to bear.

The Riverlet Diversion Project had made the ideal outdoor laboratory. The success of his experiments there had convinced Sam that he would become a famous scientist one day. And not just the average, white-coated, spectacled, head-stuck-in-a-book kind of scientist either. Sam's career was going to have flair. He would be part academic and part pirate: the daredevilling, swashbuckling, adventuring kind—a zoologist, botanist, biologist, and inventor of neat stuff, all rolled into one. Rare plants and undiscovered species of animals and insects would be advised to keep themselves well hidden, because Samuel Henry Middleton had a mission!

Sam had decided to keep his plans to himself for now, or at least until he had successfully navigated his way past the sixth grade. No one would have guessed from his quiet, cautious exterior that a fearless explorer lurked beneath the surface. It was probably just as well that he had given himself some time to prepare. A few things still had to be worked out before he packed up and ventured off. These were the usual host of worries: tornadoes, comets from space, monsters in the attic, that sort of thing (and now, in light of his unpleasant airplane journey, flying too).

Sam turned over in his sleeping bag and let out a long, sad sigh. There would be no going back home now, no matter how hard he wished. Except for an old, dusty bookcase in one corner that had been left behind by the previous owner, Sam lay alone in the empty bedroom, surrounded by moonlight. The bookcase's lower shelf had tipped awkwardly to the floor, and an old copy of *The Complete Short Stories of H.G. Wells* lay trapped underneath, torn and covered in cobwebs.

The house had apparently belonged to a professor of ancient history from the local university. Sam's mother said that he was an explorer, often dashing off to the other side of the world on the heels of some discovery. This time, however, it appeared that he had planned a trip with no intention of returning. That's how the old house had become available. One day, soon after the professor had vanished to parts unknown, the house had suddenly appeared on the market, its contents sent into storage. To Sam, it was particularly frustrating that the most intriguing aspect of this gloomy house (namely its former occupant) was no longer there, and with a fleeting wish that he could vanish to parts unknown too, he stared blankly across the room. That professor would have been really interesting to talk to, Sam thought. He was probably off on some expedition in a remote part of the world—just the kind of place Sam imagined exploring one day. Maybe the professor would even have been interested in seeing his insect journal.

Sam's eyes wandered from one dark corner of the room to another. The moonlight was casting a row of prison bar lines on the walls as it shone through the squared panes of the window. Sam shuddered. A distinctly moldy smell also seemed to permeate the room, and Sam was convinced that it was growing stronger by the minute. In an attempt to filter out this unpleasant odor, Sam shuffled further down into his sleeping bag. He pressed his nose against the soft, fluffy lining and inhaled. It was a noticeable improvement over the room's aroma and well worth the extra effort required for breathing.

Feeling comforted, Sam shuffled down a bit further, until the tips of his toes hit the ridge of the sleeping bag's bottom seam. Sam's mother had told him that the house had been in the professor's family since before the turn of the last century. At that moment, Sam felt a surge of sympathy for the man. He knew just how the professor must have felt. *His* parents had probably forced him to live in this awful, smelly house too. Sam let out another long sigh. Well, at least one of them had managed to escape.

Slightly breathless after several minutes within the confines of his sleeping bag, Sam decided to brave the outside elements once again. He wriggled back up to the top and, holding his nose, cautiously popped out his head. He discovered that by breathing in short bursts, the moldy smell wasn't as bad. Sam reached for the magnifying glass that always dangled from a string around his neck, and turned his attention to the floor. An interesting pattern of pinholes in the hardwood flooring had become sufficiently illuminated by the moonlight to invite further investigation. Termites, perhaps. Sam was filled with hope.

A few moments later, as he scratched at one of the holes with his fingernail, Sam detected a faint rustling sound. He lifted his head and listened carefully. There it was again, and this time it was considerably louder. It sounded like someone was crinkling paper somewhere close by. Sam was certain that the sound was coming from the corner of his room nearest the door. He strained his eyes to see through the half-light. Another whispered crinkle and then a quick flash of light shot across the room. Something was scampering over the floor and heading directly for the bookcase!

"Oh, great," thought Sam, "dusty, musty, and creepy, and it has mice too! Mum's going to just *love* this!"

Since it didn't look like he was going to get much sleep, Sam resigned himself to counting the scurrying rodents in his bedroom. He fluffed up his pillow and then nestled down to watch and wait. At first there was nothing but silence. But Sam's many experiences with shy and reclusive insects had taught him that patience had its rewards. After a few more quiet moments, the rustling sounds resumed.

Sam turned his attention towards the old bookcase. The flash of a pencil-thin beam of light suddenly shone out from beneath its bottom shelf. This was accompanied by the sound of what seemed very much like muffled talking. The hairs on the back of Sam's neck stood on end. There must be a rational explanation. Sam held his breath and listened carefully again. The sounds continued.

"Hmm, maybe the professor left a clock radio on a timer, or something," he thought. "Yeah, that's it."

Sam quietly pulled himself out of his warm sleeping bag, and crept across the floor to peer under the bookcase. What he saw caused him to gasp in astonishment. Rubbing his eyes and then blinking them open and shut several times, he tried to make sense of what was in front of him. On the floor, with its back to him, sat a little brown mouse. It was muttering and shaking its head as it studied a piece of paper in the glow of the tiniest flashlight Sam had ever seen.

Sam, who had been leaning heavily on one arm to get a closer look under the bookcase, suddenly lost his balance and fell sideways, landing with a soft thud on the hardwood floor. The muttering suddenly stopped and the small, brown body froze. The mouse slowly turned its head and for a second Sam looked straight into a pair of dark, twinkling eyes. Then the mouse let out a gasp of its own and, stuffing the paper under its arm, dropped the flashlight on the ground and darted out from under the bookcase. It scurried across the room as fast as its legs would carry it.

Sam lay upon the ground, his heart pounding heavily in his chest. Minutes passed before he could collect himself enough to sit up. His mind was racing. Maybe his eyes had been playing tricks on him in this strange room of moonlight and shadows. Maybe he was hallucinating. Maybe breathing through the thick sleeping bag had caused some kind of oxygen depletion to his brain. He leaned forward and peered under the bookcase again. The miniature flashlight, still casting a beam of light, had rolled toward the back wall. Sam reached underneath the bookcase and picked it up carefully between his thumb and index finger. It looked just like the one that his dad kept in the glove compartment of their car: shiny black metal with a rubber-coated switch and a wrist strap at the end. But the flashlight that Sam was holding was no bigger than the eraser top on a pencil. The wrist strap wasn't even wide enough to hold the tip of his baby finger. Sam shone it in front of him and began to inch forward into the shadows where the mouse had disappeared.

"Please come out, please. I won't hurt you," he said.

Sam tried to speak in the softest voice he could manage,

hoping to calm the little mouse. There was no response, though, only silence. Then something moved again in the shadows across the room. With a trembling hand, he managed to shine the tiny light against the far wall.

There, desperately pulling and twisting to free itself, was the little brown mouse. Its fur was snagged on a large splinter protruding from the old, wooden baseboard. On the floor, a short distance from the struggling creature, the crushed remains of Sam's lime green candy lay glistening in the moonlight. There was also a long, slimy skid mark on the ground, leading up to the wall. It looked as if the mouse, in his desperate attempt to escape, had slipped on Sam's discarded candy and slid straight into the splintered baseboard. Sam crawled over and gently lifted the mouse from the wooden spike. As soon as it was free, it dropped to the ground and lay very, very still. He scooped up the limp body and cradled it gently in his hand. When he saw the blood on the mouse's hind leg, his heart sank. Looking at the motionless creature in his hand, it seemed that this was indeed the final straw—a miserable end to a miserable day. A tear began to trickle its way down his cheek.

"I'm sorry," he sniffed. "It's all my fault. If I hadn't come after you and scared you like that..."

Sam lowered his head and began to sob. Suddenly, two little black eyes flashed up at him and once again he heard the sound of a voice.

"Oh dear, please don't cry. I'm really all right you know. I just thought that if I played dead for awhile, you'd go away."

Sam's sobs grew louder.

"There, there...it's nothing...please! You're getting my fur all wet. It's a minor flesh wound, that's all, see?"

The little mouse wriggled his leg back and forth. Gently,

Sam set him down on the ground and the mouse tried putting some weight on his leg, gingerly at first, then bouncing up and down confidently on both feet.

"There, I do hope you'll stop crying now."

Sam sniffled, wiping his nose with the back of his hand, and nodded.

The mouse continued. "In all my many years, this has been one of the most exasperating days that I can remember. Nothing has gone right from the start, and now, for the first time ever, I have been apprehended! Usually I am able to rely on the resident rodent population for assistance in these situations, but their digs seem to be quite deserted and their mouse holes have been sealed shut."

A shudder suddenly passed over the mouse. "You haven't had the exterminators in, have you?" He turned his black, beady eyes on Sam.

"Uh, no." said Sam slowly. "Unless that big white truck with the plastic cockroach on the roof..."

"Well, I certainly hope that everyone was able to escape unharmed!" cried the mouse. "This is most distressing! To make matters worse, I'm having technical difficulties. I can't seem to contact anyone for assistance."

The mouse kept babbling, his dark eyes darting back and forth across the room, barely taking a breath between sentences. He appeared to grow increasingly agitated with every word.

"Where is the professor's study? His research notes?" He kicked at the crumpled roll of paper that lay against the wall. "And this floorplan is of no use at all! Where is everything? And where, for that matter, is Professor Hawthorne?"

"He moved," said Sam quietly. "I live here now."

"Moved! Where?"

"I'm not sure," replied Sam. "Somewhere far away, I think."

The mouse threw his paws into the air.

"That's it! In this day and age you would think that I could have been provided with up-to-date information. What makes this situation all the more challenging is the fact that this was not originally intended to be my assignment at all. What bits of files that I do have are in a dreadful mess! Someone is going to hear about this. Moved, indeed!"

At that, the mouse dropped to the floor in frustration and sat there, resting a whiskery face on two furry, knobby knees.

Sam stood up and brushed the dust from his pajama legs.

"I could try to help you," he suggested hopefully.

"Well, help is what I truly need right now, but unless you know where the professor is, I doubt that you could do much to assist me," replied the mouse brusquely.

Sam shuffled his feet and stared at the floor. The mouse looked up. Another tear was welling in Sam's eye.

"I'm afraid I've been rather rude. No excuse for that!" The little mouse jumped up and held out his paw. He spoke in a more refined voice now. "Mr. Goodfellow's the name. Delighted to make your acquaintance."

Sam crouched down and nervously held out his hand. The mouse placed a tiny pinkish paw on one of his fingers.

"Pleased to meet you, too. I'm Sam."

Mr. Goodfellow sat down and eyed Sam thoughtfully, all the while twirling the long whiskers at the side of his face. Every instinct was telling him to run away, as fast as his injury would allow. He could slip into the shadows, and (if he had his bearings right) back out the same hole in the window frame he had entered through. The next morning, he would simply be a figment of the boy's imagination, or a weird dream—the result of eating too many potato chips with creamy dill dip just before bed. But something about Sam was

strangely familiar. Perhaps he would stay just a bit longer.

As Sam waited for Mr. Goodfellow to speak, he thought about this strange little creature. From the nature books that he had read, Sam was aware of many bizarre species in the animal kingdom, not to mention the strange mutations that frequently popped up as well. He was quite sure, however, that he had never come across anything like a talking rodent. But then again, the world *was* a strange place—discoveries were being made all the time. Maybe he had found a new species! Or, then again, maybe it was the oxygen depletion thing...or stress. That was probably it! His parents were *always* talking about stress and the effects it could have on you. The move must have taken more of a toll on him than he imagined. Whatever it turned out to be, Sam decided that he would try and look on it as logically and scientifically as he could.

The unmistakable sound of a gasp drew Sam's attention back to his new acquaintance. Mr. Goodfellow was pawing frantically at his wound. Assuming the little mouse must be in some pain, Sam leaned forward to offer assistance.

"Are you alright, Mr. Goodfellow? Don't be scared. Let me take a look at that," said Sam, as he reached toward the mouse's leg.

Sam was trying to sound reassuring, like his father did when he was removing an old, well-stuck bandage from one of Sam's many cuts and scrapes. But Mr. Goodfellow clamped his paws over his injury. Sam, determined to help, gently moved them aside. As he did so, fragments of tangled fur floated softly to the ground. Sam feared that a piece of the wooden splinter had lodged itself into the mouse's wound. He bent to examine the injury more closely. There was some blood, but most of it had dried into the surrounding fur. Peering at the pinkish flesh beneath, Sam could see a long gash, but it appeared to be clean and, thankfully, free of splinters. Oddly, though, there was a rather strange looking layer of material that was neither fur, nor skin, surrounding the cut.

"What's *this*?" Sam asked, as he gently prodded it. Mr. Goodfellow's eyes were wild with horror. Sam moved in for a better look, but the little mouse fell forward quite suddenly and buried his head in his knees. He looked up from time to time during his lament.

"That's it!" he cried. "I've had it! What other disaster can this wretched day possibly bring? This is most unusual, you know. I have always prided myself on being in complete control at all times. After all, proper planning is the essential ingredient for a job well done. But it would seem that whenever Goodfellow and Hawthorne come together, an element of doom awaits! It's a curse, I tell you! A curse! Oh…the humiliation!"

The little mouse appeared to be working himself into a state of great agitation once again. Sam leaned forward and gently patted his head. It was all he could think to do and after a moment or two it appeared to be having some positive effects. Slowly, the mouse began to regain his composure. He looked up at Sam and spoke in a slightly calmer voice.

"Please forgive my outburst," he sighed, rubbing his head. "I have been on the road for the last few days and I fear I may be suffering from a touch of exhaustion. I'm not generally inclined to such hysterics, but the frustrations of this day have been challenging, to say the least. And, alas, it would appear that I am no closer to finding Professor Hawthorne either."

"Is the professor a friend of yours?" asked Sam.

"Well, I suppose you *could* call him that. In a manner of speaking, that is. He doesn't know me, though, of course. Do *you* know the professor, my boy?" asked Mr. Goodfellow.

There was such a sense of hope in the gentle voice, that Sam thought carefully before he answered.

"Well, I know a bit about him, I guess. He's kind of a scientist and explorer, isn't he? I'll bet he's gone on an expedition. Maybe he told somebody where he was going or left a note or something."

"Yes, of course. You're quite right, my boy," said Mr. Goodfellow, rubbing his head more vigorously now. "I've got to knock the fog out of this old brain and get back on track somehow."

Sam's gaze fell to the mouse's injured leg again. Though Sam had never seen the inside of a mouse before, he was quite sure that there was something strange about this one.

Mr. Goodfellow slumped forward again with exhaustion and resignation, not even attempting to hide his leg this time.

"It's no use," he mumbled into his knees. "I have stayed too long and now, I fear, the ruse is up."

Sam had no idea what the mouse was talking about. He leaned forward to pat the tiny head again. This had, after all, been successful the first time.

"Oh, woe is me!" Mr. Goodfellow groaned, "for I am undone, indeed! Communications are down, my mouse assistants have been banished, and there is nowhere else to turn. Thankfully, you do appear to be an intelligent and sensitive young man," he continued. "Perhaps you might be able to assist me with this confounded Hawthorne case. After all, I am in a monumental pickle...."

He lifted his head from his knees and stared into Sam's eyes. After a few moments of reflection, Mr. Goodfellow suddenly sprang to his feet.

"I'll be right back."

2

You Can't Judge a Book by Its Cover

With a wave of his pink tail, Mr. Goodfellow trotted across the room and disappeared behind the bookcase. Sam heard a great deal of scuffling and shuffling until the small brown body appeared again, pulling a tan-colored box behind it. The box appeared to be a miniature traveling steamer trunk, the kind old-time actors had used to transport their costumes and stage makeup. It was rectangular in shape, much like a wardrobe, with handles at each end. There were two latches at the front and a pair of wheels on the bottom. Mr. Goodfellow set it down carefully and heaved a great sigh.

"I suppose I really should spring-clean this old thing," he panted, mopping his brow with a furry arm. "But it is full of all sorts of interesting bits and pieces," he reflected, "and there is an old saying that if you keep something for at least seven years, you'll find a use for it eventually."

Sam nodded in agreement, and made a mental note. He wanted to remember that for the next time his parents asked him to throw out any of his stuff. Sam stared at the trunk. It was covered, from one end to the other, with dozens of stickers. Some were old and wrinkled, and almost worn through. Others were newer, with bright colors and glossy finishes. They read like an adventurer's itinerary: London, Paris, Rome, New York, Amsterdam, Vienna, Bombay, Singapore, even Katmandu. Sam couldn't take his eyes off them—he never would have imagined that the life of a mouse could be *that* exciting.

Mr. Goodfellow fiddled with the latches of his trunk and then opened the doors as wide as they would go. Sam peered inside. On the left were four blue drawers decorated with a golden pattern of leaves and flowers. Set above these was an oval mirror in a beautifully carved gilt frame, and beside that, a map of the world, dotted with multi-colored pins. Mr. Goodfellow opened the bottom drawer and took out a folded wooden stool. He set it up in front of the drawers, sat down, and opened the top one. Inside lay an array of combs and brushes, an assortment of bottles and jars, neatly labeled and arranged alphabetically, and a tiny computer. The little mouse gave the last item a sideways glance and shook his head.

"It's down, you know. Utterly useless. Rather ironic really, considering all those years I spent with..." He stopped suddenly and waved his paws about.

"Never mind, never mind, no sense going down that road. Suffice it to say that it doesn't always work."

He rolled his eyes as he opened the second drawer, pointing to a dusty old journal and fountain pen that were nestled in one corner. Sam stretched forward and, squinting, read the words "Journal" and "Fountain Pen." They were written in black ink, in precisely executed handwriting.

"I suppose I will have to resort to my old friends here if I am to continue with my daily entries," the little mouse muttered. "Had I known I wouldn't be able to use my computer, I would have polished up my cursive writing skills. I fear I may have grown a little rusty in that department."

He sighed. Then, still perched upon his stool, he took out a tiny tortoiseshell comb (labeled "Comb") and began to brush his whiskers, slowly counting off 25 strokes for each set, before returning the comb to the drawer.

While Mr. Goodfellow was engrossed with his grooming, Sam took the opportunity to look more closely at the strange trunk. The right side of it looked more like a closet. It had a long metal rod across the top from which dozens of variously hued fur coats, hanging on tiny gold hangers, were arranged from lightest to darkest. Hung on hooks beneath them were several pairs of what appeared to be matching feet and paws. Sam scanned the neat row of perfectly crafted mouse suits. Then he turned to study the figure of Mr. Goodfellow again. Back and forth Sam's gaze went, from the suits, to Mr. Goodfellow, and back again. Finally, the mouse began to chuckle. He stood up, lifted his chin and searched with his paw until he found the end of a metal tab. Sam heard a "zipping" sound as Mr. Goodfellow pulled the tab from under his chin, past his stomach and all the way down one leg. Sam's eyes grew wider. Furry arms and paws fell away, furry feet were pushed aside, nose mask and teeth were removed, until, at last, a little man stood before him, dressed in a blue checked shirt and beige baggy trousers held up by bright red suspenders. He brushed himself up and down where strands of loose fur had stuck to his clothes. A pair of colorful argyle socks finished off his ensemble. He took another comb from his shirt pocket and began to tidy his hair, which was graying and somewhat sparse on top. Then he ran the comb through his whiskery moustache (twenty-five strokes exactly), his dark eyes twinkling with the same light that Sam had seen in the glow of his flashlight. The little figure stepped forward and held out his hand. Sam held out a finger.

"Goodfellow is still the name, my boy. Very delighted to make your acquaintance again!"

Sam was finding it difficult to speak. A talking mouse had been, well, rather a shock, but a talking mouse that was actually a tiny, miniature person, disguised as a mouse, was really just too much.

"Uh...uh...very p-p-pleased to meet you again, too," Sam stammered. He felt the little hand give his finger a friendly squeeze.

Sam stared. "This is *some* dream," he said.

"Oh, it's not a dream, Sam. I'm quite real." Then he paused. "We all are."

"We? There's more of you?"

"A few," said Mr. Goodfellow, suddenly looking uncomfortable. "This is most irregular and I've probably revealed more to you than I should have already. If it hadn't been for this blasted mix-up!" He paused for a moment just then and stared thoughtfully at the floor. "It wasn't his fault at all, you know," he suddenly murmured.

"Whose fault?" asked Sam.

"My dear brother's," whispered Mr. Goodfellow. "How I wish he were here to counsel me now. Filbert was, after all, the one who'd dealt exclusively with the Hawthorne family for years."

The little man looked squarely at Sam.

"I do hope you can be trusted!" he suddenly snapped.

"Oh yes, of course!" said Sam, as earnestly as he could.

Mr. Goodfellow eyed Sam's face intently for a moment. Then he stooped down to pick up the mouse suit that lay in a heap on the floor. He studied the spot of blood on the leg.

"With a bit of overnight stain remover and a stitch or two, I'll have this as good as new," he announced.

He lifted an empty coat hanger from the closet rod and carefully hung the suit from it, fastening the zipper all the way to the top.

"The newer ones have Velcro, of course," he remarked. "Very convenient, indeed, particularly when a speedy costume change is required. But that's more for the younger folk. I'm a button and zipper man myself. You can't always teach an old dog new tricks!"

Rolling up his pant leg, Mr. Goodfellow then bent to examine the injury on his leg. After piercing through the layers of fur and pant material, the wooden baseboard spike had torn into Mr. Goodfellow's flesh, leaving a gash that ran up the side of his leg between his ankle and knee. It was not a serious wound, but deep enough to bleed through the fur suit. Sam noticed a few older scars in the same area. There was probably an interesting story behind each one of them. Mr. Goodfellow took a bandage half the size of a paper clip out of the second drawer and placed it neatly over the cut.

"There," he said at last. "Now I'm as good as new."

Mr. Goodfellow then took a long-handled brush from the drawer and began to carefully groom all the coats that hung in the trunk.

"It's very important, Sam, to keep one's equipment in tip-top shape."

As he continued to brush, he counted off twenty-five strokes for each suit, front and back. The coats became sleek and glossy.

"These new suits are really something to look at," he said. "If it wasn't for this infernal molting problem." He picked at a few strands that were still sticking to him.

Sam admired the coats. "They're beautiful. Are they real?"

Mr. Goodfellow stopped brushing and shook his head vigorously.

"Oh goodness, no, no, no! The mice wouldn't stand for that!"

He returned to his brushing. Well, thought Sam, fake or not, they sure looked real. There were various shades of brown or gray, some with a lovely reddish hue. Others were white or cream or piebald mixes of black and white.

Sam could contain his curiosity no longer.

"But *why* do you dress up in mouse suits?"

Mr. Goodfellow smiled.

"It's really quite simple, Sam. Mice are the perfect disguise. They are everywhere and exist in every time. They have populated most of the earth's surface for millions of years and live in every type of climate, from northern cold to desert heat. And, as you may have noticed from the trunk, I do travel quite a bit. When I am disguised as a mouse, I can be relatively inconspicuous, especially in a group of other mice. And mice can be quite a helpful sort too. They're excellent hosts, devoted to family and friends, and always willing to take part in a crowd scene. I've had more than a few close calls in my time when I've suddenly felt strong paws on each arm and been whisked through a hole in the wall to safety. I've spent many delightful evenings in the company of mice." His eyes glistened. "I gave a lovely bride away once, you know." Mr. Goodfellow's voice grew quite serious. "Mice are ... well, sadly, they're rather misunderstood fellows. They really are the most gentle and pleasant of creatures."

Mr. Goodfellow stopped his brushing again to look at Sam.

"There is something very familiar about you, Sam, but I can't place it. Well, maybe it will come to me later. You seem a trifle pale, my boy. A spot of tea, perhaps? Always a welcome pick-me-up I find, especially after a shock."

The little man opened the third blue drawer. Sam could see a miniature china teapot peeking from under a wrinkled towel.

"No, but thank you anyway," Sam replied politely.

Mr. Goodfellow looked disappointed as he closed the drawer again.

"Later then, perhaps," he remarked, hopefully. "You know, I have a particularly strong conviction that you're a trustworthy lad. I suppose you may as well know the rest. In for a penny, in for a pound I always say my boy!" He took to his brushing once again.

"Oh, bother!" he said waving his brush in the air. "How many was that now? I've lost count."

"Thirteen," said Sam.

"Ah, yes...thank you my boy...fourteen...fifteen...You see, Sam, as a mouse I can go about my business and tend to my assignments without being noticed. I'm part of the woodwork you might say," he chuckled, "or, at least, part of a mouse hole in the woodwork."

"But what kind of work do you do?" asked Sam.

"I suppose you could say that I, or we, help people. Special people. People who are on the verge of discovering, or creating, or inventing something and who struggle to achieve greatness. With a well-placed whisper of encouragement in the ear, we are that 'little voice' of inspiration that helps people to continue with their work. Maybe they've hit a dead-end, or given up hope, or lost their way and just need a push in the right direction. That's where we come in."

"But what are you? Where did you come from?"

Mr. Goodfellow plunked himself down on his miniature stool and sighed.

"I'm not sure I know all the answers myself, Sam. I can tell you we are known as The Sage and that we've been here a very long time. What we do is something we have always done and, in my family in particular, it's a tradition that carries with it a great deal of honor and responsibility. Projects of the utmost importance have always been assigned to the Goodfellow family. We accept our roles with great pride, as do all The Sage families. A Governing Council, comprised of our most revered elders, oversees our work. Following the ancient laws and prophecies that they have been entrusted with, the Governing Council's role is to assign to each Sage a number of gifted ones, as we like to call them. It is then up to us to watch over these individuals throughout their lives and, whenever necessary, provide guidance and inspiration to them. The Governing Council matches us with gifted ones to whom we share a bond of sorts, a 'soul mate,' if you will. It is called the Sacred Seal. Our assignees are unaware of either our presence or our mission, of course. It is our role to ensure that the gifted ones fulfill their destinies, and that their 'gifts' benefit all of mankind."

"Is Professor Hawthorne a gifted one?" asked Sam.

"You're quite perceptive! Indeed he is, my boy, as were a number of his illustrious ancestors. My brother Filbert provided inspiration to generations of gifted Hawthornes."

Mr. Goodfellow stared quite deliberately at Sam for a second or two before he continued.

"You see, Filbert's last assignment, Dr. Elijah Hawthorne, the great-grandfather of the current professor and a dabbler in the antiquities, was the first Hawthorne to be linked to a mysterious scroll. Perhaps you've heard of it? I understand that the legend of the Hawthorne scroll is well known in these parts."

"No," said Sam. "I haven't. But then, we only got here yesterday."

"Yes, of course," said Mr. Goodfellow.

"What does this scroll thing look like?" asked Sam.

"No one really knows, my boy. I imagine that it would be a rolled up length of parchment or some similar material containing lines of script or symbols. Legend has it that the scroll was found a number of centuries ago, encased in ice, on a remote mountainside somewhere in Turkey. The scroll is reputed to be very powerful. Its precise location was kept secret by the local Turkish tribespeople for many years after its discovery. According to the legend, the scroll possessed a strange kind of energy that could only be unleashed when it was removed from its protective casing. A few years before the turn of the last century, this scroll somehow fell into Elijah Hawthorne's possession."

"But what's the big deal about the scroll? Why does everyone want it?" asked Sam.

"It may be very important, my boy. And though it might be nothing more than a fantasy, rumors have continued to circulate about it for centuries. I'm inclined to believe that 'where there's smoke, there's fire.' My brother, Filbert, who was Elijah Hawthorne's Sage, would have known for sure. But with Filbert gone, whatever information the scroll contained, or, indeed, whether it ever even existed at all was lost when Elijah Hawthorne passed away 120 years ago. Some believe that Elijah may have hidden the scroll somewhere in this very house. When I found out I was coming here, I'd hoped to locate the scroll and see, perhaps, if it could explain the fate of my dear brother Filbert. You see, he disappeared around the same time that Elijah Hawthorne passed away. I would give anything to find him again."

With this last declaration, Sam noticed Mr. Goodfellow's shoulders begin to shake. He reached into his shirt pocket and removed a clean, neatly folded white handkerchief. He dabbed at his eyes first, then he gave his nose a short blow and, with a deep breath, continued.

"With both Elijah's death and Filbert's disappearance, the Hawthorne case lay dormant for many years. When the Governing Council suddenly reactivated everything as a result of the present Professor Hawthorne's work, I pleaded with them to grant me custody of the Hawthorne files. In situations where a Sage cannot complete his assignments, it is quite commonplace for the Sacred Seal to be transferred to a family member. I was not about to let one of my pushy cousins take over, so I immediately applied to the council and was granted the files. What I didn't know, however, was that most of the information about Elijah Hawthorne and what he was working on had disappeared along with Filbert. And so here I am today with very little to go on, hoping that the work of the current Professor Hawthorne might lead me to Filbert, or, at least, to some understanding of the fate that befell him. Of course, Professor Hawthorne's discoveries are also of grave importance, not only to me but to mankind as well. That is why it is critical that I find the professor as soon as possible. I owe that much to dear Filbert."

With this last line, Mr. Goodfellow was forced to reach for his hanky again.

"Oh dear," he said, blowing his nose, "there I go again, I'm afraid. I must apologize, my boy. It's quite out of character, you know, and most embarrassing. The nature of our work certainly doesn't encourage sentimental displays, but thinking about Filbert tonight seems to have unleashed a wellspring of emotion in me. I can't explain it. I must be suffering from the effects of fatigue. By the way, what is that interminable humming noise? Are you running an electrical appliance of some sort in here, my boy—an air cleaning apparatus or a humidifying machine?"

"No," said Sam. "I don't hear any humming noise."

"You don't? How curious. It's really most annoying."

He tipped his head from side to side. "Perhaps I have acquired a disturbance of my inner ear," he murmured.

Mr. Goodfellow opened and closed his mouth in a wide yawn as he attempted to clear the blockage.

"It's no use," he said, giving his head one final shake. "It may be helpful if I focused on something else for awhile."

Crinkling his forehead into a series of deep furrows, Mr. Goodfellow stared at his trunk. Holding his hands in front of him, he drummed his fingers together in a slow, steady rhythm until a smile began to form at the corners of his mouth and his eyes widened with excitement. Suddenly, he thrust his head between the rows of hanging mouse suits and began to rummage around.

"Ah, here it is! I haven't taken this out for ages. I think you will find it most interesting, my boy."

Mr. Goodfellow emerged, holding a flat, black book that was nearly as big as himself. He lay it down on the floor before him, untied the long, silk ribbon that held it shut and, with a wave of his hand, beckoned Sam to come closer. Sam crawled forward, shining the miniature flashlight in front of him. Mr. Goodfellow carefully lifted the heavy black cover and turned to the first page.

The album was full of photographs. At first glance it looked just like any other family album. But when Sam pulled out the magnifying glass from around his neck to take a closer look, he could see that these were anything but ordinary pictures.

The photographs were mounted on sheets of thick black paper and each had an inscription beneath it, beautifully written in gold ink. Sam pointed to the first picture.

"Wow! You've got a photograph of Albert Einstein!"

"Oh, yes," Mr. Goodfellow replied. "I'm quite proud of that one."

"What's that fuzzy little blob in the corner?" asked Sam, as he moved the magnifying glass back and forth across the page.

"Why that's me, my boy!" cried Mr. Goodfellow. "I set my camera on time delay. If you look even closer, you can see some of the chalk crumbles I've arranged on the floor there."

Sam squinted as he read slowly. "E equals..."

Mr. Goodfellow lowered his voice. "He was a little stuck that day, you know. Just needed a bit of inspiration and voilà! Such a brilliant man."

Sam turned to the next picture and read the inscription. "Charles Lindbergh—Solo Flight, 1927."

"Ah, yes, 'Lucky Lindy,'" said Mr. Goodfellow. "Lucky, indeed, to have someone sing into his ear and keep him awake on that long flight across the Atlantic. He was quite an eccentric sort, really. Did you know, Sam, that he insisted on taking exactly five sandwiches with him on that historic flight—no more, no less." Mr. Goodfellow smiled sheepishly. "I have always thought it must have perplexed that poor man to no end when he could only find four and a half."

"Alexander Fleming, 1928," read Sam. "I think I remember him from school last term. Wasn't he the one who discovered penicillin, from some kind of mold or something?"

"That's right, my boy! Most fortunate that someone had the foresight to leave that old cheese sandwich sitting around in his laboratory." Mr. Goodfellow gave Sam a wink.

"You seem to know a fair bit about these things for a lad of your years."

"Well...I'm going to be a scientist too," said Sam quietly.

"Really?" said Mr. Goodfellow. "That's most admirable, my boy." He gave Sam another one of his long and thoughtful looks.

There were many other pictures in the album too. Sam read out the names as Mr. Goodfellow carefully turned each page.

"Marie Curie, Edmund Hillary, Thomas Edison, Amelia Earhart, Albert Schweitzer, Alexander Graham Bell, Florence Nightingale."

The list was as impressive as it was lengthy. The last few pages of the album held some beautiful pen and watercolor sketches.

"These are my greatest treasure, my boy," said Mr. Goodfellow solemnly. "They chronicle some of my most prestigious assignments."

Sam recognized all of the names written below the sketches: Beethoven, Galileo, Newton, Rembrandt, Handel, Gainsborough, and Franklin.

"If you helped all of those people, you must be really old!"

Mr. Goodfellow nodded proudly. "I'm 902 actually. The tales my father could tell you are the most amazing, though, my boy. He accompanied Marco Polo, you know. Turned 1320 on his last birthday. He's retired now and has a lovely place in the country. Quite the adventurer! But that, my boy, is another story."

"Wow," said Sam as he stared down at the pictures, "this is amazing!"

Mr. Goodfellow smiled to himself. He watched as the boy stared solemnly down at the photographs and sketches in the album. It was quite satisfying to see that he was beginning to lose his sad countenance.

"These pictures have a real knack of helping you forget your troubles, don't they? And for all of my disasters today, Sam, I suspect that you were having an equally bad time of it too. Am I right? You know what they say: 'a trouble shared is a trouble halved.'"

Sam nodded. It wasn't easy for him to share his feelings. He was reluctant to talk about his problems, even (to their great dismay) with his own parents. But there was something compelling about the little man and the way that he spoke that, this time, Sam could not resist. He took two deep breaths and began to tell Mr. Goodfellow about his old house, and this new one, the old garden, then the new one, and every sad and lonely feeling in between. When he got to the part about finding Mr. Goodfellow, Sam was smiling. Maybe the little man was right about the trouble-halved thing.

Leafing through the album as he related his problems, Sam suddenly stopped to stare at one page in particular. He moved his magnifying glass to the bottom of the picture.

"There are two fuzzy blobs in this photo. Who's that standing next to you?"

Mr. Goodfellow looked a little puzzled at first.

"I thought that you worked alone," said Sam.

"I usually do, my boy...I usually do." Furrowing his brow, Mr. Goodfellow stooped over the photograph in question. As Sam had stated, there were two figures in this picture, one slightly smaller than the other. Behind them were lush green fields and a clear blue sky. When Mr. Goodfellow checked the date below the picture, his face suddenly brightened.

"July, 1936...of course! It must be Edgar! The 'Summer of Edgar,' I always called it. Quite a remarkable time."

"But who is Edgar?" asked Sam.

"Why, he's my nephew, my boy," said Mr. Goodfellow. "My goodness, I haven't thought about those days in quite some time."

Mr. Goodfellow gave Sam another one of his long, thoughtful looks.

"I think you would have liked Edgar. And I am certain that Edgar would have liked you. Come to think of it, if anyone could genuinely sympathize with your predicament, it would surely have to be Edgar. That boy certainly had his own share of troubles."

"Was Edgar my age?" asked Sam.

"Well, around your age, I imagine. Let me see now...back in '36 Edgar would have been, oh...about 105."

Sam's eyes flew wide open.

"You see," explained Mr. Goodfellow, "we Sage age about one year to every fifteen of yours. So in your years, Edgar would have been about seven."

Sam nodded, his fingers moving across his other fingers as he counted under his breath.

"I get it. It's sort of like double dog or cat years, only in reverse, right?"

Mr. Goodfellow seemed taken aback by the comparison.

"Well, I've never thought of it in those terms before, Sam, but I suppose that would accurately sum it up."

"What was the 'Summer of Edgar'?" asked Sam.

Mr. Goodfellow shook his head. "Oh, it's a rather long and involved story, my boy, with considerable twists and turns. I don't think I could..."

"Please!" pleaded Sam, "there's no way I'll be able to go to sleep now anyway! Pleeease!" When he turned to look at Mr. Goodfellow's face, the little man's eyes suddenly began to fill with tears once more.

"Oh dear, it's happening again." Mr. Goodfellow reached for the now crumpled hanky and lifted it to his eyes.

"What is it? What did I say?" asked Sam with concern.

"Please don't blame yourself, my boy. It's just that this talk of Edgar's adventures seems to have set me off again. It is a magnificent story, but sadly it's a tale that's end remains unwritten. I can't honestly say if there will be a happy ending, or an ending at all for that matter." He blew his nose again and took a deep, cleansing breath.

"Maybe it would help to talk about it," said Sam. "You just told me that a trouble shared is a trouble halved. Please, tell me about Edgar."

Mr. Goodfellow sighed and attempted a trembling smile. "Ahh, it was the grandest of times, Sam. It truly was." He wiped a remaining tear from his cheek. "I suppose we *could* use a little distracting. It's been a rather trying day for both of us, hasn't it? And I suppose neither of us will be getting any sleep just now, will we?"

Like an actor preparing to take the stage, Mr. Goodfellow cleared his throat noisily and, with one great gulp, expanded his lungs with air.

"Let's see now, Sam . . . If you'll bear with me, I'll just take a moment to gather my thoughts. It has been quite an exhausting day."

With a determined expression, he blew vigorously into his handkerchief and then reached up to undo the top collar button of his shirt and then the two buttons that fastened each cuff at his wrist. Then he rolled his sleeves, very neatly, all the way up to his elbows.

"I would suggest you get comfortable too, my boy. This is quite a long story. I suppose I should start at the beginning, when Edgar and I were first, shall we say, 'thrown' together."

As Mr. Goodfellow prepared to tell his story, Sam retrieved his sleeping bag and pillow from the other side of the room. Propping the pillow up against the wall, he thumped it a few times to fluff it and then climbed into his sleeping bag. There was just enough space at one side of his pillow for a much smaller head, which soon joined his. In fact, Mr. Goodfellow's entire body fit quite nicely onto this spot, conveniently close to Sam's ear.

Whispering into the ear of a person was nothing new to Mr. Goodfellow, of course. However, the fact that this person was fully aware of where the words were coming from was an altogether unique experience. He was quite certain that this kind of relationship between Sage and human had never occurred in the annals of the Goodfellow family (or any of the other Sage families, for that matter), and he knew he was going to have to answer to the Governing Council for it one day. However, Mr. Goodfellow had the distinct feeling that telling Sam the story of Edgar Goodfellow's summer adventures was the right thing to do.

"It was in England in the late spring of 1936," began Mr. Goodfellow, "when I was summoned to Pebble Hall, the home of my Great Uncle Cyrus. He is, at the grand age of 1498, the oldest living Goodfellow, and a respected member of the Governing Council. He is responsible for assigning the apprenticeships of young Sage in our family. You see, it is common practice for each young Goodfellow, as it is in other Sage families, to apprentice by the side of an older, more experienced member, usually a father. But Edgar's father, my elder brother Filbert, had tragically disappeared during the Elijah Hawthorne case when the lad was little more than a toddler. Now that Edgar had come of age, it would fall to another Goodfellow to take the boy in hand and teach him the ways of The Sage. The Governing Council determined that Edgar would benefit from a younger influence, and since the other male members of our family were a great deal older, the council unanimously decided to have him apprentice with me. Naturally I was flattered. I had been overseas for some time completing a number of assignments and I was, in fact, quite flush with success. And now I had been summoned to mold this young fledgling. I did not take my responsibility lightly. With enthusiasm, I set out to meet Edgar. I had seen him only once before, as a little tyke in the arms of his mother, Hazel. It would be just Edgar and me; Edgar and his Uncle Jolly."

"Hey, wait a minute!" Sam's voice suddenly intruded. "Your name is Jolly? Jolly Goodfellow?" Sam chuckled loudly. "Your Mum and Dad must have been playing a joke when they named you!"

Mr. Goodfellow lifted his head and rolled his eyes.

"Really, Sam. I'm over 900 years old, remember? I'm the original."

"Oh," replied Sam. "Sorry."

"But, I digress." Mr. Goodfellow sank his head, once again, into Sam's pillow. "Back to the story at hand, my boy! However, it takes more than a good teller to make a good story, Sam. It takes a good listener, too. You must let yourself enter the tale, lad."

Sam had no trouble with that. He closed his eyes and he could see Great Uncle Cyrus' house clearly, from the stately green fern fronds that lined the long path, to the tall pebble columns that framed the entrance.

3

Follow the River and You Will Find the Sea

M r. Goodfellow stood before the large wooden door, his hand reaching up to a heavy brass doorknocker. The ever attendant drizzle, hallmark of an English spring day, had subsided for a brief period. There was a soft, cool breeze, and the delicate scent of flowers floated in the air. The much stronger aroma of freshly brewed coffee wafted out of the hallway when the door was opened. Mr. Goodfellow lifted his fur-clad foot to step inside.

"Come in, Jolly, come in! So glad you've finally arrived!" An elderly gentleman, with fluffy gray sideburns and a wonderfully long handlebar moustache, beckoned him inside.

"Hello, Uncle Duncan. Better late than never, I suppose!"

"I see you're still collecting those old sayings, Jolly!"

"Why, yes, Uncle Duncan. In fact, while I was abroad I managed to acquire some of the lesser known ones. I'm hoping to publish them one day." He fumbled about his mouse suit. "I've got a notebook on me somewhere...."

Uncle Duncan patted him on the arm. "Later, Jolly, later. We really must make up for lost time."

"Oh, of course!" Mr. Goodfellow stepped over the

threshold and onto the expanse of black and white marble tiles that covered the hallway floor. It had been years since he had been in this house, but it was just as he remembered it. A beautiful crystal chandelier hung from the ceiling and exquisite paintings lined the walls. Mr. Goodfellow's mouse nails clicked across the marble tiles. The only other sound was the steady ticking of a grandfather clock in one corner.

"Let's hang up your suit, Jolly."

As Mr. Goodfellow began to unzip his fur front, he glanced toward the closet along the far wall. A row of handsome mouse suits hung from a long line of brass hooks—sleek dark browns and blacks, some flecked with gray. A much smaller, lighter brown suit was hanging well away from the others on the very last hook in the closet. When Mr. Goodfellow moved forward to take a closer look, he suddenly understood why the smaller suit hung alone. It was quite unkempt, in need of a good brushing, and, oh dear, what was that? Prominently displayed, directly at chest level, was a half-eaten, bright red candy embedded in the fur. Mr. Goodfellow shuddered. If this was Edgar's suit, and he guessed that it was, he would have to have a very strongly worded discussion with the lad about cleanliness and grooming. Mr. Goodfellow quickly removed his four paws and whiskered nose mask, struggled for a moment to extract his protruding teeth, then stepped smartly out of his suit and hung it on a hook, as far away from the small, offensive garment as he could. He was wearing his usual attire of shirt, trousers, and suspenders, but on this day he had also worn a necktie and his best houndstooth jacket.

"This way, Jolly. They're waiting for us."

Uncle Duncan took his arm and guided him through another narrower hallway that led to an elegant study.

Mr. Goodfellow looked into the room. They were all here:

Uncle Caleb, Uncle Everett, his elder cousins (the twins) Bradford and Borden, Cousin Hamish, and sitting in an imposing wing chair in an almost regal pose, walking stick by his side, was Great Uncle Cyrus. He had never admitted it to anyone, but ever since he had been a child, Mr. Goodfellow had felt just a little nervous in the presence of the old man. He straightened his tie, dusted off the arms of his jacket, and walked in.

In the middle of this rather intimidating assembly of Sage, looking utterly lost within the velvet folds of a big brown settee, sat a young boy. There was a tall glass of lemon drink on the table beside him, but it had not been touched.

The group raised their cups from their saucers and saluted Mr. Goodfellow as he and Uncle Duncan entered.

"Good to see you, Jolly!" "Wonderful of you to come." "How is your father progressing?"

Mr. Goodfellow's father, in fact, was the only adult male family member not present that day.

"Much better, thank you. They say he should have the cast off in another week or so."

The month before last, Mr. Goodfellow's father had had the unfortunate experience of falling down an abandoned, partially obscured mole hole at the bottom of his garden, and breaking his leg.

Cousin Bradford turned and whispered into Borden's ear. "Excellent timing, if you ask me. It's a good job he's not here, you know. We'd never have gotten away with this."

Mr. Goodfellow looked over at them. Borden gave Bradford an elbow in his side and the two quickly straightened up. Although Mr. Goodfellow hadn't heard what Bradford had said, he was beginning to feel suspicious. In an effort to distract him, Uncle Caleb shuffled over and pushed a cup of coffee into his hands. On its way across the room, the contents had slopped over the sides of the cup and into the saucer. It was going to be quite a challenge, thought Mr. Goodfellow, to drink it with dignity now. He wasn't even that fond of coffee. Tea was much more civilized. What he wouldn't give for a cup of Earl Grey right this minute.

"Come, Edgar... come and meet your Uncle Jolly!" chirped Uncle Duncan.

Mr. Goodfellow watched as Edgar shuffled off the settee and onto the floor in front of him. He was a slightly built boy, with delicate wisps of reddish hair floating in the air above his head. Distinguishing him as a Goodfellow were the oversized and somewhat protruding ears which framed each side of his face. He wore a white shirt and a striped blue and red school tie. Below his gray flannel shorts were two bony knees, covered almost entirely with dozens of bandages, each of differing age and size. A bright, yellow yo-yo had been stuffed into one of his shorts pockets. Its string, soiled and knotted, dangled to the floor.

Uncle Duncan turned to Mr. Goodfellow and whispered into his ear. "How do I put this, well, delicately? You're our last hope."

"Ouch! I say! What was that for?" Uncle Duncan, apparently in some pain, rubbed at his leg. Uncle Everett, standing on the other side of him, was giving him a wide-eyed glare.

Edgar stood shyly in the center of the group, kicking at the carpet with a pair of scuffed oxfords. Everyone in the room looked down at him. One blue sock and one gray sock peeped above the rim of his shoes. Uncle Duncan gave Mr. Goodfellow a sideways glance and patted him on the shoulder.

"Good luck, my boy."

Mr. Goodfellow's anxiety over the situation was beginning to grow considerably, but he managed to smile kindly at Edgar in any case. He was about to ask him if he had another pair of socks like that in his drawer at home, but Edgar looked up at him with such hope in his eyes that he could not bring himself to do it.

Mr. Goodfellow was not aware that Uncle Everett had left the room for a moment. But he returned now, carrying with him a blue suitcase. A length of sleeve trailed on the floor behind it. Before Mr. Goodfellow had time to get a word out, Uncle Everett shoved the suitcase into his right hand and Cousin Hamish attached Edgar's hand to his left.

"There now, you're all set!" said Uncle Caleb. "Don't they look wonderful together, Uncle Cyrus?"

The old man, who had not budged throughout this exchange, suddenly grunted and nodded his head in approval.

Mr. Goodfellow cleared his throat.

"I really didn't think we'd be off so soon. I thought perhaps in a week or two, once I've had time to make some plans, arrange things..."

"No time like the present, my boy!" said Uncle Duncan, as he shepherded the two of them into the front hall. He laughed nervously. "What do you know, Jolly, it looks like I'm picking up those old sayings of yours!"

Uncle Caleb, who had rushed into the hall ahead of them, stood by the open door. Mr. Goodfellow's coat and accessories were laid over his arm. Hanging from his other hand, which was stretched as far as possible from his body, was Edgar's grubby suit.

As the two climbed into their outfits there was a great deal of backslapping and choruses of "Have a wonderful time" and "Look forward to hearing from you at the end of the summer!" Mr. Goodfellow barely had time to zip up the top portion of his suit and adjust his nose mask, when he and Edgar suddenly found themselves standing outside on the front step, alone. The big wooden door had closed behind them. Mr. Goodfellow quickly turned back to the door, dropped the suitcase on the ground and lifted his hand to the brass knocker. He was just about to give it a loud knock when, out of the corner of his eye, he noticed Edgar looking up at him with that same hopeful expression he'd seen earlier. He let his arm drop to his side and leaned down to pick up the suitcase once again. Turning slowly, he took a few deep breaths of fresh air (while counting to ten) and then spoke to the little boy beside him.

"Well, Edgar, it appears that we are bound for adventure, you and I."

"Oh, yes, Uncle Jolly, yes, please!"

Edgar was smiling for the first time since they had met that day. Mr. Goodfellow continued.

"The first thing we're going to do is get you cleaned up a bit. Let's make our way back to my flat and see if we can't have a go at that suit. Then we can decide what the next course of action will be."

It had started to rain and there was a fresh and delicious smell of growing things in the air. As they began to walk down the long, shaded pathway, Mr. Goodfellow felt Edgar's small paw creep back into his own. Even though it looked decidedly sticky, he gave it a comforting little squeeze.

When they had traveled as far as the big country road, Mr. Goodfellow suddenly stopped and put his hand up to his ear. He motioned for Edgar to be quiet and still.

"I do believe I hear our ride home approaching. Come along, Edgar!"

He scampered closer to the side of the road. Edgar followed behind. A few moments later Edgar heard a noise too: a low, steady rumbling in the distance. It grew louder and louder

until the shape of a green farm tractor pulling a hay wagon behind it appeared in the distance. Edgar looked a bit anxious.

"Don't worry, my boy. These farm vehicles move at a snail's pace. Just take my paw and be ready to jump when I say."

The low-lying wagon was within range.

"Ready, Edgar?"

"Ready" replied a rather nervous little voice.

"Here we go, then . . . jump, Edgar!"

Tossing the blue suitcase up first, Mr. Goodfellow leapt onto the wagon and landed with a soft thud, holding tight to Edgar's paw the whole time. He coiled his other arm around a thick length of hay.

"There, that wasn't so bad, was it?"

He turned back to look at the boy and gasped in horror. He was still holding Edgar's paw, but Edgar's hand was not in it. Peering over the mountain of hay he saw a lonely little figure standing by the side of the road, waving at him frantically with one brown paw and five pink fingers. Mr. Goodfellow immediately jumped down to the ground, the blue suitcase in hand, and ran back.

"Edgar, didn't you attach your paw properly?" Mr. Goodfellow asked sharply.

The figure lowered its head and mumbled, "Sorry, Uncle Jolly."

It seemed an eternity, to both of them, until the next hay wagon finally came along.

Utterly dejected, Edgar sat in silence, barely lifting his head for the rest of the trip home. Mr. Goodfellow made a concerted effort to be more patient. He had no idea, however, how long he had been chattering away to the boy, but when he next turned to look, Edgar had fallen fast asleep in the hay.

A few miles later, Mr. Goodfellow nudged Edgar awake.

They jumped down and walked further through the woods and into a clearing.

"Ah! Here we are, home at last!" Mr. Goodfellow announced with relief.

Mr. Goodfellow's "flat" was actually a hole dug into the earth on the side of a riverbank. It was quite a modest abode, with clay walls that had been painted a charming periwinkle blue (his favorite color). There were a few pieces of antique furniture, the odd painting here and there, and in one corner, an old tan trunk, covered with an array of stickers. It was a plain, but comfortable place, and for a bachelor who spent more time away from his home than in it, it was ideal. When he did have time to relax, the front porch afforded a lovely view of the water. There had been the occasional evening when Mr. Goodfellow had sat contentedly in his old wicker rocking chair, serenaded by a choir of bullfrogs and crickets, watching the world go by.

After they had entered his home, by way of a series of stone steps built into the bank and carefully concealed by the overhanging vegetation, Mr. Goodfellow wasted no time whatsoever. He trotted over to a great iron cooker that stood against the back wall and removed one of its round, heavy lids with a charred poker. While feverishly stoking the coals inside, he stretched his other arm across to a series of low shelves from which he retrieved a rather battered old teakettle. After checking the water level, he plunked it down on the now sizzling cooker lid, and then reached for a much larger tin bucket. The sound of a gently bubbling kettle was (in Mr. Goodfellow's studied opinion) one of life's greatest comforts. In times of trouble and uncertainty, he always tried to make it the first order of the day. He felt a similar affection for crisp, clean bed sheets (no crumbs or crinkles). Indeed, a steaming cup of perfectly brewed tea and a pristine sleeping station were, to Mr. Goodfellow, a foolproof recipe for certain bliss.

With the task of tea-making well underway, Mr. Goodfellow now proceeded to fill the larger bucket from a water pump by the front door. At one end of the noisy pump, a thick, rubber hose had been pushed outside through a hole in the wall, where it snaked its way down the steep bank and into the river. When the bucket was nearly full, Mr. Goodfellow took three different bottles from a nearby cupboard.

"Let's see now. Which one? Stain remover, disinfectant, fur restorer..."

Edgar had already removed his mouse suit. Mr. Goodfellow took it from him and lowered it, gingerly, into the bucket. He carefully studied the labels on the bottles in front of him while Edgar looked down, mesmerized by the pathetic sight of his floating suit.

"Hmmm, let's just put them all in, shall we?" said Mr. Goodfellow finally.

He began to liberally pour the contents of each bottle into the water. Then he picked up a walking stick he kept by the door and began to stir the concoction round and round.

"There now, Edgar," he said, trying to make the boy feel more comfortable. "We'll just let that soak for awhile."

There was an awkward silence for the next few moments as the two of them stared into the bucket. Mr. Goodfellow's inexperience with children was beginning to make him feel nervous. In an attempt to keep the boy entertained, his mind scrambled about frantically for something to say. His eyes fell on the string dangling from Edgar's pocket and he decided to remark on that. Edgar was delighted at his uncle's interest. He whipped the yo-yo from his pocket and began to spin it up and down.

"Can you do any tricks, my boy?" asked Mr. Goodfellow a little hesitantly.

"Well, I've just started practicing this new one," replied Edgar eagerly.

At that, he snapped the yo-yo back up towards him, whereupon it hit Mr. Goodfellow squarely between the eyes. Edgar was mortified.

"Oh, no! Uncle Jolly!" he wailed.

"It's quite alright, Edgar," said Mr. Goodfellow, rubbing at his forehead where a great big pinkish lump was beginning to form. Struggling a bit to keep his balance, he pointed across the room.

"Why don't you have a seat over there?"

Edgar gladly obliged, but had only made it halfway across the room when the toe of his shoe suddenly met with a bulge in the rug. Edgar shot forward, grabbing onto the first thing his arms could reach—a beautiful antique side table (one of the few truly collectable pieces that Mr. Goodfellow possessed). It held a lovely glass bowl, filled with water and containing some fragrant plate-sized rose petals. There was, of course, a terrific crash. And then...

"Sorry, Uncle Jolly."

Mr. Goodfellow grimaced. In the middle of a big puddle of water, amidst slivers of glass and pieces of petal was a lone, exquisitely carved table leg.

Mr. Goodfellow pointed across the room to the bed in the corner.

"Perhaps you would be safer over there Edgar, while I clean this up."

As Mr. Goodfellow searched through the cupboard for a dustpan and brush, Edgar made his way, successfully, to the bed, where he now sat, swinging his legs back and forth. He soon grew bored with this though, and so he began to bounce up and down, gently at first and then with increasing vigor. There was another clatter, followed by a faint yelp, when Edgar suddenly disappeared behind the back of the bed's wooden headboard. Only the lower part of his legs, with mismatched socks and scuffed shoes, laces dangling, could be seen waving above it.

"What on earth! Edgar, are you alright?"

"Yes, I think so," came the muffled reply. "But I'm afraid I may have broken something else. Sorry, Uncle Jolly."

A small watercolor painting of the Scottish Highlands, which had been hanging above the bed for the last few hundred years, now lay on the floor beside it. There was a jagged diagonal line across the glass, and its gold plaster frame was chipped and cracked.

"Never mind, Edgar...never mind." Mr. Goodfellow clenched his teeth as he reached once again for the dustpan and brush. "But please Edgar, do up your shoelaces before you have another accident!"

Once Mr. Goodfellow finished cleaning up the mess, he turned his attention to Edgar's suitcase. He lifted it onto the bed next to Edgar and snapped open the two locks. As he was stuffing the dusty sleeve back inside, he spotted a letter perched on top of the other clothes. It was addressed, in a lovely scripted hand, to him. He lifted the letter out and stared at it.

Edgar looked up.

"Sorry, Uncle Jolly. I think I was supposed to give that to you."

Mr. Goodfellow carefully tore open the envelope, which was decorated in a colorful border of hearts and flowers, and removed the matching letter.

"Dearest Jolly," it read.

I was so thankful when I learned that Edgar would be apprenticing with you this summer. It's been very difficult for him, spending so much time each weekend with his great Uncles and cousins. They haven't seemed to bond with him at all (I do hope they won't be reading this letter, but just between you and me, Jolly, they are a bit old and stuffy, in my opinion). They tell me that you are wonderful with children. This is a great relief. I'm sure that you will have better luck than they have. Please look after my dear Edgar. He has promised me faithfully that he will be a good boy.

Your loving sister-in-law,
Hazel
P.S. XOXO. A kiss and hug for you, and one for Edgar too!

Mr. Goodfellow opened his fingers and let the letter float down to the bed. He was utterly perplexed. What was this "wonderful with children" part? He had never married and never had any of his own children. In fact, he had had, for the most part, very little to do with children at all. They were a clever lot, his uncles and cousins. He was beginning to understand that he had just played into a very crafty conspiracy. "Lovely to see you, Jolly!" "So glad you could come, Jolly!" It had all been part of their cowardly plot to unload the boy.

The old teakettle, which had been boiling away for some time now, began to emit an ear-piercing sound from its whistling spout. Mr. Goodfellow, lost in thoughts of anger and exasperation, seemed oblivious to its screech. It took another loud crash from Edgar's general direction to finally jolt him to attention. This was immediately followed by a phrase that was becoming very familiar.

"Sorry, Uncle Jolly."

A pottery table lamp lay in tiny shattered shards on the floor. Edgar stood next to it, looking glum, a loose shoelace tangled in the electrical cord.

Edgar had only been in the flat for one half-hour. In that short space of time he had managed to destroy a large percentage of Mr. Goodfellow's personal belongings. What on earth was he going to do with this young lad—this walking disaster in short pants?

Mr. Goodfellow stood and pondered the issue as he surveyed the destruction around him. Close quarters were definitely not a good idea for the accident-prone Edgar. What was needed were wide open spaces. A thought suddenly twigged in his weary mind. What could be more wide and open than the sea? An ocean voyage—how perfect! He would take Edgar to America, where there were even more wide and open spaces than the mind could fathom. He might even be able to arrange for a few minor assignments over there, just to let Edgar get his feet wet. There were other reasons why America seemed a prudent choice at the moment. Dark clouds of conflict and uncertainty were forming over Europe, and the shadow of war was not far behind. Mr. Goodfellow could feel it in his bones and he was almost never wrong about this sort of thing. He knew that whenever fear and hatred filled the hearts of mortal men, shadows of another sort, attracted by the scent of corruption and evil, would also be in attendance. Now that he was solely responsible for his nephew's welfare, Mr. Goodfellow felt a great urge to protect him from these dangers. And so it was decided. Edgar Goodfellow's young life was about to be launched in a very different direction.

4

WHEN ONE DOOR CLOSES,
ANOTHER ONE OPENS

"SAMUEL MIDDLETON! ARE YOU STILL UP?" Mr. Goodfellow's story came to an abrupt end when the door to Sam's room suddenly swung open. Light from the hallway chandelier pierced the darkness. Sam's mother stood in the doorway, her arms folded, peering awkwardly into the moonlit room.

"It's almost 1:00 in the morning, Sam! I thought that we'd talked about this sort of thing before," she said sternly. She paused for a moment before taking a step into the room towards him. "I could have sworn that I heard talking...."

Sam quickly reached towards the bookcase, and grabbed a corner of the old book that lay trapped beneath the bottom shelf. What was left of its flimsy paper jacket tore as he struggled to pull it loose. Once it was free, he lifted it for his mother to see, holding up Mr. Goodfellow's tiny flashlight in his other hand.

"Just looking at this book, Mum. Guess I must have been reading out loud, too." He hoped he sounded convincing.

Sam's mother squinted at the little flashlight. "Where on earth did you get that from? It's so small! Collecting miniatures is one thing, but really, Sam, you'll ruin your eyes with that!"

Sam smiled meekly. "Sorry, Mum."

"Turn it off now, alright dear? We all have a lot to do tomorrow."

She had already begun to pull the door closed when she popped her head back inside again.

"And don't forget, Sam. We have that reception at the university later in the afternoon, too. Your father and I would really like you to come along. It could mean a lot for the gallery and it will be a good chance for us to meet some new people. Promise me you'll get some sleep now. It won't be at all polite, dear, if you're yawning your head off in the middle of everything."

"Do I *have* to?"

"Yes, Samuel!" replied his mother sharply.

"Oh, alright. Yes, Mum. I promise."

As soon as the door closed, Sam pointed the miniature flashlight toward the other half of his pillow. The only thing there was the tiny, almost perfect impression of Mr. Goodfellow's body. Sam peeked underneath the pillow anxiously, praying that he had not been leaning his elbow down too heavily. But there was nothing beneath the pillow either. His heart began to race with panic until he heard a familiar voice from behind the bookcase.

"What's this I hear about a 'do' at the university, my boy?"

After he had breathed a sigh of relief, Sam explained that his parents had been invited to attend a reception and fundraising auction at the university. It was to be hosted, he thought, by the Fine Arts Department, and it had something to do with his parent's new art gallery. The fact was, the art faculty had shown some interest in working jointly on several of the exhibitions that Sam's parents were planning. Sam's parents were hoping that this event would help them to establish a presence and make some connections in town. Influential members of the community, some local politicians, and the university faculty had also been invited to the reception, along with their families. Naturally, Trevor and Peggy Middleton were anxious to make an appearance and a good first impression.

Mr. Goodfellow's dark eyes twinkled at this news.

"What a particularly fortunate turn of events, Sam!" His excitement began to grow. "You must attend with them, of course!"

Sam groaned loudly, but Mr. Goodfellow ignored this and carried on.

"When one door closes, another one opens, my boy! Free access to the university grounds is a most welcome opportunity indeed. It should be easy enough for you to slip away in such a large crowd. Then you could locate Professor Hawthorne's office for me, and you might even be able to garner some clues as to his present location. Heaven knows, I'm not having much luck here!"

Mr. Goodfellow mumbled something under his breath about messy files again and looked at Sam expectantly. He couldn't help but notice that the boy was not terribly excited. He stared off into space for a few minutes, searching for a solution. He suddenly turned back to Sam.

"I have just had a rather interesting idea, my boy, concerning your troubles. In fact, ever since you mentioned how sad you were to leave your home and backyard, I have been considering how I might be of some assistance to you. I do have extensive knowledge of the natural world. Before you leave for the reception we might have time to give that new yard of yours the once over. I'll warrant there's more to it than first met your eye. A quick search of the professor's office in return for the Goodfellow garden tour—a fair exchange, wouldn't you say?"

Sam nodded his head, but not as enthusiastically as Mr. Goodfellow would have liked. Perhaps events were moving along too quickly for him—the prospect of espionage might be distressing the lad. Mr. Goodfellow tried a different tack.

"On second thought, Sam," said Mr. Goodfellow thoughtfully, "perhaps we should both attend this reception. Yes, of course! I could travel quite comfortably in your pocket. Though I'm not used to having human help, perhaps in this case two minds are better than one." He rubbed his hands together in anticipation.

This version of events, however, which had Sam skulking around the university with a little man disguised as a mouse hiding in his pocket, failed to make the boy feel any better. Mr. Goodfellow, on the other hand, was positively beaming and Sam could not bear to disappoint him. He swallowed bravely and tried to smile.

"We're all set then," Mr. Goodfellow said enthusiastically, "the university it is, my boy! Now we really should follow your mother's sound advice and catch some winks. We can carry on with the tale another time." He let out a great, noisy yawn. "I am really much more tired than I realized."

"Hey! Wait a minute!" Sam protested, "if you expect me to help you out tomorrow, then at least you could finish telling Edgar's story!"

Sam begged and pleaded relentlessly until the little man

raised his hands to cover his ears in mock protest. He could see that the boy would not settle just yet.

"All right! All right, my boy! Against my better judgment, I will tell you one more episode. But after that, you will have to wait. Agreed?"

"Yes, yes!" said Sam. "I promise."

Thinking that he must be a truly gifted storyteller, Mr. Goodfellow suddenly found his second wind. After puffing out his chest, he graciously continued with his story.

"Shortly after I had been entrusted with young Edgar, I managed to secure a transatlantic passage for us. We soon found ourselves standing under a dock in Southampton, me with my traveling trunk and Edgar with his blue suitcase. Edgar was looking considerably neater in his freshly cleaned attire. After soaking it overnight in the chemical brew, I had hung his suit on a twig by the front door for a whole day. The river wind had dried and fluffed it back to its former self. If you looked closely you could still make out a faded red blotch on the fur front, but all in all, I considered it a job well done. And now we stood, side by side, looking up through the wooden slats of the dock to a most wondrous sight. Edgar, I believe, was quite awestruck. It was a great ship, the *R.M.S. Queen Mary*, a vision of loveliness in bright new red and black paint; her decks busy with noise and activity; her maiden voyage just hours away.

"What astonishing timing, I thought to myself. I had been reading about this ship for months, longing to go on her first crossing. Now I had the luxury of time and the perfect reason to go—the education of a young Goodfellow! What incredible luck! I was just about to emphasize our good fortune to Edgar, when..."

It hadn't taken long for Sam, eyes tight shut, to fall back into the story. As Mr. Goodfellow's words filled his imagination, Sam's reality shifted once again. The smell of engine fuel mixed with the freshness of ocean air filled his nostrils. The sound of machines and crowds and the screech of seabirds filled his ears.

5

WORSE THINGS
HAPPEN AT SEA

"Isn't the ship magnificent Edgar? I say, Edgar?" Mr. Goodfellow spun around. "Edgar! EDGAR GOODFEL-LOW! Great Heavens! Where *is* that boy?"

A group of young mice stood huddled in a corner, squeaking and chattering excitedly. In the middle of them stood Edgar, in the midst of a very animated conversation. He, like all young Sage, had been able to converse with mice since he could toddle. It was very important, a matter of survival in fact, for all Sage to be bilingual in mousespeak.

Edgar looked up upon hearing his name, said his goodbyes quickly, and made his way back to Mr. Goodfellow. The group of young mice, squeaking happily, scampered off. One of them, it appeared, was wearing Edgar's blue and red school tie.

Mr. Goodfellow looked aghast.

"Edgar, no! What were you thinking? You can't give mice those sorts of things. What if someone sees them? Really, Edgar! It would be all over the front page of one of those dreadful tabloid newspapers by the end of the week! It's a cardinal rule. No trinkets for mice!"

Edgar looked at the ground, his lip quivering.

"Now, now... it's alright, Edgar." Mr. Goodfellow gave his shoulder a pat. "It was very generous of you, I suppose. I do hope you have another tie at home."

Edgar sniffled and nodded. "Lots. Something always seems to be happening to them, so Mum keeps extras."

Mr. Goodfellow turned Edgar back in the direction of the departing mice.

"Now just run after them, my boy, and remind them..."

Edgar quickly scuttled off.

Mr. Goodfellow had to shout his last instructions.

"It's all right, but they must tell their parents. And they must remember to always wear anything like that in the privacy of their own holes!"

Edgar ran back to Mr. Goodfellow presently, a little breathless, but confident that he had conveyed to the young mice the need for absolute discretion.

They both stood now and watched as the *Queen's* mighty cranes loaded the ship's stores and provisions, and what seemed like endless mountains of bags marked ROYAL MAIL.

"It's her maiden voyage, Edgar," explained Mr. Goodfellow. "It would be quite a coup for a stamp collector somewhere to receive a letter 'postmarked at sea' on such an auspicious occasion."

Mr. Goodfellow tapped Edgar's arm.

"Ah well, no more time to waste, my boy! We should be able to easily slip onboard with all this activity about. As soon as we have boarded, we'll make a point of securing appropriate and safe accommodation."

He struggled a bit as one of his trunk's tiny wheels snagged on a stone.

"I shall have to stow this thing as soon as possible. If we could be so fortunate as to find any mice aboard..."

At that, Edgar piped up.

"The mice I was talking to said they had come down to see some relatives off to America."

"Splendid, Edgar! What excellent news! We must locate them at once."

Edgar beamed at the knowledge that he might actually have been a help to his Uncle Jolly. He happily gazed up at the grand ship. With blue suitcase tightly in hand, he was ready for adventure and eager to begin the voyage and education of a lifetime. If only he could move his feet forward. What was that tugging at his behind?

Mr. Goodfellow was far ahead of his nephew by now, still mumbling away about mice and trinkets, when he turned and called.

"Edgar! Do catch up!"

"I can't, Uncle Jolly. I . . . I think I'm stuck!"

Mr. Goodfellow sighed, then returned to examine the situation.

"It seems that someone has tied your tail to this stump of wood," he said, as he attempted to loosen it. "And they've put quite a knot in it, too! Who could have done such a thing? Surely not the mice. It's a very unmouselike thing to do."

"I don't think it was the mice, Uncle Jolly," said Edgar. "Maybe that mole that was with them came back and . . ."

Mr. Goodfellow threw his hands into the air.

"Well, that explains it! Fraternizing with moles! They're dreadful pranksters. Really Edgar, you should be more careful. I certainly hope he doesn't get hold of that tie of yours!"

He picked away at the knot.

"Please, Edgar, don't twist about so. You'll pull out all the stitching. There, I think I may have it now. You're free at last!"

Edgar uttered a quiet "thank you." His newfound

confidence had now all but melted away. Looking glum once again, he trotted obediently behind the tan trunk toward the big ship, suitcase in one hand and slightly twisted tail in the other, casting mournful glances behind him all the way.

They moved as swiftly as possible up the passenger walkway, zigzagging their way through the jumble of swinging bags and shuffling feet until they reached the great doorway that led into the ship.

"Quickly, Edgar!" Mr. Goodfellow urged. "We mustn't stay out in the open like this for too long. It's far too risky."

"Coming Uncle Jolly...coming," panted Edgar. His feet were becoming hot and sore inside their two furry mouse shoes, and his blue suitcase felt much heavier than when they had first left home.

They stopped a moment to catch their breaths, then darted down a hallway.

"I did have the opportunity to study some interior plans of the ship that recently appeared in the press. If I'm not mistaken, Edgar, this corridor leads to a stairwell that will take us down to the service areas. I suspect we will find the mouse passengers there."

Which indeed they soon did. As is usually the case with mice, they were received most warmly and with great excitement and flourish. Since food was an almost obsessive concern in the mouse world, the two newcomers were immediately led to view a vast array of edible items. All of the food had been proudly laid out on a red cloth napkin.

"Been exploring the kitchens, I see," said Mr. Goodfellow.

The mice smiled and nodded in unison.

"Well, it looks like an unparalleled feast!" he continued.

One of the mice took Mr. Goodfellow aside and began chattering in the very animated manner that mice are known for.

Mr. Goodfellow returned to Edgar.

"The mice have very kindly invited us to dine with them, Edgar, but I have politely declined—for this evening at least."

Edgar could not hide his disappointment. He had been fighting off hunger pangs all day.

"But, Uncle Jolly," he whined.

"Now, now, it's not everyday that one gets a chance to sail on the maiden voyage of such an impressive vessel, Edgar. I have a plan. There is a small element of risk involved, but I think that with a little care we can pull it off. Such a rare opportunity is rather hard to resist. It's the Captain's table for us tonight, my boy!"

Oh, well, that sounded all right, thought Edgar. He did not even try to imagine how his uncle was going to arrange it. Mr. Goodfellow wheeled his trunk into a quiet corner and set it down. He placed Edgar's blue suitcase squarely on top.

"Well, Edgar, we have a comfortable spot to set up our cots and the company of kind creatures. I'd say we've made quite a good start!"

There was a sudden blast from the *Queen Mary's* whistles and an announcer's voice was heard crackling over the ship's loudspeakers. "All ashore that's going ashore!"

Mr. Goodfellow's eyes twinkled.

"That's it, Edgar! We're off!"

A little while later, the ship jerked slightly and the sound of cheering could be heard in the distance.

A few moments after that, Edgar's face began to turn a rather unusual shade of green.

"Uncle Jolly, I don't feel so well."

"But we've not even left the dock yet, Edgar!"

Edgar groaned and swayed.

"Nonsense, my boy! It's all in the mind you know!"

Mr. Goodfellow had not wanted to return to the crowded decks so soon, but Edgar's "mal-de-mer" was beginning to visibly worsen.

"We'll have to get you out into the fresh air for a few deep breaths—until you get your sea legs!"

He took Edgar's arm to steady him, and led the way back up through the maze of ship's corridors and finally out onto one of the vast teak decks.

"Follow me, Edgar. I believe I know a place where we might rest safely."

They darted from post to post, under stairwells and into cubbyholes, finally scrambling up a huge davit that secured one of the many lifeboats hanging above the sundeck. Then they leapt down from their perch and landed on the lifeboat's canvas cover. This covering, tightly stretched across the top of the lifeboat, acted like a gigantic trampoline and Mr. Goodfellow and Edgar bounced up and down several times before they were able to regain their footing. This was of no help to Edgar's condition, of course, and he staggered about until Mr. Goodfellow caught him and helped him duck beneath the lifeboat's cover. There they were able to snuggle down, popping only their mouse heads out to view the start of their grand journey. Mr. Goodfellow convinced Edgar to keep his eyes fixed on the distant horizon and he soon began to feel less queasy.

From their position high above the deck, Edgar and Mr. Goodfellow now had front row seats to a magnificent show. Though he would never tell the boy, Mr. Goodfellow was secretly delighted that Edgar's unsteady stomach had caused them to ignore the risk of discovery and return topside.

Hundreds of little boats surrounded the huge liner, escorting her downriver to the vast ocean beyond. Several airplanes circled overhead, while on the dock, well-wishers by the thousands pushed forward to get a closer look. A marine band next to the spectators played a rousing rendition of "Rule Britannia." Many of the almost 2,000 passengers had crowded onto the *Queen*'s decks, waving and cheering as the great ship pulled away.

All the excitement had succeeded in taking Edgar's mind off his turbulent stomach, and he settled down comfortably to watch the proceedings. As the music of the marine band faded into the distance, the ship's orchestra, which had been tuning up at the stern, started to play.

Edgar dozed off. It had been a long and tiring day. When he awoke sometime later and peered out again, he was sure that he could see land up ahead. He rubbed his eyes in disbelief, but the figure sitting quietly beside him had seen it too.

"It must be Cherbourg, Edgar. We've crossed the channel to France. I expect we'll pick up a few more passengers there and then it's out to sea again and on to New York!"

Mr. Goodfellow inched forward and squeezed his body out from under the lifeboat's canvas top. He held up the edge and waited for Edgar to shuffle out.

"We really should be getting back to our quarters now, my boy."

Edgar and Mr. Goodfellow carefully made their way down through the ship again and to the safety of the mouse encampment below. Their new traveling companions, sitting excitedly around a red napkin, had wasted no time tucking into a massive feast. They raised their heads for a second and exchanged a hearty greeting with the newcomers.

Mr. Goodfellow walked directly to his trunk and began to unlock it.

"Come, Edgar. We must dress for dinner."

Thoughts of food still made Edgar's stomach lurch, but he offered a brave smile anyway. Mr. Goodfellow sorted through his row of mouse suits then removed the most beautiful formal attire that Edgar had ever seen. It was shimmering black fur, with white chest and cuffs. Edgar sighed with admiration. He was speechless, however, when Mr. Goodfellow reached into the trunk again and took out an identical suit in what appeared to be Edgar's very own size.

"Do please try to keep it clean, my boy. It has rather a sentimental value. It was given to me by my Granddad (your Great Granddad), when I was not much older than you, on the occasion of my own apprenticeship. I have kept it all these many years."

Edgar stepped out of his own light brown suit and nervously reached for the elegant black one. He struggled with the row of pearl buttons that ran up the front. The paws attached to the coat with another row of buttons and, at this, he was forced to call for assistance. Mr. Goodfellow obliged and then turned him round and round, smoothing the sleek black fur as Edgar twirled. Somewhat dizzy from the motion, Edgar swooned momentarily, but Mr. Goodfellow stepped forward to catch him.

"There you go, my boy. My goodness Edgar, what a transformation!"

It seemed to Edgar that his uncle was going to an extraordinary amount of trouble dressing them up in suits that no one else (apart from the mice, of course) were supposed to see. The mice, who were crowding about him, were lavishly praising Edgar's transformation, and it was beginning to make him feel rather uncomfortable. But when he saw his reflection in the trunk's gilt-framed oval mirror, Edgar was overwhelmed by his appearance. The image that stared back at him was completely different from his own familiar, rather sloppy exterior. This Edgar looked older, self-assured, even handsome. He was thrilled.

"Thank you, Uncle Jolly."

"Don't mention it, my boy," said Mr. Goodfellow as he did up the last few buttons of his cuffs.

"There, we're all set."

Together, they stood before the mirror.

"Aren't we a grand pair?"

Mr. Goodfellow suddenly ran back to his trunk.

"Just one last thing, Edgar!"

He searched through his closet, eventually removing a tube-shaped canvas sack (labeled Dining Supplies) that he slung over his shoulder. He beckoned to his nephew and, once again, they were on their way, back up through the layers of ship.

Mr. Goodfellow had plotted out the safest route to the First Class Dining Room. When they reached the huge carved doors that led inside, they peeped through to the massive room where bustling crew members were preparing dozens of round tables with an assortment of china and cutlery.

Mr. Goodfellow and Edgar made their grand entrance into the dining room on the bottom shelf of a silver serving cart, hidden within the folds of two swan-shaped napkins. As they approached the Captain's table, which was set slightly apart from the others, Mr. Goodfellow whispered instructions to roll when the cart came to a stop beside it. They tumbled out from under the cover of the napkins to a cover of another sort—a big, white tablecloth, its crisp folds cascading over the table's edge and down to the floor. Once safely hidden beneath the billowing cloth, it was as though they had entered a huge circus tent. They made their way to the center of the floor, where Mr. Goodfellow removed a small folding table and two matching chairs from the canvas sack upon his back. He then unrolled a white tablecloth of his own which held a selection of cutlery, plates, napkins, and cups and, for added effect, a miniature vase of colorful paper flowers. After he had finished setting their places, Mr. Goodfellow removed one last item from his sack. It was, to Edgar's surprise, a collapsible fishing rod complete with line, reel, and a curious looking three-pronged hook. Edgar had no idea what this rod was doing amidst Mr. Goodfellow's dining supplies, unless his uncle was intending to engage in a spot of after dinner fishing from one of the decks. He was slightly concerned at the thought of Mr. Goodfellow matching his strength against the sizeable fish in these waters.

"And now, Edgar," said Mr. Goodfellow, carefully propping the fishing rod against the edge of the table, "we sit back and await an evening of world-class cuisine, set in an atmosphere of truly regal elegance."

Edgar sat down in anticipation, his black paws clasped tightly in his lap. By now, his tummy had settled down enough to actually welcome a bit of food.

The clinking of glasses and cutlery finally faded away. A few moments later the sound of footsteps and excited chatter would break the silence. The head table diners, handpicked by the Captain, were soon seated with appropriate ceremony. Shiny black shoes and tuxedo legs, long elegant ballgowns and satin pumps all took their place around two considerably smaller, but equally well-attired dinner guests. Beautiful wraps and beaded evening bags were slung over chairs. Then the Captain himself, in full dress uniform, arrived and the sumptuous affair began.

An endless line of serving carts, filled with a variety of

exquisite morsels, pushed past the hidden diners. As each cart stopped, Mr. Goodfellow cast his fishing rod from beneath the tablecloth and hooked an assortment of treats from the bottom shelves. He then reeled in the fare and placed it on his and Edgar's plates. Edgar was delighted. It was a wonderful and most satisfying meal.

When he felt that he couldn't possibly manage another bite, Mr. Goodfellow leaned back on his chair, loosened a couple of pearl buttons, patted his stomach, and sighed. It was a sigh not only of contentment, but of relief, too. The evening had gone without a hitch.

Facing Edgar, but behind Mr. Goodfellow's back, a lovely beaded evening bag had slipped from its mooring and snapped open as it tumbled to the floor. A bright, sparkly and very familiar flash of red immediately caught Edgar's eye. Shimmering before him was a large, red candy, his favorite kind: shiny, sticky, and very, very close. Now, Edgar was not a disobedient or reckless boy. He was, admittedly, prone to accidents, but he was generally thoughtful and eager to please. When it came to candies, however, Edgar Goodfellow lost all reason. He could not steal his eyes away from the crinkly wrapper and the sparkling red orb within it. He looked at Mr. Goodfellow, but his eyes had closed. Edgar slipped from his chair and sidled up to the bag. Reaching in, he gave the sweetie a little tap. He would try to knock a tiny, unnoticeable piece of it off. He pushed his paw beneath the crinkled wrapping, but the candy suddenly dislodged itself and fell further down into the depths of the bag. Edgar pulled the bag open a little more, glanced back at his snoozing uncle, then gingerly climbed in to retrieve his prize. There was a snapping sound and Edgar found himself enclosed by darkness. At the same time, Mr. Goodfellow was jolted from his catnap. He turned

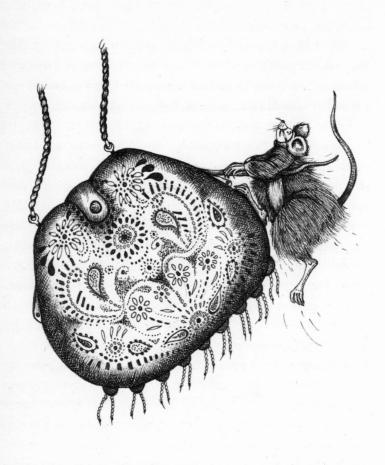

around just in time to see a large hand clutching a glittering, purple evening bag as it was lifted from the dining room floor, a pink tail hanging between its metal clasps.

He spun around.

"Edgar! Edgar!" he whispered frantically.

In the split second that followed, Mr. Goodfellow lunged for the trailing appendage, tugging and pulling at it until he fell backward with a thump. The evening bag disappeared and Mr. Goodfellow sat alone and bewildered on the floor, holding onto the remnants of Edgar's tail, broken stitches and all.

What on earth had that boy been up to? The gravity of the situation was only just beginning to sink in. The face of Mr. Goodfellow's dear brother Filbert flashed before him. And what would he say to Hazel? She would never survive the news! Oh, this was just too dreadful!

He ran to the edge of the table and peered out from beneath the cloth, to assess the situation. The evening bag, hanging over the arm of a rather large woman dressed in flowing purple was presently floating out through the dining room doors. Tossing caution to the wind, Mr. Goodfellow flung himself onto a passing dessert cart, crouching between a baked apple and a slice of meringue torte. Suddenly, the dessert cart changed direction, turning down one hallway as the evening bag sailed off down another. Mr. Goodfellow waited for his chance, then rolled off the cart and into the temporary safety of a four-inch doorframe. Never letting himself lose sight of the swinging bag, he began to dart skillfully from doorway to doorway, then down a grand staircase and along a very long passageway, until, thankfully, the bag's owner finally stopped at one of the First Class stateroom doors.

As the door opened, Mr. Goodfellow raced between two large feet and into the room. He scurried across the floor and under one of the single beds. As he sat down to catch his breath, he heard the sound of the door closing and locking behind him. There was a faint clicking noise too, and the room was immediately illuminated. From his vantage point, Mr. Goodfellow watched as chubby ankles in purple satin pumps made their way back and forth across the room. Then they disappeared altogether. The mattress springs groaned and sagged above his head. He waited, hardly daring to breathe, until the steady sound of snoring began to fill the air. Then, carefully lifting the draped bed skirt, he poked his nose out and scanned the room. No sign of the evening bag. Tiptoeing out into the open, Mr. Goodfellow scrambled up an oversized chair to afford himself a better look. Ah! The evening bag was perched precariously near the edge of the bed, wiggling ever so slightly. Well, at least the lad is still moving, thought Mr. Goodfellow.

The bag crept closer to the edge of the bed. Finally it plunged over the crest, hit the floor and snapped open. The sudden thud had roused the lady from her after dinner nap. Mr. Goodfellow shot over the arm of the chair while a dazed Edgar tumbled from the bag and ran for cover. When they encountered each other beneath a writing desk, Mr. Goodfellow grabbed the boy and gave him an emotional squeeze.

"Oh, Edgar. I thought I'd lost you for good! Here, let me look at you, my boy!"

He released him from his grip and took him by the shoulders. Edgar's mouse mask and whiskers were encrusted with a sticky red goo.

Mr. Goodfellow shot his nephew a disapproving glance.

"Well, I see that you managed to keep yourself busy for the duration of your imprisonment, while I risked life and limb!"

"But, Uncle Jolly, I was hungry."

"Hungry! Good gracious, Edgar! You've just finished a seven-course meal!"

"Well, I *was* hungry. But, right now I feel a bit sick again."

Mr. Goodfellow shook his head as he took a handkerchief from under his suit and began to clean Edgar's face.

"Well, at least you are safe and sound, my boy. That's the important thing." He glanced down at Edgar's eveningwear. "And the suit doesn't look too worse for wear either, considering the time it has spent trapped in a lady's evening bag."

"Yes, I tried to be careful," replied Edgar, nodding earnestly.

(It would be much later, while Mr. Goodfellow was smoothing down the lovely black fur and preparing to reattach the tail, that he would cringe in horror at the sight of a very large and very red makeup stain on Edgar's suit bottom.)

There was a loud yawning noise and a great creak of the mattress as two purple-pumped feet suddenly swung from the bed and hit the ground. Edgar and Mr. Goodfellow retreated further into the shadows beneath the desk. After flinging off the purple pumps, one of which landed dangerously close to Edgar, two large stockinged feet stumbled across the floor and into the bathroom, where a continuing stream of yawns was soon accompanied by the sound of running water.

Mr. Goodfellow began to ponder how he and Edgar might escape from the locked stateroom. It would be a challenge, considering that there were no mouse holes about. He was still deep in thought when the lady returned and began to sort through her luggage.

Mr. Goodfellow's eyebrows suddenly arched in revelation. "Come quickly Edgar! Follow me! An intriguing idea has come to mind and I think it just might work!"

Mr. Goodfellow raced into the bathroom, with Edgar close at his heels.

"Now if I recall the ship's plans correctly, each of these bathrooms is equipped with a panel next to the tub. I believe that the red button summons a steward and the green one, a stewardess."

Edgar looked confused.

"I know that it may seem rather odd, my boy, but first class passengers are quite used to, and indeed expect, assistance with their bathing."

Edgar wrinkled his mouse nose.

"In any case, Edgar, this may well be our way out of this predicament."

He looked behind them. The large purple lady was occupied with her wardrobe.

"Climb up onto my shoulders, Edgar. Reach up and give the green button a push, my boy!"

Edgar struggled onto Mr. Goodfellow's back, his clawed feet digging into his uncle's shoulders. Mr. Goodfellow wobbled under the strain of Edgar's weight.

"Hurry, my boy...hurry!" he croaked.

Edgar obliged, stretching his furry arm up as far as it would go.

"Did you push it, Edgar?"

"Yes, Uncle Jolly. I've pushed it. The red one."

"Edgar, no! I distinctly said green!"

Mr. Goodfellow wobbled more uncontrollably now and the two suddenly descended into a furry ball of black and white fur, four arms, four legs, and one tail. After untangling themselves, they dashed out of the bathroom and back to the relative safety of the writing desk. It was not a moment too soon either, as the lady, now clad in a blue silk robe, strolled back into the bathroom and closed the door firmly behind her.

Mr. Goodfellow and Edgar crouched by the stateroom door and waited. Soon the sounds of swishing and splashing began to emanate from the bathroom. At the same time, heavy footsteps approached from outside the room.

"Get ready, Edgar. This window of opportunity will be a small one indeed."

The door was unlocked and a young man, carrying an armful of fluffy white towels, entered the room. He walked to the bathroom door and began to turn the knob.

"Steward, sir. May I assist you?"

"Now Edgar! Run!"

Edgar scurried behind his uncle and out the open door to freedom. They were halfway down the passageway before the sound of an ear-piercing scream reached them, but even then they did not stop until they had safely arrived back at their mouse haven.

After he had related the tale of their dining escapades to the astonishment and admiration of the attending mice, Mr. Goodfellow excused himself and retired to his trunk for the evening. Edgar, however, had become quite popular among the younger mouse set. Chattering and squeaking, they danced about him excitedly, then lined up for piggyback rides. And although they tugged and pulled at his hair and clothes repeatedly, Edgar never lost his patience once. He reached into his pockets and distributed tiny pieces of red candy to each one of them. When they demanded a story, he managed to somehow gather them all at his feet with barely a whisper between them.

Mr. Goodfellow, sorting through his trunk, watched from a distance. Without a doubt, the boy was a calamity waiting to happen, but he did possess some unusual qualities. Mr. Goodfellow rummaged a little more, then removed some paper, a box of paints, scissors, and a tiny bottle of glue. When he glanced up again, he couldn't help but smile. Edgar was making shadow puppets in the half-light to the enchantment of his audience.

Barely lifting his head for the next half an hour or so, Mr. Goodfellow sat on a little stool at his trunk—painting, cutting, and gluing. He finally looked up, waved an arm, and called out across the room.

"Edgar, over here! I have something rather interesting to show you."

Edgar stood up and left his band of admirers squealing in delight as they tried to make their own shadow puppets on the wall.

Mr. Goodfellow was standing next to his trunk when Edgar approached, patting something down with his hand. He stood aside and proudly displayed a new, freshly painted sticker. It was oval in shape, with the words *R.M.S. Queen Mary* at the top and the ship's image at the center. It was quite a reasonable likeness of the much larger stickers that adorned the trunks and suitcases of the paying passengers.

"I do believe I have captured this one rather well. What do you think, my boy?"

"It's very nice," said Edgar softly.

"Well, then, I have a surprise for you. Wait until you see this!"

Mr. Goodfellow bent down and reached behind his trunk. When he popped back up again, he had Edgar's blue suitcase in his hand. There was one freshly painted sticker right in the middle.

Mr. Goodfellow beamed. Edgar looked sadly at the floor.

"Don't worry, my boy. It may not look like much right now, but before long, it will be festooned with stickers from your adventures all over..."

He let his words trail off. Edgar looked even more distressed.

"What is it, Edgar? Are you feeling ill again?"

Edgar quickly wiped a sleeve across his eyes and shook his head.

"Well, what on earth is it then, my boy?"

Edgar looked up.

"I just know I'll never be any good at this, not ever. Not like you, Uncle Jolly."

"Nonsense, my boy! You're a Goodfellow, remember? It's one of the finest pedigrees around. All you need is practice and some time to adapt. You've had an unsteady start, that's all."

Edgar hesitated.

"But, well, it's not just that, Uncle Jolly. I don't think I like traveling. I keep feeling sick and my head hurts and I make mistakes all the time, and..." He clasped his hands together and took a deep breath, "and, I want to go home," he announced.

Mr. Goodfellow gasped.

"There, there, my boy! No need to be so dramatic. It will all turn out right in the end. When we reach dry land, you'll feel much better about things, I'll wager."

Mr. Goodfellow was determined not to let this setback defeat him. Edgar had become his mission. He'd show those scheming uncles and cousins of his. He would bring back a polished, refined and capable young man, worthy of carrying on the Goodfellow tradition—if it was the last thing he did.

"Stiff upper lip! Right, Edgar?"

Mr. Goodfellow gave his nephew a comforting pat on the back. Edgar did his best to look reassured. But later that night, as his uncle snored peacefully, he lay awake upon his cot. Under a blanket of darkness, and as quietly as he possibly could, Edgar cried himself to sleep.

The next couple of days brought an abundance of fog that slowed the crossing somewhat. This was disappointing news for those on board who were eager to see the *Queen* take the Blue Riband trophy for fastest Atlantic crossing on her maiden voyage. It was rather welcome news to Edgar and Mr. Goodfellow, however, as it provided them with more opportunities for outings up on deck. The brisk, fresh air was also a great help in subduing Edgar's occasional bouts of malaise. It was a break for Edgar, too, from the continual attention of his adoring mouse fans. Mr. Goodfellow was pleased by Edgar's popularity. He had never seen a young lad show as much patience and kindness to such demanding creatures. He could certainly teach his great uncles and cousins a thing or two about tolerance. The best thing of all about the cover of fog, though, was that it afforded the opportunity to partake in one of the greatest of ocean liner rituals (and a particular favorite of Mr. Goodfellow's): afternoon tea. At precisely 1600 hours, stewards began to maneuver down the long decks, holding tiered plates in both hands, each brimming with delicious looking teacakes and sandwiches.

"How absolutely delightful, Edgar," whispered Mr. Goodfellow, as the two huddled in the fog beneath a deck chair, helping themselves to the tasty morsels parading by.

Mr. Goodfellow was in his element. He was so tickled, in fact, that he hardly flinched when Edgar, failing once again to properly fasten his appendages, lost a paw inside a passing cucumber and cheese sandwich. Thank goodness his mother had thought to pack several spare paws in the event of just such an occurrence.

When they had both had their fill of treats, Mr. Goodfellow announced that it was time to make their way back below deck. Edgar turned to take one last look through the fog and noticed that the purple lady from the First Class Dining Room had been sitting in the deck chair above their heads during their whole tea. He was just about to point this coincidence out to his uncle when he observed her plump hand reaching for the furry paw, cucumber and cheese sandwich. Edgar turned sharply and ran instead.

"Wait for me, Uncle Jolly!"

Considering the events that had surrounded their first supper at sea, Mr. Goodfellow decided to play it safe and dine as guests of the mice for the remainder of the voyage. On their final evening onboard, they were treated to a particularly wonderful feast. Mr. Goodfellow couldn't begin to imagine how they had gotten their paws on the exquisite chocolate truffles that were left by the stewards each night on the First Class passenger pillows, but he decided not to make inquiries. After all, everyone was having a delightful time and it was a fitting farewell for both Goodfellow and mouse.

In his ongoing attempt to be more flexible and sensitive with Edgar, Mr. Goodfellow had allowed the boy to borrow his beloved paintbox and supplies after their last dinner. Surrounded by his admirers, Edgar set about doing mouse portraits for his friends. The mice then ran off with the rolls of paper under their arms, promising Edgar faithfully that they would only display them in their rooms at home. When Mr. Goodfellow finished conversing with the elder mice, he walked over to watch the young artist at work. He was taken aback when he saw Edgar's beautiful paintings.

"These are absolutely amazing, my boy! You have quite a talent!"

Edgar smiled shyly and grew a deep shade of pink.

"I really like to draw and paint, Uncle Jolly."

"Yes, I can see that you do."

In fact, Mr. Goodfellow was astonished at Edgar's skill. He was loath to admit it, but it made his own artistic attempts look decidedly amateurish. This was, indeed, a lad of unusual talents.

6

EVERY CLOUD HAS A
SILVER LINING

Mr. Goodfellow paused for breath. His mouth had become parched, too. Giant cups of tea were dancing in his head. When the faint whisper of his voice suddenly stopped, Sam was jolted back to reality. The little man leaned over toward him.

"Do you like the story so far, my boy?"

Sam was silent at first, his mind a bit fuzzy. But slowly his thoughts slipped back to reality and he began to babble excitedly.

"It's fantastic! It's just like being there!"

Mr. Goodfellow was flattered.

"Well, I'm glad you're enjoying it, my boy."

"Please, don't stop right now. Keep telling the story!" Sam implored.

"Well, all right, but I was hoping we could have a spot of...oh, never, mind."

Mr. Goodfellow reached into his shirt pocket and pulled out a tiny pocketwatch.

"Good heavens, my boy! It's almost 2:30 in the morning! Have I been talking this long? This will never do, you know.

Neither of us will be of any use at the reception tomorrow at this rate—we've got to get some sleep!"

With that, Mr. Goodfellow patted the pillow beneath him, beckoning Sam to lay his head down once again. Then he rolled himself off and onto the floor. Sam heaved a disappointed sigh at Mr. Goodfellow's retreating figure.

Mr. Goodfellow returned to his trunk and opened up the third drawer. He took out a folded canvas camp cot, which had a red flannel nightshirt tucked inside, and made preparations to settle down for the night. Before lying down on his cot, he removed the tiny journal and fountain pen from the second drawer of his trunk and spent a few moments putting his thoughts on paper.

Though disappointed, Sam also tried to settle down. The faint scratching of Mr. Goodfellow's fountain pen floated up from behind the bookcase. He would have given anything to know what the little man was writing. Sam couldn't help but feel that some of the words must be about him. Mr. Goodfellow popped his head up now and then and gave Sam some rather thoughtful looks. Sam struggled to keep his eyes open, but the continual tapping of Mr. Goodfellow's pen had a hypnotic quality to it, and soon his thoughts came to a standstill as sleep overcame him.

Golden beams of sunlight were streaming onto the floor of the empty bedroom by the time Sam began to stir again. It was almost 9:30 in the morning. Out of the corner of his eye Sam could just glimpse the edge of the miniature traveling trunk from beneath the bookcase. His nighttime adventure had not been a dream after all. A voice suddenly called out to him.

"The full moon brings fair weather, Sam. It's a glorious morning."

Mr. Goodfellow, who was methodical about his personal grooming, had been up for some time already. He had washed, shaved, dressed, brushed his hair and moustache thoroughly, and was at that moment neatly rolling his nightshirt back into the folds of his portable cot.

"Come, on, Sam, my boy! Let's get out into this wonderful day. I promised to help you explore that new garden of yours, remember?"

"But the Edgar story," Sam pleaded.

"Later, I promise. Anyway, I believe we have a full day ahead of us. You haven't forgotten our other plans, have you?"

"Oh, *great*," said Sam, as recollection flooded back to him. "That thing at the university."

"Look on it as an opportunity for adventure, Sam, as will our foray into the wilds be, if you'd only get yourself moving. I'll wager I can show you things you never even imagined were there. You can't always judge a book by its cover, you know. Just give me a moment to finish preparing. Let's see, I think I'll wear the field mouse this morning," he said, and he began to rummage through his closet.

That flat, boring yard that stretched out from behind the new house was hardly "the wilds," thought Sam. But Sam supposed that it wouldn't hurt to go along and see what Mr. Goodfellow had to show him. Once they were both ready, Sam picked him up and, on the little man's instructions, slipped him into his shirt pocket.

"Are you all right in there?" asked Sam, concerned that Mr. Goodfellow might be a bit cramped.

"Quite all right, my boy," he replied as he shuffled himself around in an attempt to find the most comfortable position. "Actually, these accommodations are luxurious compared to some of the ways I have been forced to travel in the past. One has to be adaptable in this line of work, you know. A fair number of drafty musical instrument cases come to mind, along with some shipping crates, paintboxes, saddlebags, and the occasional beast of burden. I remember one mountain journey in particular where I spent the better part of a week clinging to an elephant tusk. Lovely creature as I recall, and quite the conversationalist, but the constant dust and interminable swaying were most distressing. Had Edgar been along, he would have been inconsolable!"

Sam was just about to open his bedroom door when the sound of gentle tapping drew him over to the room's window. Tiny droplets of water were trickling slowly down the surface of the windowpane. It couldn't possibly be rain, the sun was still shining. Mr. Goodfellow popped his head out of Sam's pocket.

"A sun shower," he proclaimed. "How delightful!"

"It's raining," groaned Sam. "I can't believe it."

Sam turned his back to the window and slid down the wall to the floor.

"Stupid weather—now we can't go in the garden."

"Nonsense, my boy! I'm going to have to teach you a thing or two about looking on the bright side of things. Every cloud has a silver lining, Sam, and this cloud is going to make that garden of yours a veritable paradise. There's nothing like a spot of water to liven things up a bit. It makes things brighter, richer, and fresher. It's the essence of life itself, isn't it? The scientist in you should know that, Sam."

"I guess so," Sam said slowly.

"That's the spirit, my boy. The rain will pass soon enough and then we'll see nature in all her glory. I don't suppose that until then you'd care to discover what Edgar's been up to?"

"You bet I would!" said Sam, his eyes lighting up.

Sam dashed across the floor, with Mr. Goodfellow clinging to the rim of his shirt pocket, and dove into his sleeping bag. Taking a moment to gather his thoughts and accept an apology from Sam for the overly bumpy nature of his journey across the room, Mr. Goodfellow picked up Edgar's story where he had left off.

Nestled in the folds of his sleeping bag, atop the wooden floor of his empty bedroom, Sam was transported back onto the deck of the *Queen Mary*, lulled once again by the gentle sound of Mr. Goodfellow's words.

"Our last day at sea was the first of June. The *Queen Mary*'s historic arrival in New York harbor was heralded long before any sighting of land. Several hours before we were to dock, when the ship was still a considerable distance out to sea, we heard the sound of an airplane circling overhead. Passengers were informed over the ship's loudspeakers that an aircraft piloted by World War I flying ace Eddie Rickenbacker, known more intimately to my cousin Hamish, I believe, and carrying a contingent of photographers and newsmen, had arrived to welcome us all to America.

"As there was still a lingering fog about, Edgar and I were able to make our way back to the deck to watch. On one of the plane's passes, the cargo doors suddenly opened and thousands of white carnations floated down onto the ship. The *Queen Mary*'s elegant teak decks were awash with fragrant blossoms. Edgar complained when one of them landed on top of his head and dislodged his mouse mask—but it gave me a wonderful idea. Holding carnations above us, we were able to move freely about the ship. Gusts of wind occasionally shifted the flowers so we looked like two more blossoms in a great moving bouquet. We remained topside for the rest of the approach to New York."

If it was true that it took a good teller *and* a good listener to make a good story, then Mr. Goodfellow had found in Sam the perfect partner. Hanging on to every word, Sam felt as though he, too, was mingling with the excited passengers on the deck of the *Queen Mary*. He imagined he could smell a combination of coffee and roasted peanuts, mixing with the sweet scent of carnations, and hear a steady hum of people and machines. Unfathomable shapes loomed out of the mist, becoming more familiar as they drew nearer. They sailed past the Statue of Liberty and up the Hudson River. Flotillas of boats surrounded them and planes circled overhead. The ship's orchestra had appeared on deck once again, this time playing a song composed especially for the end of the voyage. Other bands, from smaller boats that had pulled alongside, played their own musical salutes as the *Queen* made her way to Pier 90. Across her decks and down the companionways, a stream of passengers flowed out of the ocean liner. The excitement of arriving in New York City was electric and Sam felt, at that moment, that he could reach out and touch it.

7

TAKE HEED OF THE WORDS

OF THE WISE

Taking advantage of the flurry of activities that followed the ship's arrival, Edgar, Mr. Goodfellow, and all of the mice aboard gathered their belongings and disembarked. They quickly made their way to the safety of the world beneath the docks. Mouse relatives were on hand to greet the travelers. It was a touching scene. Mice can be quite emotional, as Edgar had recently learned, especially at reunions and farewells. When it came time for Edgar and Mr. Goodfellow to bid adieu to their traveling companions, there was a great flood of tears. Clutching their souvenir portraits, the younger mice hugged Edgar relentlessly. It did calm them down somewhat when he promised to look them up for a visit once he returned home.

The members of the American branch of the mouse family were particularly honored to make Mr. Goodfellow's acquaintance. His reputation had preceded him. They mentioned that some close mouse friends were presently hosting two Sage under Grand Central Station. Mr. Goodfellow was delighted to hear this news, as it was not all that common to cross paths with others of their kind. It could be a grand opportunity for the socialization of young Edgar. The mice believed that the guests had been preparing to leave New York shortly. Where they were headed was not known, but if Mr. Goodfellow and his nephew hurried, they might be able to catch them.

After determining the fastest route to Grand Central Station, Edgar and Mr. Goodfellow soon found themselves on a street corner by the pier, huddled beneath two wilted carnations. This proved to be a rather brilliant disguise as the white flowers had managed to find their way everywhere. They languished in bunches atop carrier bags, poked out from lapels, hats, and hairdos, while others could be found floating tranquilly along the waterfront. Mr. Goodfellow, watching and listening carefully, peered up through the frilly petals at the people around him.

"We must pick just the right one, Edgar," he whispered, as he scanned the crowd.

A man with a train ticket tucked in his jacket pocket moved in next to them on the pavement.

"This may be it, Edgar. Get ready, my boy!"

"Taxi! Taxi!" shouted the man, leaning into the street and waving his arms about wildly.

Mr. Goodfellow gave Edgar a gentle nudge when a big automobile pulled up sharply. While the man climbed inside, and the driver loaded his luggage, Mr. Goodfellow grabbed hold of Edgar's arm and, under their floral umbrellas, shuffled toward the rear bumper. A large grill with a spare tire upon it loomed over their heads. Edgar, blue suitcase in hand, jumped aboard first with a rope around his waist that was tied tightly to his uncle's trunk. Mr. Goodfellow followed and then, looping the rope through the automobile's metal grill, they pulled the trunk up beside them. As the taxi pulled away from the curb, the crowd may have observed a pair of dusty white carnations, sitting snugly within the rim of the spare tire. As the taxi navigated its way through the city streets, Edgar and Mr. Goodfellow made themselves as comfortable as possible.

"Just lean back and enjoy the magnificent view, Edgar, my boy," said Mr. Goodfellow, cradling his head in his furry paws as he gazed up. Tall buildings of stone and glass towered above them.

But Edgar, of course, was not content to do this. There was too much to see at street level. There were more people and cars than Edgar had ever seen before, not to mention buses and pushcart vendors. The latter were of particular interest to Edgar. Loaded with roasted corn and chestnuts, baked potatoes and frankfurters, lemonade and (dare he dream it) candy, they were almost irresistible. He leaned forward to take a closer look.

"I really think you should refrain from leaning out so, Edgar," warned his uncle. "These vehicles do have a reputation for erratic behavior."

But it was too late. Since leaving the docks, the taxi had been steadily accelerating. It now began to move at an alarming speed, weaving between vehicles and pedestrians. Edgar felt his feet lifting off the tire just as he grabbed for the metal grill. The taxi then made a wide turn and Edgar, still clutching the grill, suddenly swung out behind it. Mr. Goodfellow sprang to his assistance.

"Hang on, my boy!" he cried, trying vainly to pull him back in by his mouse ears and praying that once, just this once, Edgar had remembered to fasten his paws securely.

When the taxi came to a screeching halt at the train station, Edgar finally lost his grip on the grill and tumbled to the ground below. Dusty and bedraggled, his mouse mask pushed crookedly to one side of his head and pieces of carnation

welded to his fur, Edgar staggered away, unaware that he had just been introduced to one of the city's more colorful features—the heart-stopping New York cab ride.

After hurriedly composing themselves beneath the taxicab, Edgar and Mr. Goodfellow quickly made their way to the safety of the train station's dark recesses. The mice at the docks had provided Mr. Goodfellow with detailed directions and they were soon able to locate the home of the station mice. They were welcomed with open arms, as is the way with mice of course, and immediately invited to set up their cots and make themselves at home. Their other visitors, they explained, had decided to stay on for an extra day or two to see a bit of the city, but were expected back at any moment. Mr. Goodfellow took the time to tidy up his trunk and Edgar was happy to rest quietly on his cot after all the excitement. Mr. Goodfellow, searching through his closet for a coat hanger, was just preparing to remove his mouse suit when he heard the sound of footsteps.

He looked up to see a figure coming towards him through the long dark tunnel. He was suddenly struck by the way it moved, a strange gait that seemed to float from side to side. It was an ancient memory, but he knew that walk. Of course, Beatrice Elderberry! He hadn't seen her for years. Never in his wildest dreams would he have imagined that he would meet her again.

Beatrice Elderberry was the only daughter of Branston and Bronwen Elderberry. She had been adored and indulged as a child, the apple of her father's eye. The Goodfellows and Elderberrys had been neighbors for many years and their children had played together. After apprenticing with her father in Europe, Beatrice had staked out a modest career for herself, taking on a number of small but varied assignments throughout the world. She had always been a headstrong, romantic girl—stubborn, carefree, and a bit inclined to frivolity. In fact, she was everything that Mr. Goodfellow was not. She was far too flouncy, flighty, and opinionated, and though he would never admit it to anyone, he had loved her, hopelessly and completely, since they had both been seven.

Mr. Goodfellow felt the blood rush to his face and his hands immediately began to tremble inside his suit as she drew closer. He put a paw on his waist in what he hoped was a debonair pose, and smiled. Just at that moment, his two protruding mouse teeth loosened and dropped noisily to the ground.

"Confound these things!" he whispered.

He was down on his hands and knees, fumbling around for the wayward teeth when a soft, familiar voice addressed him.

"It can't be!"

He froze, then looked up in embarrassment.

"Why, Jolly, it is you! I can't believe it! It's been centuries!"

He jumped up, trying to compose himself, and held out his paw. Unfortunately it was the one that held his teeth. He quickly pushed them at Edgar, who had thankfully just arrived at his side, and stepped forward.

"Why, if it isn't Beatrice Elderberry. How are you? Wonderful to see you again."

Mr. Goodfellow felt slightly light-headed as he breathed in the sweet fragrance of lavender that surrounded Beatrice. She was just as he remembered her. Although the little strands of black hair that peeped from beneath her mouse cap were flecked with silver now, her dark brown eyes were as lovely and deep as they had been years before.

"It is a small world, isn't it? Bumping into you here after all these years!"

She looked behind Mr. Goodfellow. "And who might this young man be?"

Mr. Goodfellow turned and placed both his hands squarely on Edgar's shoulders.

"This is my nephew, Edgar, Filbert's boy."

A look of sadness filled Beatrice's eyes, at the mention of Filbert's name.

"Oh yes. I was so sorry to hear about Fil..."

Beatrice's words were interrupted by the arrival of another smaller figure, which had been trailing along behind her. Beatrice took the figure by the arm and pulled it closer.

"This is Charlotte Sparrow, of the Boston Sparrows. She and her family are living in California now. You remember my cousin Edwina, don't you, Jolly? We were more like sisters, really."

Mr. Goodfellow couldn't recall who Edwina was at all, but nodded politely anyway.

"Well, this is her granddaughter! Can you believe it? Charlotte's parents have been on assignment in a remote part of South America for the past few months and since they were always quite keen on exposing her to new educational experiences, Edwina suggested she spend this last school term with me in England. We've had such a delightful time together, too, haven't we Charlotte? We arrived here last week, and the mice have been enormously kind and helpful, so we decided to take a bit of a holiday and do some sightseeing before I take Charlotte back to California. It's been quite wonderful!"

Charlotte had wandered off towards a group of young mice playing in the corner. Edgar followed by her side. He smiled at her, but she returned him a most unpleasant glance.

Dinnertime was fast approaching and the mice were busy preparing a delicious repast, which included some interesting local delicacies. The four guests were led to two separate dining tables. These were, in reality, rather crude groupings of wooden blocks (what the mice lacked in decorating skill they made up for with commitment to the culinary arts). There was a small seating arrangement just for the children (to Charlotte's great consternation) and another more intimate setting, off in a secluded corner, for the grown-ups.

Mr. Goodfellow was delighted at the setup, but when he noticed Beatrice blushing openly, he became equally embarrassed. Oh dear, he thought, the mice have misinterpreted our relationship completely. He hoped that Beatrice didn't think he had anything to do with this. It was most inappropriate. They hadn't seen each other in years, after all. But it wasn't terribly surprising, considering mice were such hopeless romantics. There was half a birthday candle glowing at the center of the table and a little pile of crushed flower petals to the side (carnations, in fact, and white ones at that). There was also, to Mr. Goodfellow's surprise and delight, a small bottle of domestic wine next to them. Mr. Goodfellow pulled out one of the little wooden blocks and Beatrice graciously took her seat.

"What an extraordinary coincidence!" said Beatrice, as she studied the bottle of wine.

She went on to explain. Apparently, Charlotte's grandfather, Hartland Sparrow, had sustained a serious back injury during a mission and had been forced to retire from the field a number of years ago. He had resettled in northern California and established a ranch/spa famous for its mud baths. It was becoming a popular retreat for stressed and weary Sage. In an effort to diversify, Hartland had begun to dabble in winemaking. This bottle of wine, as it appeared by the label, was from his reserve stock, "Soaring Sparrow." The national mouse network must be a far-reaching one indeed for the bottle to have found its way across the continent. A fascinating story said Mr. Goodfellow to Beatrice. Privately, though, he couldn't help but doubt the prudence of allowing alcohol to fall into mouse paws. He had always found them to be excitable enough.

The four guests proceeded to dine on a variety of items the city was famous for. There were hot, salted pretzels from nearby street vendors, rich succulent cheesecake from Lindy's restaurant and Waldorf salad from the Waldorf-Astoria Hotel, just blocks away. It was always risky acquiring this sort of item, but it was brand new and irresistibly trendy.

Charlotte seemed anxious to escape the company of Edgar and after gobbling down her meal, asked permission to leave the table. She could be heard, to Beatrice's great embarrassment, "harrumphing" quite openly when Edgar trailed behind her.

Demurely sipping her wine as she watched the children scurry off, Beatrice leant towards Mr. Goodfellow.

"She calls me Nana Beatrice," she said proudly. "I never settled down and had a family of my own, you know. Always too busy, I suppose."

Mr. Goodfellow's ears pricked up at this very interesting bit of news.

She continued. "It's lovely at our age, isn't it, to have the young ones about?"

"Hmm," replied Mr. Goodfellow, vaguely. He wondered if Beatrice would have said that had she seen the state of his home after Edgar's visit.

"I've heard, from time to time, Jolly, that you have had some remarkable successes."

He blushed at the flattery.

"Oh my, well, thank you. And, you too, Beatrice!" he stammered, in reply.

"Oh, no, no, Jolly. Mine were always, shall we say, a little flamboyant, but not nearly as important as your contributions. I always admired you, Jolly. You're the consummate professional, rock solid and dependable."

Mr. Goodfellow flinched. She would not have said that had she seen the near disaster in the First Class Dining Room only days before.

"All of our projects are important, Beatrice, even the smaller ones. Inspiration is in short supply these days."

"You're right of course, Jolly. And I can't complain. My life has been quite full. But, just once, I would like to inspire one lasting, significant thing." She looked fondly at Charlotte. "Something to be remembered by. Perhaps a splendid work of art or a medical breakthrough, or a great, stirring speech. Actually, that's why I am quite eager to return to England, once I've safely delivered Charlotte. There's so much happening back home and I have a lead on a rather interesting assignment. Perhaps I can put myself to some good use."

A troubled look crept across Mr. Goodfellow's brow.

"A great storm is about to sweep over the world, Beatrice. I can feel it in my bones. And you know what that means."

Beatrice smiled and squeezed his arm.

"Dear Jolly, you haven't changed a bit. Always worried about something. I can look after myself, you know. Anyway, when it's all over, I would be more than happy to slow down a bit, perhaps even an early retirement. A little cottage at the seaside would be just perfect. I do love the ocean so."

Mr. Goodfellow tried to smile through his concern. He didn't want to alarm her but he could not, in all good conscience, let her ignore the dangers.

"Whatever you decide to take on, Beatrice, promise me that you will be careful." He lowered his voice. "You don't know them like I do. You might not be aware that they are watching, but watch you they will. They will follow you too, if they think they can disrupt an important mission. You cannot be too prudent in these matters. They will stop you if they can."

Beatrice tossed her head in defiance.

"Well, just let them try! I've never had much trouble with them anyway, as I'm sure you can imagine, Jolly. I suppose they've never been interested in sabotaging my little jobs. That's why it's all so perfect, really. I'm the last one they'd ever think of."

Her tone became more serious.

"But you, Jolly, with all of your special work, you must have had your share of troubles over the years."

"Yes, I suppose I have, from time to time. But, I think with experience I've learned how to keep one step ahead. It is strange though; I have been feeling a rather ominous presence ever since we docked. You do tend to get a bit of a sixth sense about these things after awhile. I can't imagine why they would be lurking after me now. I am, after all, on a bit of a sabbatical this summer."

He paused, taking Beatrice's hand in his own.

"I wouldn't dream of stopping you from doing what you feel called to do, Beatrice. You know your heart better than anyone. But, if you ever find yourself in peril, try to seek the company of other Sage. They rarely attack a group. They seek out the weak and will do all they can to get you alone. We can never be too vigilant. And try, if you can, to remember one final thing: they know much more than you think and are infinitely more devious than you could ever imagine."

"Who's infinitely more devious, Uncle Jolly?"

"Oh, dear," whispered Mr. Goodfellow, slowly turning around.

Edgar and Charlotte had been listening to enough of the conversation to warrant more than a casual explanation. Mr. Goodfellow turned back to Beatrice for guidance but it was apparent by the glazed look in her eyes that she, too, did not know how to handle this situation. They were both hopeless, childless novices. Mr. Goodfellow felt trapped. This was, after all, a subject best handled by a child's mentor and...alas, exactly the type of information that should be sensitively imparted at this very moment. Taking Edgar and Charlotte each in hand, he guided them over to Edgar's cot and sat them down. Charlotte gave Edgar a quick sideways glance and then shuffled to the opposite end. Mr. Goodfellow looked over at Beatrice and she looked sadly back at him. How he wished that Edgar and Charlotte didn't have to hear what he was about to tell them. But the time, it seemed, had come. He prayed for the appropriate words to find him as he cleared his throat.

"Now, I want you both to be quiet and to listen carefully to what I have to say," he began. "I suppose you are old enough to know the facts now, especially you Edgar, apprenticing as you are, my boy. Both of you are aware that we Sage have noble missions to perform here."

Edgar and Charlotte nodded their heads, earnestly.

"It is a calling that our families accept with the greatest pride and one which we undertake with respect and honor."

The children nodded even more earnestly.

He paused for a moment and glanced across at Beatrice. Well, that was easy enough. The next part was going to be more difficult. He hoped he wasn't going to alarm them too much. It was time perhaps for Edgar, but Charlotte's apprenticing days were still to come. Beatrice, trying to bolster his confidence, or perhaps just relieved to be a silent observer at the moment, sent him a most encouraging smile. He loosened the button at his neck, which had suddenly become unbearably tight, and plunged ahead.

"What you don't know is that there are other beings who oppose our work. Beings who would stop at nothing to disrupt our missions and, if possible, destroy all that we stand for. We must never underestimate their power."

He looked sternly at Beatrice when he said this last line. Well, he had managed to get the most important news out, and not too badly at that, he thought. Edgar raised his arm to speak. Mr. Goodfellow paled. He had not anticipated questions.

"Are these others like us, Uncle Jolly?"

"Uh, no, not exactly, Edgar."

Mr. Goodfellow paused, searching for the right words. He looked at the two trusting faces before him. The whole truth was perhaps the best route to take.

"They are dark and shadowy creatures, Edgar. They have a distinct presence, if they get near enough to you. It's like a cold wind on a warm day that comes from nowhere, and chills you to the bone. They wear coal black cloaks that conceal them so well it is almost impossible to tell where their bodies end and the shadows that always surround them begin. But they do exist—I can assure you of that. I have been as close to them as any Sage would care to get, although no Sage has actually seen one of them face to face and returned to tell of it, I'm afraid."

He could see by the strange look in his nephew's face that his last words may have gone too far. Edgar's eyes suddenly filled with tears.

"Uncle Jolly, did, did they...take my Dad away?" Edgar's voice quivered.

"Oh, dear, Edgar, well, no. Probably not. I don't know. I don't think so." Mr. Goodfellow floundered. "It was probably, most likely, an accident of some sort."

He sat down on the cot beside Edgar, tipping it slightly to one side, and swallowed nervously.

"The truth of the matter is, my boy, no one really knows. I wish I could tell you that they had nothing to do with it, but I simply don't know."

Edgar's head fell to his chest and his shoulders shook. Mr. Goodfellow put an arm around him. Beatrice dabbed at her eyes with a frilly handkerchief. Even Charlotte, who had made it quite clear to Edgar that she resented his intrusion on her holiday, looked upon him with sympathy and moved closer to the center of the cot. Beatrice offered one of her lavender scented hankies to Edgar, as Mr. Goodfellow continued.

"The Goodfellow name and reputation, amongst others, is one that they know well, Edgar. Trying to disrupt our work is only a part of what they do, however. They have a mission here, too. And they will remain here, I'm afraid, for as long as is necessary to carry out their hideous plans. They hide in the darkest of corners, on the edge of shadows, and whisper sly and evil words to anyone who will listen. They know who to seek out, too. As long as there are people on this earth driven by greed, jealousy, and revenge, the kind of people who hunger for riches and power at any price, they are sure to have a most attentive audience."

Mr. Goodfellow could see that his words had sent waves of fear through them all. He tried to convey a more hopeful message.

"You may be the more fortunate of us. They may never choose to bother you."

At that moment he couldn't help but look straight into Beatrice's dark, brown eyes.

"If you find yourself following a path in life that you feel particularly strong about, however, take care. For it is then that you pose a threat to their evil work. Then they will nip at your heels and torment you every step of the way. Whatever fate befalls us, it is our duty to see that these dark creatures never succeed. Our work must continue. We will fight them always. We will fight them on the seas and oceans; we will fight them on the beaches, on the fields and in the streets. We shall fight them in the hills. We shall never surrender!"

Beatrice blew her nose delicately into her hanky.

"Oh, Jolly! What wonderful, inspiring words! They have such an unusual ring to them. I just can't explain it. Would you mind terribly if I wrote them down right now?"

She pulled a notebook and pencil from inside her coat.

"No, my dear, of course not. Please, use them some day, if you will. I would be most honored."

Edgar's eyes were still red and moist, but he was determined to ferret out as much information as he could. He raised his hand once again.

"The dark ones, Uncle Jolly. Do they have names? Where do they come from?"

"Well, Edgar, the most powerful of their kind have names, I believe. But none of them have proper family names, as we do."

He looked about cautiously and spoke in a quieter tone.

"They are known as The Fen."

Edgar's mind reeled. He was sure that he had heard that word before! When he was very, very young, Great Uncle

107

Cyrus and several of the other great uncle Goodfellows had come to pay his mother a visit. They had gathered solemnly in the small front room to take tea, and Edgar had peered in from the hallway. He could vaguely remember eating warm blackcurrant scones that day and sipping his first ever cup of tea. His most vivid recollection of all, though, was the whispered word Fen and then his mother's soft weeping.

"As for their origins, my dear boy," continued Mr. Goodfellow, "their past seems to be as sketchy as our own, although..." At this he lowered his voice considerably. "I don't know how much truth there is to this, but legend has it that in the very distant past, at the beginning of time itself if you will, we were all one and the same creatures. Brothers, in fact."

The children gasped. Beatrice shot him an icy stare. He had gone too far this time.

"No one quite knows for sure, of course!"

Beatrice tutted openly. "Really, Jolly, scaring us all with that nonsense. I've never heard of such a silly thing!"

Mr. Goodfellow held up his hands in defense. "I'm not making this up, you know. But you must remember, it's only a legend, after all."

He gave the children as confident a smile as he could, then turned and whispered in Beatrice's ear.

"I can't believe you've never heard of this before, my dear."

"I have indeed," she whispered back, "but please, Jolly, I think the children may have heard enough for one evening."

He looked at the two charges in front of him and nodded his head in agreement.

Edgar and Charlotte sat quietly on the cot for some time. Their years of sheltered, carefree childhood had come to an abrupt end. The world looked very different to them now. New responsibilities and concerns had fallen heavily on their young shoulders. It was certain that things would never be quite the same again.

Edgar had trouble falling asleep that night. He lay awake, his mind a jumble of thoughts and memories, not so much of himself and home, but of the father he had hardly known. How he wished that he could remember more about him, but he had been only three when he disappeared. His mother and the other members of his family had always spoken of his father in the most glowing terms, but it wasn't the same as a memory. Edgar tossed and turned. When he was finally able to fall asleep, he took comfort in the thought that his father must have been just like Uncle Jolly.

Beatrice and Mr. Goodfellow spent the remainder of their evening reminiscing about old times and old friends. But the conversation soon returned to a familiar topic.

"They're close, Beatrice—I can sense it—but keeping well enough back. You can't feel it then?"

"No, I'm afraid not, Jolly. I suspect I am not as sensitive to them as you are, with all your years of experience."

"Well, perhaps it's best. It really is quite an unpleasant sensation. On the other hand, it would probably be in your best interests, Beatrice, to try and become more intuitive about them. It can be learned, you know, with time. I would be most happy to..."

"You're being quite silly again, Jolly. I really don't think I have any cause for concern. I've already told you that they've never had any interest in me at all."

Mr. Goodfellow shook his head in disappointment. Fortunately, the opportunity had presented itself for a proverb.

"You know, Beatrice, when you have been at it as long as I have you know the signs. He who lives a long life must pass through much evil."

Beatrice smiled sweetly and took his hand.

"But remember, dear Jolly—a good heart will always over-come evil fortune."

Mr. Goodfellow's heart fluttered.

"Beatrice! You're a collector of sayings. Never!"

"Well, just a few, really," she replied. "It's recently become a bit of a hobby."

"Mine too! How extraordinary!"

He sighed dreamily. For all their differences, wouldn't it be wonderful if they were kindred spirits after all?

8

UNDER THE THORNS
GROW THE ROSES

"Sam! Sam!" Mr. Goodfellow tapped his furry paw on the arm beside him. "I believe that the weather has finally improved, my boy. Time to get a move on. We really must catch the magnificent effect of the rain before it's too late!"

Sam sat up and shook his head. When he looked down he noticed that the little man had wasted no time crawling back into his shirt. He was now staring intently at Sam and drumming his fingers along the edge of the pocket.

"But what about you and Edgar and Beatrice and Charlotte?" Sam asked, looking around cautiously. "And The Fen," he whispered into his chest.

Mr. Goodfellow leaned out of Sam's pocket.

"I will finish the tale for you as soon as possible, dark creatures and all! I promise you faithfully, my boy, and you will find that I always keep my promises. And there's no need to worry. I have placed a mental bookmark in our story. Up we go!"

Sam rose to his feet and shook the last remnants of Edgar's adventures from his mind. He opened the bedroom door and trailed down the stairs into the empty kitchen, past his mother and father. They were sitting on two cardboard boxes, sipping tea from paper cups and eating toast they had made under the oven's grill.

"I think that we all needed a bit of a sleep in this morning, didn't we? Have a good first night, dear?" asked his mother.

"Yeah, great!" Sam replied.

His parents looked at each other and raised their eyebrows.

"Want to take a walk down to the park, Sam? Look what I found in the attic."

Sam's father tossed a well-worn football at his son. Sam made a sincere effort to catch it but it tumbled away from him and rolled toward the fridge.

"Thanks, Dad. Maybe later. I'm going to check out the backyard."

"The yard? Really? I'm so glad to hear you've had a change of heart," said his mother.

"Well, I'm going to give it another chance. You can't judge a book by its cover, you know, Mum."

As Sam raced out the door, his startled mother pushed a piece of toast and jam into his hand. The screen door slammed behind him.

Sam's father sighed. "He's still into that bug stuff, isn't he, Peg? I thought he'd have outgrown that by now."

"This move's going to be a big adjustment for him, sweetheart," said his mother. "Maybe we should just let him be for now. You know what kids are like. He'll probably lose interest after a while."

Trevor Middleton nodded and sighed. A pleasant vision of his son sprinting down a football field on his way to a touchdown, wearing the bright purple and gold colors of his alma mater, had already begun to fade to gray.

Sam walked down the lane at the side of the house and

stopped in front of a low picket gate that led to the backyard. Covered in curling flakes of old white paint, the gate was hanging on by a single hinge. When Sam moved to swing it open, it clattered off its remaining hinge and into a large, freshly formed puddle, spraying mud all over Sam's shoes and across his pants. Sam climbed over the fallen gate and stopped to look at the unappealing view beyond. Several clumps of dead and dying grass, a large pile of rotting leaves and three discarded tires were spread out in front of him. The rain had intensified the rather pungent odor that emanated from these items. Sam crinkled his nose. Surely this couldn't be the wonderful effect that Mr. Goodfellow had been talking about. Sam wasn't sure that he was interested in going any further, but with Mr. Goodfellow prodding at his chest from inside his pocket, he reluctantly plodded ahead. There were many opportunities for Mr. Goodfellow's proverbs here and he reeled them off with relish; a man (or presumably, a yard, either) is not known by his looks; do not judge by appearances; under the thorns grow the roses. The list went on and on. As they moved farther into the interior, Sam began to notice a change in their surroundings. Tufts of wildflowers were lying in small puddles and poking valiantly through the wet soil. As Sam picked his way through the debris, he suddenly found himself knee-deep in a colorful mixture of snapdragons, daisies, and day lilies, all dripping with fresh rainwater.

The pungent aroma had given way to a fresh, sweet, earthy fragrance. Birds were chirping loudly. Sam dropped to his knees when he noticed a beetle scurrying under a leaf and then counted dozens of ladybugs, spiders, butterflies, and even a dragonfly.

Tucked at one end of the property, and all but hidden behind an old wooden shed, was an extensive rock garden.

There was even a chipped stone birdbath, though the basin had tilted off its mooring. A collection of forest gnomes and clay animals lay scattered in the grass at its base. The possibilities for redevelopment were endless. Behind the safety of the garden shed, Sam carefully lowered Mr. Goodfellow to the ground. The little man bounded over rocks and crevasses, stopping to point out unusual plants and coaxing bugs out for Sam to study. With Mr. Goodfellow as his guide, and his magnifying glass glinting in the sun, Sam discovered a wonderful natural world. In no time at all he had chosen the ideal spot for another multi-tiered Popsicle stick habitat, and this time (with the help of Mr. Goodfellow) he would receive the total cooperation of the insects.

It was a perfect morning marred only by one unfortunate incident. In his enthusiasm to begin renovations, Sam had first set out to adjust the tilted birdbath. As it stood now, the angle of the basin allowed only a small amount of rainwater to collect, a pitiful bath for any bird that happened along. Sam took hold of the big, stone basin and slowly rotated it until it sat flat atop the pillar's base. As the basin scraped against the pillar, a small piece of concrete broke loose and tumbled towards Mr. Goodfellow, who was standing directly below. The falling fragment of stone, though minute by Sam's standards, knocked Mr. Goodfellow clean off his feet and onto a pile of jagged rocks. He struggled back up, wincing as he rubbed his left arm. There was a small tear in the furry suit just below the elbow.

"Good heavens! Not the field mouse this time," he complained. "I fear I am becoming exceedingly accident-prone. It's a good job I've thought to keep up my sewing skills, isn't it?"

Mr. Goodfellow removed his mouse paws and began to roll up his damaged sleeve. The rough stones had scraped a layer of skin off his arm. He glanced up at Sam who was staring down at him with a look of despair.

"What is it, my boy?"

"I've done it again, I've hurt you."

"Nonsense, Sam. It was only an accident. If anything, I was standing too close to the proceedings. Think nothing of it," he said, as he dabbed at the raw skin with his hanky.

Sam began to rummage about in his pants pocket, finally producing a rather grubby looking Band-Aid and a slightly cleaner piece of tissue. One end of the Band-Aid had lost both its paper backing and its stickiness and the middle bit was definitely questionable from a sanitary point of view. The other end, however, had remained intact and relatively dirt-free. Sam tore this end off as well as a tiny square from the tissue and reached toward Mr. Goodfellow. The little man held up his arm helpfully.

"That looks as if it just might do the trick, my boy."

Sam carefully placed the piece of tissue onto Mr. Goodfellow's skin then wound the Band-Aid around it, then once around again.

Just then Sam's mother called from the back door. Sam stood up as Mr. Goodfellow pulled a pocketwatch from inside his suit.

"It must be getting late! I'm afraid we'll have to continue our field trip another time."

Mr. Goodfellow stood at Sam's feet, impatiently tapping his own as he waited to be lifted up. Sam was careful not to press heavily on any part of the little man as he slipped him into his pocket. On the third and shrillest call from his mother, Sam trailed reluctantly back into the house. His mother was waiting for him in the kitchen, but not nearly as irritated as he had feared.

"Your Dad and I have been talking, Sam, and seeing how the move here has been a bit difficult for you, well, for all of us I expect, we have decided that we don't want to force you to go to this reception. We know how much you don't want to go. I'm sure there will be lots of other chances for you to meet people. You'll be starting at the new school tomorrow, after all and..."

The blood drained from Sam's face—school!

"Really, now, it's perfectly alright Sam. My, you're looking rather wan, dear. Too much running about outside, I imagine. Come and rest here for awhile," she said, as she dragged a cardboard box over for Sam to sit on. "I've telephoned Mrs. Stanwyck and she would be happy to pop over and sit with you this afternoon while your Dad and I are at the reception."

"The real estate lady? No way!" exclaimed Sam, rather abruptly.

Sam had not yet forgiven the real estate agent for finding this creepy, old house in the first place. She had also become, in Sam's mind at least, the prime suspect in the extermination of Mr. Goodfellow's mouse friends.

There was a sharp jab against his chest.

"I want to go with you, Mum, really," said Sam, forcing the words out.

This sudden change of heart came as a most pleasant surprise to his mother.

"Well, alright, dear, if you insist," she said smiling. "Actually I'm quite thrilled that you've decided to come along. A few of the professors and their staff will be there and I understand some of them have children your age." She leaned down to give Sam a hug. "Now that you're coming, dear, why don't you put on that lovely new blazer that Nana bought for you last month?"

Sam grimaced. He was just about to change his mind when another sharp jab from inside his pocket convinced him to keep his mouth closed.

"Sure, Mum."

Sam's mother looked down at her watch.

"It's almost a quarter to twelve now and the reception starts at two. I expect they will have some sort of refreshments there but it does seem rather a long time to wait, doesn't it?"

She reached for a paper plate from the counter and opened up the old fridge, picking through an assortment of leftover take-out food and airline snacks until she had created an odd but appealing luncheon. Peering over her shoulder with great interest, from the top of Sam's pocket, Mr. Goodfellow clasped his paws together and prayed that she would think to throw in just one or two of those irresistible roasted almonds.

"There you go, dear," she said, placing the plate in Sam's hands. "This should keep you going until this afternoon. It might be a good idea to have a rest too, if you can. That *was* a late night."

"Sure, Mum. I'll try."

Sam bolted up the stairs to his room, balancing the plate in his hands. This forced Mr. Goodfellow to do some balancing of his own in order to remain right side up.

"I cannot stress the point enough, my boy. You really must try to remember that you are a passenger carrier now. A little less turbulence, if you please!"

"Sure," said Sam, plunking himself down onto his sleeping bag. He placed the plate of food on the floor in front of him. "Sorry."

"It's quite all right. The nausea has almost passed now. Perhaps you would be so kind as to pass me one of those

117

roasted almonds. A spot of lunch followed by a quiet rest sounds just perfect."

Sam, who had worked up quite an appetite in the fresh outdoor air, heartily attacked his meal. He passed morsels of egg roll, a cracker with cheese spread and the tip of a shortbread cookie to Mr. Goodfellow, who had decided to climb down from Sam's pocket to stretch his legs. They cleared everything on the plate until only one roasted almond remained. Sam's hand reached for it, colliding in mid-air with a much smaller, slightly furry one. The situation called for a compromise.

"An almond for a story," Sam offered.

"I was afraid of that."

"Please! I just have to know what happens to you and Edgar and everyone!"

"Very well then," sighed Mr. Goodfellow with an air of resignation. "If you could bear with me for a moment, I will attempt to get comfortable."

Sam had already stretched himself out on the sleeping bag and moved his head to one end of the pillow. Mr. Goodfellow climbed up beside Sam's ear, turning this way and that as he nestled down like a strange little bird.

"Close your eyes, Sam," said Mr. Goodfellow, forming his words with some difficulty as he tried to swallow a large morsel of almond at the same time. "Hear my voice and let yourself imagine. Drift back to Edgar and Charlotte and Beatrice, back to New York and their haven, underground."

Sam, his eyes tightly shut, took several long, deep breaths, in and out, in and out, all the while listening to Mr. Goodfellow's quiet voice.

"Remember, Sam?"

And with one deep breath Sam fell under the spell of Mr. Goodfellow's adventures once again.

THERE'S ALWAYS A CALM
BEFORE THE STORM

C harlotte had inherited her dark hair and lovely brown eyes from Beatrice's side of the family. She spent a great deal of time, each morning, brushing her long hair and adorning it with silver slides and colored bows. These were hidden beneath her mouse cap if she was venturing out, of course, but it did succeed in making her feel pretty.

The next morning she followed her usual routine. She also spent a little extra time tending to her mouse suit. It was her favorite one: a silky brown coat with auburn highlights. They were, after all, in one of the most exciting cities in the world and she wanted to look her best. She had just finished preparing herself when Edgar approached. Charlotte looked him up and down as he beamed back at her. His light brown suit had been groomed that morning until it practically shone, but under Charlotte's observant eye a few bald patches were still visible. How strange, she thought, that the shade of the front paws did not quite match the rest of the outfit. There was an odd twist to the tail too. She didn't even want to think about the stains. She removed herself from Edgar's stare and sidled over to Beatrice.

"Do I have to stand next to him?"

"Oh goodness, Charlotte, please try to be civil. He really is a very nice young man."

"But Nana Beatrice," she whispered in her ear, "he smells of...disinfectant."

"Well, perhaps he is just a very nice and a very clean young man, dear. Anyway, Jolly is an old friend of mine and I would like you to treat his nephew accordingly, Charlotte," Beatrice replied sternly. "Please try to be pleasant."

Charlotte folded her arms, rolled her eyes and sighed. This was going to be a very long day, she thought. When Beatrice looked disapprovingly at her, she tried to smile sweetly at the awkward boy across the room. He waved back excitedly and returned her a most admiring glance.

Before Edgar and Mr. Goodfellow's arrival, Beatrice and Charlotte had planned to spend their last day in New York strolling through Central Park. They also wanted to visit the top of the Empire State Building. Mr. Goodfellow was adamant they continue with their original itinerary, assuring Beatrice that he and Edgar would be only too happy to tag along and spend the day in the company of such delightful ladies. He did suggest, however, that they avoid traveling by taxi.

In no time at all, the station mice were able to plot out an underground route of their trip. It would be somewhat less direct, but safer in the long run, especially for a group of four. Clasping their paws and chattering noisily, the mice implored them to return before sunset. Since it was going to be their last night in the city, they were to be the guests of honor at a lavish dinner later that evening.

Promising to be back on time, Mr. Goodfellow, Beatrice, Charlotte, and Edgar made their way through the dark, tunneled labyrinth beneath the city streets. Mr. Goodfellow led the way, illuminating a small, hastily drawn map with his flashlight. Beatrice and Charlotte followed along behind, with Edgar bringing up the rear. Edgar was trying to make a good impression, even though the previous evening's revelations and his sleeplessness had given him a heavy heart and made him very tired. In light of the fact that they would be spending the entire day with the ladies, Edgar was determined to let no embarrassing mishaps occur. He had taken extra care dressing that morning, making sure all the buttons attaching his paws to his coat were tightly fastened. He had checked for broken stitches too, and finding his twisted tail a bit loose (no doubt a result, he thought, of that dratted mole's meddling), he had decided to add an extra security feature. Using a discarded metal staple he'd found in one of the station's tunnels, Edgar managed to create a clamp, attaching his tail to his suit.

The little group made their way due north first, towards Central Park. After traveling a considerable distance, they began a slow and steady ascent through one of the vertical pipes toward a street grate. Mr. Goodfellow popped his head out to get their bearings and was delighted to find that he had calculated their whereabouts with typical accuracy. In a flash, they were through the grate and under the safe cover of some nearby bushes. From there they began their sojourn through the park. They were, unfortunately, too late to witness the renowned blossoms of the cherry and magnolia trees, but their lovely scent still lingered in the air. Clusters of bright spring flowers lined the paths that wound through the woods, leading the way to soft green meadows beyond. Squirrels and marmots scampered over and under a carpet of leaves, while orange orioles and bright red tanagers flitted between branches of maple and oak. The loud screech of blue jays mingled musically with the gentle cooing of mourning doves. The underbrush offered an extensive amount of cover for the four sightseers and they were able to move about freely, unencumbered by crowds and traffic.

They had stopped by a pond to observe a handsome family of ducks when Mr. Goodfellow suddenly looked down at his watch. He rubbed his hands together and looked about.

"I suppose we should think about a spot of lunch," he announced.

"Oh yes, please!" said Edgar and Charlotte, in unison.

With the endless mouse advice and directions, they had not left the station until quite late into the morning.

"I don't suppose you have any ideas?" asked Beatrice, scanning the area for signs of refreshment.

"It's a very good job, indeed, that you've decided to bring me along," laughed Mr. Goodfellow, as he reached into his bulky suit and produced a shapeless package, wrapped neatly in brown paper and tied with white sewing thread.

"I suppose I can't take all the credit, though. It was my idea at first, but once the mice got wind of it, they shooed me out of the way and took over entirely. They have crafted, I'm sure, a picnic luncheon that will be quite memorable."

"Oh, Jolly, you think of everything! How wonderful!" Beatrice gushed.

They all gathered round him as Mr. Goodfellow untied the thread and folded back the layers of paper. There were some pieces of pretzel from the night before, a sizeable chunk of orange cheddar (extra old, Mr. Goodfellow hoped), slices of apple and pear, two large pecans, some crumbles of petit four cake (white icing and sugar flower intact), and last, but not least, a miniature flask of tea (well-milked and sugared, as it should be). There was also an assortment of containers for drinking, and four squares of red and white cloth to serve as placemats.

Edgar lunged at his lunch with gusto. His tummy had been rumbling for quite some time. Pretzel crumbs began to tumble down the front of his suit, followed by dribbles of tea. Charlotte grimaced and turned away. There were going to be a few more stains on Edgar before the day was through. Mr. Goodfellow looked up.

"Edgar, it's really not like your Mum to forget to pack you an extra suit, my boy."

Edgar, twiddling his thumbs, hesitated a bit.

"She did pack one, well, two actually, Uncle Jolly. Plus the extra paws. But, I'm afraid they're back at Great Uncle Cyrus' house. I couldn't bring them, you see. They'd become a little messy and..." Edgar began to explain.

Mr. Goodfellow cringed and waved his paws about. He didn't really want to know what had befallen them.

"Never mind, Edgar, never mind."

He didn't want to cause Edgar any further embarrassment either, so he leaned over and spoke softly to him.

"If you sustain much more damage to that poor suit, Edgar, you'll end up finishing the trip in your formal attire. Please try to be a bit more careful, my boy." He patted him on the back and Edgar nodded his head.

"Yes, Uncle Jolly. Sorry Uncle Jolly."

Edgar wanted to avoid that situation at all costs. Attractive as it was, the black suit was unbearably hot and much too tight at the neck, especially when one was trying to enjoy a meal.

When he had had his fill of sweets and savories, Mr. Goodfellow lay his head back in the soft grass and looked up at the sky. The picnic had been up to the usual mouse standards. They were all well fed and most contented to find themselves in such lovely, peaceful surroundings. Beatrice and Charlotte were chatting happily, and Edgar was still nibbling.

It suddenly occurred to Mr. Goodfellow, as he watched the clouds float overhead, that Edgar had not met with a significant catastrophe for some time now. Their dinner last night, the expedition through the tunnels, their walk through the park, and now luncheon, had all been pleasant and incident free. He wasn't quite sure what to make of it. Could it be that the lad was beginning to find his rhythm? Or, he dreaded to think, would there be one gigantic disaster when they least expected it? Time would ultimately tell.

Mr. Goodfellow had grown quite fond of Edgar. Despite his inclination towards mishap, and his retiring nature, Edgar had some admirable Goodfellow qualities. His heart was in the right place and his intentions were good. The challenge to develop Edgar's full potential was not to be taken lightly. Mr. Goodfellow was more determined than ever to do just that. It was simply going to take more time. He closed his eyes and let his thoughts drift. He could see Edgar in Paris, Edgar in Rome, Edgar in London—one successful campaign after another. Edgar Goodfellow, master Sage, whispering words of inspiration into the ears of the brave, the gifted, and the visionary. He would be unseen counsel to the great peacemakers and they, though they would never know, would have him—J. Goodfellow, teacher and mentor extraordinaire—to thank for it. Edgar's contribution to the world would be monumental!

Mr. Goodfellow was soon carried away by his thoughts and it was only the rumble of distant thunder that broke through his daydream. He opened his eyes. The puffs of wispy, white cloud that had scudded past just moments before had swelled into an ominous mass of dark gray. A large drop of rain hit his nose mask, followed by another, and another. He sat up and looked around. Beatrice and Charlotte were already folding the red and white cloths while Edgar was grabbing at the last morsels of food. They stood up and raced to the edge of the meadow, taking refuge under an arched, stone bridge that forded a tiny stream. It took them a moment to catch their breaths.

"Grand timing, I'd say," panted Mr. Goodfellow.

"A spring rain is quite refreshing, really," offered Beatrice.

At that moment, the skies opened up and a torrent of raindrops began to fall. The rain pounded the pebbles by the side of the stream and bounced up and down on the surface of the water. The children "oohed" and "aahed" as streaks of lightning lit up the sky. It was like watching an enormous fireworks show. As the thunder grew louder and the lightning intensified, Beatrice, Charlotte and Mr. Goodfellow backed farther under the bridge.

"Edgar, do move back in a bit. There's a good lad," said Mr. Goodfellow. "And, by the way, what on earth is that shiny thing on your tail?"

Edgar turned to look behind him. Suddenly, there was a tremendous crack of thunder and a great flash, followed by a puff of smoke. With a high-pitched squeak, Edgar fell to the ground. The back of his suit was smoking, and orange flames danced around the base of his tail.

Mr. Goodfellow leapt forward.

"Edgar! Good gracious!" he shouted frantically, as he rolled him back and forth in the dirt. "Are you hurt, my boy?"

Beatrice and Charlotte rushed forward to circle Edgar and his smoldering suit.

"I think I'm alright, Uncle Jolly," Edgar replied weakly as he staggered to his feet.

"Oh, the poor, dear boy!" cried Beatrice as she clasped her hands to her face. "We must take him home, at once!"

"No, please," said Edgar. "I don't want to ruin anyone's day. I'm fine, really."

He looked plaintively at Mr. Goodfellow, who could see that he was desperate to redeem both himself and the rest of the outing. Mr. Goodfellow decided to champion Edgar's cause. Once everyone had calmed down, a prolonged discussion ensued and it was decided that they would press on as long as Edgar continued to feel up to it. They would have to undertake a few hasty repairs to the suit, though, as there was now a rather large hole in the back just above the twisted and charred tail. Beatrice searched about in the little handbag she kept under her mouse suit until she found a miniature pin. Then she gathered the frayed edges of what was left of the suit bottom and fastened them together as securely as possible. It looked a little strange, but she assured Edgar that once they returned to the station, she would be able to make a better job of it.

Edgar, in the meantime, had removed the staple clamp from his tail and shoved it beneath his coat, hoping that it would be forgotten in the excitement. He hadn't intended it to attract the power of nature.

When the suit repairs were complete, Beatrice insisted Edgar rest a bit more, until he felt completely recovered. After that, they were on their way, back down through the grate and into the complex pattern of tunnels beneath the city. It had been decided that Beatrice and Charlotte would follow behind Edgar to make certain he stayed steady on his feet. Though she felt great sympathy for Edgar in light of his ordeal, Charlotte was mortified to find herself traveling in such close proximity. The smell of disinfectant was nothing compared to the odious aroma of his singed suit.

Following their mouse map once again, Mr. Goodfellow led the way south now, towards their next destination: The Empire State Building. Certain that they were traveling beneath 5th Avenue, Mr. Goodfellow plotted the last few steps carefully. When he felt confident they were in range of their target, he popped his head through a street grate. Eureka! There it was in all its splendor, towering up toward the clouds, with a long lineup of eager visitors trailing out the door and onto the sidewalk.

From their vantage point beneath the grate, they carefully studied each person who shuffled by. Two young ladies carrying large round hatboxes moved into view. This looked hopeful, Mr. Goodfellow thought, provided the tops of the containers could be dislodged. He was just about to conduct a quick test when something interesting caught the corner of his eye. It was a metal baby buggy, complete with a blanket-lined wire basket at the bottom. Perfect! Mr. Goodfellow motioned to the others to move closer and listen for his signal. When the buggy moved into position beside the grate, they all squeezed through on Mr. Goodfellow's count of three. Mr. Goodfellow threw himself into the wire basket, then reached down and pulled each of the others in as well. They landed, quite comfortably, on top of a fuzzy blue blanket. Charlotte, in particular, could not have been more thankful. She buried her nose in the blanket's folds and inhaled the sweet powdery scent. There was a rattle in one corner, which they avoided for fear of jostling it, and a trio of stuffed animals in another. These last items would provide the perfect cover. If anyone in the milling crowd happened to look a little closer, they would not be in the least surprised to see a family of mouse toys peeping out from the collection. Edgar had already located a discarded teething biscuit and was inquiring if anyone wanted to share.

Once through the building's front doors, they found themselves in an opulent, marble-lined lobby. Their buggy proceeded rather slowly, and it was some time later before they were pushed into one of the many elevators. The elevator doors closed with a swoosh. Three Sage braced themselves, but Edgar, still preoccupied with his biscuit, was unprepared for what came next. The sudden rush to the 86th floor was an unexpected and violent assault on his poor senses. His ears plugged and his stomach tumbled. It was a sensation not unlike the one he had experienced onboard ship. By the time they had reached the top, Edgar wanted no more of the elevator or the famous building. While the others chattered excitedly, making plans to obtain the best possible view as they were wheeled out onto the observation deck, a shaken Edgar refused to move from the basket. Viewing the city from these dizzying heights was the last thing on Edgar's mind. How he wished he had never seen that wretched biscuit.

Mr. Goodfellow, with Beatrice and Charlotte close behind, jumped from the basket and moved into one of the sheltered corners of the observation walkway. Mr. Goodfellow took a small oval hand mirror from under his suit and tied it to a long length of thread. After just two tries, he successfully looped it over a metal brace on the ledge that held a viewing map and maneuvered it into position. By jiggling the mirror back and forth, he provided them all with a panoramic view of the city below. Ever conscious of the time, though, Mr. Goodfellow was adamant that they return to Edgar before too long. If they missed the ride down, it might be difficult to procure the next one. Charlotte trotted ahead, while Beatrice sidled up to Mr. Goodfellow. She linked her arm through his, to Mr. Goodfellow's great delight.

"What an exhilarating sight, Jolly! It's such a shame that Edgar is missing it all. That poor boy does seem to have more than his fair share of misfortune. Considering his recent encounter with the random forces of nature, it may be best that he not hear this anyway. I wouldn't mention it at all really, except that I do know you have more than a passing interest in the wonders of science. I read somewhere that the enormous build-up of static electricity on top of this building can cause, well, a significant spark when two subjects... kiss." At this, she raised her face to his and closed her eyes.

What an awkward situation thought Mr. Goodfellow. Was it just to be a simple science experiment, or could this notoriously romantic venue have cast a spell upon Beatrice?

"Well, of course, my dear, for the sake of experimentation," he said, closing his eyes and wondering what to do with his infernal mouse mask.

They were no more than a fraction of an inch apart, when a gust of wind suddenly swept over them, blowing them into the air. A few paces ahead, Charlotte was nearly carried aloft but for a quick thinking Beatrice, who grabbed her foot with one hand and the wire basket of the buggy with the other as they both floated by it. Mr. Goodfellow had blown past them to one of the buggy's front wheels. He clung to the wheel as bits of torn newspaper and chocolate bar wrappings flew over his head and into the sky. Just then, Edgar, who had been catnapping in the basket, was jolted awake by a most disturbing feeling. It was a chilling presence, not the bracing chill of the wind, but something quite different, and in fact, quite sinister. Edgar caught the whiff of an unpleasant odor too, before the swirling wind carried it past him. He peered out from the basket just in time to witness his friend's distress. Alert now and called to action, Edgar braced his legs against the metal wires, and with the help of Beatrice and Charlotte, who had managed to pull themselves in, he took a firm hold of Mr. Goodfellow's suit and tail and dragged him inside too. The four of them, frightened and breathless, lay silent for a time, catching their breath. Then the buggy began to move. Edgar hardly noticed the elevator ride down, so concerned was he that his beloved uncle had come so close to disaster. Edgar did not want to discuss the ominous feelings he had experienced in front of Beatrice and Charlotte. He was certain they were viewing the episode as an unfortunate natural phenomenon, but the look he'd seen on Mr. Goodfellow's face convinced him that he too suspected there was more to it than that.

When they reached street level once again, the buggy was pushed through the lobby and out into the street. The occupant of the baby carriage decided to pick just this moment to stir from his nap. His soft chubby arm appeared over the side of his chariot, followed by the appearance of a bright, inquisitive face as he leaned over and twisted round to view the contents of the basket beneath him. Large, pink fingers groped within the folds of the blue blanket. Mr. Goodfellow and Edgar tried in vain to interest him in the big rattle, but he had his eye on something else. Cooing delightedly, he closed his hand around a very startled Edgar and lifted him out of the basket. While Charlotte gasped and Beatrice grabbed for yet another hanky, Mr. Goodfellow shouted for Edgar to freeze. Edgar, perhaps more out of fear than anything else, was happy to oblige. Beatrice began to weep as Edgar disappeared from view, but it was not for long. There was a gasp of another sort, a much bigger sort, in fact, as the child's mother, grabbed Edgar from his hand.

"What on earth is this, William? Good grief! What a filthy toy, all covered in crumbs, and such an odd smell too. You mustn't pick things up from the street, dear. You don't know where it's been!"

In the midst of this hubbub, Mr. Goodfellow, Beatrice and Charlotte took the opportunity to leap out of the basket and back down a grate. When William's mother tossed the offending article by the side of the pavement it lay quite still, until it was given the all clear by a tiny voice below the street and it scrambled, limping slightly, to safety.

On their way back to the station, Mr. Goodfellow became uncharacteristically silent. Edgar could sense that he was deeply troubled.

"Uncle Jolly, I was wondering... about the wind."

From his expression, Edgar could see that Mr. Goodfellow needed no further prodding.

"He who has a thousand friends has not a friend to spare, he who has one enemy shall meet him everywhere. You felt it too then, my boy?"

"Yes, well, I felt something. I'm not sure, really."

"It was them, Edgar, I'm certain. And, they appear to be growing a great deal bolder." He lowered his voice. "The ladies don't seem to be aware of anything untoward. If you don't mind, my boy, I would prefer it if we kept this to ourselves for now, until I can determine what it is they want from me. I must admit, they have me stumped."

Mr. Goodfellow walked on a bit farther, then spoke more cheerfully. "One thing is certain, Edgar. You're getting the knack, my boy. You're a Goodfellow through and through!"

Edgar managed a small smile at this distinction. When they finally returned to the station late in the afternoon, he was exhausted. The lightning strike and their subsequent ascent to the top of the Empire State Building, not to mention being flung onto the streets of New York City, had taken more of a toll on him than he wanted to let on. He removed what remained of his mouse suit, hid the metal tail clamp under the clothes in his suitcase, and collapsed onto his little cot where he fell fast asleep. Beatrice found a needle, brown sewing thread, and folding travel scissors in her luggage. She had asked Edgar for one of his many pairs of spare paws and she now set about fashioning it into square patches for mending. When she was finished, the back of Edgar's suit had taken on an odd, rather quilt-like appearance that was not altogether unattractive. She hoped that the repairs were adequate. There had been some singeing around the front of his suit, but at least the troublesome red candy stain was gone once and for all.

Edgar was roused from his nap by the mice, who had begun to squeak and natter in loud chorus. They had held dinner for as long as possible, they complained, and if their guests didn't start into the first course shortly, it would be ruined. Edgar tidied himself up and joined the others. The wooden blocks had been pushed together this evening to produce one large table, and Mr. Goodfellow was invited to preside over the proceedings. Groups of mice brought out a continuous stream of food, chattering about each course as it appeared. There was an enormous tureen of broccoli and cheddar soup to start, a platter with portions of fresh fruits and buttered sesame crackers, two types of salad, and then the main course, brought to the table with great fanfare—a limburger soufflé. When it was time for the dessert course, the mice swarmed around their guests again, their arms laden with an assortment of sweets and goodies. At this point, Mr. Goodfellow leaned over and whispered to Beatrice.

"It's quite amusing, isn't it, to see how much these lovely creatures are enamored with food?" he said, carefully licking every vestige of butter from his fingertips before he lunged at a morsel of cream puff.

Beatrice, still chewing, nodded in agreement. She mumbled, but in as ladylike a manner as possible. "Would you be so kind, Jolly, as to pass me one of those delicious looking chocolate drops? No, wait! Is that gingerbread over there? I'm absolutely *mad* for gingerbread, you know!"

After making a considerable dent in the mountain of sweets set before them, Edgar and Charlotte were encouraged to join the younger mice in their play area. Edgar was happy to amuse the little ones with some quick pencil sketches. Charlotte decided to keep her distance, even as the mouselings crowded round. Edgar had long since removed his offending suit, of course, but a burnt odor still lingered around him. Mice, it appeared, were not too particular about that sort of thing. Charlotte, her curiosity piqued, was forced to stand up on her tiptoes, and strain to get a glimpse of whatever it was that Edgar was doing.

Much later, when Edgar finally crawled back into his cot, he looked over at his blue suitcase set against the wall. Mr. Goodfellow must have been busy that afternoon. A brand new sticker, with a pen and ink rendition of the Empire State Building and the words "I Went to the Top," had been placed next to the first one. Edgar pulled the covers over his head, turned over on his side and sighed.

The next morning Edgar woke up later than usual. When he saw that Beatrice and Charlotte had finished packing, he jumped out of bed. Before they were to continue with their own plans for the next few weeks, Edgar and Mr. Goodfellow had insisted they see the ladies safely onboard their westbound train. Edgar found his uncle sorting through his big, tan trunk. The blue suitcase, with some hasty rearranging and the application of Edgar's weight to close it, was ready to go in no time.

When it looked as if they were almost set to go, small groups of mice began to gather. Mr. Goodfellow was dreading the next few moments. It was time for that most dramatic of mouse rituals: the fond farewell.

The mice lined up and, at first, held themselves together quite bravely. But when one of them started to weep there was rapid disintegration among the ranks and soon they had all collapsed into a heap of tears, wailing and wringing their paws. The youngest mice rushed forward and, as usual, it appeared that it was Edgar they would miss the most. He was clutched and embraced until he could hardly breathe. Beatrice and Charlotte went through a considerable number of hankies and by the time they were able to break free from their sobbing hosts, even Mr. Goodfellow's eyes looked a good deal moister.

The four of them then raced along the tracks, luggage in tow, towards the point of departure for the magnificently luxurious train *The Twentieth Century*, bound for Chicago. Once there, Beatrice and Charlotte would board another, similarly equipped transport, for the rest of their journey to California.

As is often the case with goodbyes, things felt a bit rushed at the end. Mr. Goodfellow had laid awake much of the night, thinking of just the right thing to say to Beatrice. Now he stood, feeling awkward and tongue-tied. What he eventually blurted out sounded trite and casual. Beatrice, looking deflated, smiled and waved limply from the top step of the last baggage car. He had wanted to tell her how much the last two days had meant to him, how he would cherish the moments, and how he hoped that they could resume their friendship sometime in the future. He could have kicked himself now, convinced that the opportunity was lost forever. The great Jolly Goodfellow, known amongst his Sage peers the world over for his wise, articulate, and inspirational words, was a miserable failure in the language of love. He stood forlornly beside Edgar (who was feeling a few sad pangs over Charlotte's departure), watching the train as it pulled out of the station, listening to the steady clacking of the wheels on the track and the mournful echo of the train whistle.

Beatrice and Charlotte, pressed against the back window of the baggage car, were beginning to fade into the mist ahead. There was nothing to do but turn and walk away. Mr. Goodfellow took the handle of his trunk and wheeled it behind him. Conscious that his uncle was not quite himself, Edgar trotted at his side quietly. As sensitive as he was, Edgar couldn't possibly have imagined the burden of his uncle's heartache at that moment.

When they stopped to rest some time later, Mr. Goodfellow, out of a need to feel useful and in control of his destiny once again, decided to sit down and plot out a strategy for the coming weeks. He took a pencil and notebook from his inside pocket and produced a long list of names and locations.

"We have a great number of possibilities here, my boy. Let's see now... ah yes, Atlanta. Wonderful southern hospitality and the magnolias are so, wait a minute, no, no. I took care of that one last year. I have no idea why it's still listed." He immediately crossed Atlanta out. Then he paused and smiled at the memory as he chewed on the end of his pencil. "It was a rather intriguing assignment though, involving a writer of great promise. You may have noticed the book that was littered all over our ship. There must have been an advance copy of that woman's novel on every other deck chair!"

Edgar nodded his head. How could he possibly forget? He had, after all, endured an evening inside a deep, purple evening bag, crushed up against a particularly hard copy of it. Mr. Goodfellow continued.

"I thoroughly enjoyed the time I spent with that lovely lady. She was uniquely talented, and with just a bit of redirection, highly successful too. I called it my 'gone with the breeze' project."

"But, Uncle Jolly, I'm sure that book was called *Gone With the Wind*."

"Precisely, my boy!"

Pencil poised, Mr Goodfellow turned his attention to the next few items on the list.

"What do we have here? There's experimental aircraft, underwater diving innovations, high speed automobile trials..."

Mr. Goodfellow looked sympathetically at Edgar, who was trying not to appear nauseous.

"Perhaps we should just cross out these transportation ones, shall we? Something at a slightly slower pace may be in order. Are you familiar at all with Charles Babbage and his Analytical Engine, Edgar? A fascinating computation machine. It took him forty-nine years to develop it and I was with him for most of them. Now that's something you can really get your teeth into. There's a Professor Atanasoff, in Iowa, doing some fascinating work in binary systems. I'll see if we can't swing by there and..."

He suddenly stopped in mid-sentence. Edgar looked up from the list. Mr. Goodfellow's face had turned quite ashen.

"Uncle Jolly, what's wrong? You look awful, like you've seen a ghost or something."

"I think I may have seen one, Edgar, for all intents and purposes. Or perhaps it's more the fact that I haven't..."

Edgar was perplexed.

"What do you mean, Uncle Jolly?"

"Haven't you noticed, my boy. They're gone."

Edgar, still confused, stared back blankly.

"The Fen, Edgar! There's not a trace of them. Those ominous feelings have vanished completely."

A sudden shiver crept along Edgar's spine. Mr. Goodfellow turned even paler.

"Good gracious, my boy! How could I have been so blind? It's not me they're after. It's Beatrice! It must be! Whatever she's planning to get involved in back home, they've twigged to it somehow. They'll be upon her before she knows it! She's in grave danger, Edgar, and little Charlotte too. We've no time to waste, my boy! All this will have to wait."

He closed his notebook with a quick snap and shoved it back inside his suit. Called to action once again, Mr. Goodfellow sprinted through the underground tunnels like an Olympian. The tan trunk careened behind him, its wheels speeding noisily over the long, shiny road of metal track. It was taking every ounce of Edgar's strength just to keep up with his racing uncle. Without stopping, Mr. Goodfellow called out in the darkness to offer encouragement.

"Quickly, my boy! We mustn't tarry! Every lost moment may be critical!"

To the utter delight of their still grieving hosts, Edgar and Mr. Goodfellow soon arrived back at the mouse lair. Mr. Goodfellow made it clear that there would be little time for pleasantries on this visit, though. After the mice had been alerted to the gravity of the situation, they were only too happy to offer assistance. Within minutes, Mr. Goodfellow had obtained a scribbled list of train schedules and an underground guide to the railroad terminal in Chicago, including a well-marked route to the mouse contingent there. To Mr. Goodfellow's relief, there was a hurried farewell this time around, but he did take time to acknowledge the heartfelt outpouring of mouse prayers and good wishes. How they would proceed to the Midwest now, in the fastest time possible, became their primary concern. As they hurried through the tunnels once again, Mr. Goodfellow poured over the timetables of both the passenger and freight trains.

"These schedules are somewhat spotty, Edgar. There won't be another passenger service leaving on that route for a few more hours. In the interests of time, we may be best advised to ride the rails, if you will."

Edgar didn't like the sound of that. His suit was already hanging by a thread. How would it survive a ride on the rails? The pained expression on his face must have revealed his mounting concern. He felt Mr. Goodfellow's hand on his shoulder.

"Edgar, my dear boy, it's just an expression! We'll find passage on a freight container. It won't be nearly as luxurious as baggage car digs I'm afraid, but it will be quite safe, I can assure you."

Edgar felt relieved and a trifle foolish at this explanation. He stopped now to catch his breath and rub his aching legs. When he looked up again, Mr. Goodfellow, who had not slowed his pace for a second, was disappearing around yet another corner. Edgar had to double his speed to catch up to him. Before too long they found themselves pulling alongside the westbound freight train. Edgar was only too thankful to rest now. He had developed a stitch in his side and the beginnings, he was sure, of a big blister on one toe. Mr. Goodfellow was not one to linger, though, and he insisted they climb into one of the freight cars immediately. As the steps on this transport were considerably steeper than the passenger train, they were forced to pull themselves up like mountaineers, with ropes and hooks from Mr. Goodfellow's trunk. No sooner had they hauled the trunk and suitcase up behind them then the rail car suddenly jerked ahead, rolled back a few feet, and then rolled forward again and was on its way.

"Now you must appreciate why we had to make haste!" said Mr. Goodfellow a little breathlessly as he mopped his brow with one of Beatrice's frilly hankies. "Time and trains wait for no man, or something like that," he mumbled.

He jumped up and staggered over to one of the car's corners, attempting to place his footsteps in tune to the rhythmic roll of the train.

"It's going to be a long ride, Edgar. We had best get ourselves settled."

Edgar stood up, then immediately fell over. This, he feared, was starting out rather too much like the ocean voyage. Mr. Goodfellow, in the meantime, had found a comfortable pile of straw beneath an old burlap sack and beckoned Edgar to join him. Edgar slowly shuffled over, preferring to crawl on all fours until he got his "train legs." They nestled down in the straw and watched the interior of the station roll past them through the long opening that ran down the boxcar's sliding door. They were outside in seconds, speeding past rail yards and sheds and the outskirts of the city, until they reached open ground—woods, meadows, and farmer's fields. They had both begun to ease into the motion of the train and, fortunately for Edgar, it proved to be a much more soothing sensation than the uncomfortable swell of the sea voyage.

"It's really not an unpleasant way to travel, is it, Edgar? I say . . . Edgar?"

Mr. Goodfellow looked down by his side. The steady, undulating roll of the railcar had lulled a very tired Edgar to sleep. There was little Mr. Goodfellow could do now to speed their journey along. Alone with his thoughts, he might have enjoyed the views of the passing countryside had he not been so concerned with the welfare of Beatrice and Charlotte. How he wished that she had taken more heed of his warnings! He hoped she would remember some of his advice at least.

Edgar was jolted from his peaceful sleep by a great clattering noise, followed by the clomping of giant footsteps on the wooden roof above them.

"What was that, Uncle Jolly?" he whispered nervously.

The train had been stopped at a depot for some time, but was now beginning to inch forward again. Suddenly the big side door swung open and three burly men, running alongside the slowly moving train and clinging to the floorboards, threw their legs over the car's side and rolled into the boxcar. They were dressed in old, shoddy clothes layered with a considerable amount of grime and dust. Two of them had cloth bundles tied onto their belts and all looked as if they could have used a good hot meal and an even hotter bath.

"I believe we have been joined by vagabonds, my boy," whispered Mr. Goodfellow.

Edgar slunk down further beneath the cover of burlap.

"Why have they come here, Uncle Jolly? What do they want?" asked Edgar. Not only did he resent the intrusion, but also the rude interruption of his nap.

"They must live by their wits in hard times like these, Edgar. Some are migrant workers looking westward for opportunity and others have nowhere to go. Make no mistake, though, many learned and talented men down on their luck or simply lured by the wanderlust have ridden these rails— musicians, writers, and philosophers. I have been proud to help quite a few of them in my day."

After what Mr. Goodfellow had said, Edgar looked differently at the men who were talking together as they sat on the floor of the boxcar. One of them had brought a large tin can of steaming food aboard. Each of them produced clean but slightly bent forks from their pockets and began to pass the tin around. When they had finished, the can was tossed aside, conveniently close to where Edgar and Mr. Goodfellow lay.

Mr. Goodfellow had already opened up his trunk and removed a couple of plates and utensils from one of the drawers. He crept over to the rolling can and spooned out two small servings of what remained.

"Ah, Mulligan Stew," he whispered as he returned to Edgar's side. "It's a hobo staple, my boy, that the men traditionally cook in a can with a few vegetables and sometimes, if they are having a particularly lucky day, a 'stray' chicken. This one, thankfully for us, is of the vegetarian variety. Now, eat up, Edgar! We need all our strength for the challenges that lie ahead."

Edgar looked down at his meager portion. These were slim pickings indeed compared to the gourmet meals that he had been ingesting lately. His stomach began to grumble as cream puffs and cheesecake danced in his head.

A deafening screech of metal and the sudden grinding halt of the train soon interrupted Edgar's daydreams. There was a great deal of shouting from the tracks as everyone in the railcar lurched forward. Without a word, the men in the boxcar grabbed their belongings and silently swung themselves out the door. Edgar could hear those who had settled on the roof shimmying down the side of the car as the shouts grew closer. He looked wide-eyed at Mr. Goodfellow.

"Railroad bulls, Edgar! Train detectives! They're the bane of vagabond life. We had better make ourselves invisible. No doubt they'll be searching every car, and quite thoroughly too."

They burrowed themselves into the pile of straw and waited. After what seemed like an eternity, the big door was pushed open and two men jumped inside. Edgar held his breath and Mr. Goodfellow squeezed his nephew's arm. The men walked the full length of the boxcar twice over, stopping the second time to pick up the burlap sack that covered the pile of straw. They turned it inside out and tossed it across the floor as they leapt down from the car to the tracks below.

Edgar could breathe again, but neither he nor Mr. Goodfellow felt confident enough to leave the safety of their straw cave. They waited and waited but the train had been stopped for over two hours now. They could still hear shouting in the distance and the occasional rush of footsteps outside the boxcar door. Mr. Goodfellow looked anxiously at his pocketwatch, and when it finally appeared that the search had been abandoned, he stepped out and began to pace the floor, muttering about timetables and schedules.

"This is most distressing, Edgar. We have lost a considerable amount of time with this business already. At this rate, I fear we may miss Beatrice and Charlotte altogether. We'll never catch them now, not in Chicago, at least."

The train began to chug forward once again, but at a snail's pace. When it finally rolled into Chicago's Union Station, they had missed both the arrival of the New York train and the departure of the train service to San Francisco. Edgar and Mr. Goodfellow followed the directions they had been given to the station's mouse lair, where it was confirmed that two delightful ladies had indeed passed through just hours before and had been seen safely aboard the baggage car of a California bound train. Disappointed and exhausted from their railroad ordeal, Mr. Goodfellow decided that another slow-speed pursuit by freight train was definitely out of the question.

"We need a plan, Edgar," he mused, as he plunked himself down beside his trunk, "and a good one, at that. We'd have to fly like the wind to catch up to them." He paused for a moment, lost in thought, until Edgar noticed a sly little sparkle in his eye.

"That's it, my boy! Of course!"

Mr. Goodfellow jumped up and opened his trunk, pushing

the suits aside with his nose. He emerged with a long roll of brown parchment paper.

"This was your Grandfather Goodfellow's, Edgar," he said proudly as he carefully unrolled the paper on the floor. "A souvenir of one of his most celebrated assignments. He passed this on to me on his retirement. In light of our current predicament, I'm sure that Mr. da Vinci wouldn't have minded a bit."

Looking over his uncle's shoulder, Edgar strained to see what it was his Uncle Jolly was peering at. It appeared to be an intricate drawing of some type of vehicle. It looked like a flying machine. Edgar was immensely impressed with the finely detailed work, the lovely pen strokes and the subtle shading.

"We must build one of these at once, my boy! It will have us in sunny California before the train arrives," said Mr. Goodfellow.

Edgar looked anxiously at the drawing again. He couldn't deny that it was a beautiful design, but when he imagined himself being carried aloft within its delicate frame, his heart began to sink rapidly to the floor.

"The big question now is how to secure the necessary supplies. Let's see if we can elicit the aid of the mice." Mr. Goodfellow lifted his head and waved them over.

The mice crowded round him, growing increasingly excited as he outlined his plan. He mentioned that he had observed a large group of pigeons milling about outside as their train had entered the station.

"Perhaps we can arrange a suitable trade of some sort. Food items come to mind." (He had no doubt, considering the wonderful range of fine hotels and restaurants in the area, that these Chicago mice were as well fed as the New York ones.)

In no time at all, a deal had been struck with a group of

enterprising birds. They would agree to deliver a number of wood strips of varying lengths, as per Mr. Goodfellow's instructions, along with as much twine and thread and thin wire as they could collect, all in exchange for an assortment of tantalizing mouse goodies.

"We need a point of departure, too," explained Mr. Goodfellow. "The higher the better!"

When the mice informed him that the train station had a lofty clock tower, the stage was set. It was arranged that the pigeons would deliver their loads there, where the machine could be built on sight and away from passing crowds. Mr. Goodfellow and Edgar, along with the trunk and suitcase, and a handful of eager mouse assistants, began to make their way up the long flight of stairs to the top of the tower. The climb would take them a considerable amount of time and effort.

"Isn't this wonderful, Edgar? To be able to recreate a centuries-old invention and fly to the aid of dear Beatrice and Charlotte?"

Edgar nodded his head. He felt quite unhappy, though, and it wasn't just the agonizing ascent up the clock tower that had set him trembling. Edgar had never thought about having to fly one day. What's more, the thought of setting off in a rickety homemade wooden contraption (even if it had been built by his Uncle Jolly) was almost too much to bear.

When they finally reached the top of the tower, there was already a pile of building materials awaiting them. Mr. Goodfellow immediately took charge of the project, directing the incoming flight traffic and arranging and fitting each piece according to his plan. Mr. Goodfellow had made some modifications to the original design, including an advanced pedal system that would enable better control of the giant, flapping wings. Two long strips of yellow-colored wood had been arced and lashed to the main frame to form the top of the wings. Shorter lengths of wood, with pieces of discarded silk stocking stretched between them as support netting, had been fanned out below to complete the wing assemblies. When the contraption was finished, it was an impressive sight. It reminded Edgar of the pictures he had seen of great prehistoric birds. Like a golden pterodactyl, the flying machine seemed to teeter impatiently at the edge of the clock tower, awaiting its chance to swoop down over the city.

When every piece was in its place, tied securely with lengths of thread and twine, Mr. Goodfellow made one last check for wind direction and velocity. After he had announced that they were ready to go, Mr. Goodfellow climbed into the steering position and strapped his mouse feet into the pedals. The tan trunk was secured below the left wing, with Edgar and his blue suitcase balanced off on the right. Edgar prepared for his first takeoff. He took one long, deep breath, closed his eyes as tightly as possible, and gripped the wooden bar in front of him. After he had relayed his gratitude to the circling pigeons, Mr. Goodfellow asked the attending mice to give them a forceful push off the ledge. A large group of mice gathered at the back of the flying machine and with a hearty "One! Two! Three!" (in mouse-speak, of course), they rushed forward, pushing the flying machine with all their might. Aboard the little craft, Edgar and Mr. Goodfellow soon left the top of the tower and sailed majestically into the air. The flying machine tipped from side to side and swooped towards the ground, while Mr. Goodfellow attempted to get a proper feel for the controls. Finally, he was able to gain altitude once again and they soared up into the sky.

"Look Edgar, what a magnificent view!" he cried, as he

pedaled furiously. The great wings creaked and groaned as they flapped up and down in the air.

Edgar would have preferred not to look of course, but with his uncle's continual pleading, he eventually forced himself to open one eye slightly. There was, as had been promised, a spectacular vista below, but Edgar only felt comfortable looking for a minute or two. The effects of the high altitude soon brought the now familiar dizziness, and Edgar had to close his eyes once again and try desperately to convince himself he was back on solid ground.

They traveled over forests and grasslands, rivers and fields and foothills. Sometimes they would hit a powerful wind current that carried them through the air. Mr. Goodfellow longed for these moments as it afforded him an opportunity to rest his weary, pedaling legs. He could sit back and enjoy the flight as they glided on the warm winds and refer to the map he had pasted on the beam of wood directly in front of him. It was Edgar's job to consult the compass (which had been tied securely around his neck with a double loop of string), whenever Mr. Goodfellow called for a reading.

They had no trouble following the rail tracks through the day but this task became more difficult when the light faded into night. They had been blessed, thankfully, with a full moon and Mr. Goodfellow was able to steer fairly accurately by lunar light. Nourishment on the long flight had not been forgotten either. The mice had prepared two small bundles of food and drink that had been strapped next to each of them. Edgar, of course, had to be warned repeatedly to make his portions last until they reached San Francisco. This was not at all easy for him. With nothing to do on the journey, he had quickly grown bored. He had also discovered that keeping his eyes closed was an effective remedy to his wobbly tummy, and so, to Mr. Goodfellow's dismay, Edgar's healthy appetite remained unaffected. They had not cleared the last mountain range when Edgar began to complain about his empty stores. With another stern warning to take better heed of his instructions in future and a vow that on the next flying machine he would install *two* sets of pedals, Mr. Goodfellow reached across and passed his last inch of breadstick to Edgar.

Those final mountain peaks, with their snow capped summits, were a signal to Mr. Goodfellow that they were nearing the end of their flight. After a long consultation with his maps and schedules, he concluded that Beatrice and Charlotte's train must be directly up ahead.

As San Francisco, and the blue Pacific Ocean beyond it, loomed in the distance through a curtain of fog, Mr. Goodfellow suddenly spotted the train snaking its way toward the city. Looking for a suitable place to land, Mr. Goodfellow began to pedal even faster, determined to intercept the train's arrival at the station. A soft green meadow, cradled between a couple of the city's notable hills, and not too far from their destination, would provide an excellent landing site. Mr. Goodfellow had become quite adept at handling the controls now and had begun to anticipate the shifting air currents. Like a seasoned pilot, he guided his aircraft through layers of wispy cloud and set it down with hardly a bump, right in the center of the meadow. After he and Edgar had dragged the craft from view and sheltered it with leaves, they raced to the station and located Beatrice's train. Passengers had only just begun to stir from their seats and collect their belongings, as Edgar and Mr. Goodfellow flew past the cars on their way to the last baggage compartment.

"Beatrice! Charlotte!" whispered Mr. Goodfellow, as they climbed up the steep stairway and into the railcar.

There was no reply. Perhaps they had chosen another car, thought Mr. Goodfellow. They were just about to begin the long climb down when Mr. Goodfellow spotted the tip of Charlotte's small suitcase perched on the edge of a very large duffel bag at one end of the car. He and Edgar rushed over to investigate. They found a few clothing items next to it and, stranger still, two undisturbed breakfast settings, with uneaten fruit and toast, and two full cups of tea, now quite cold.

"Oh, Uncle Jolly," cried Edgar, "Something terrible must have happened to them!"

Mr. Goodfellow studied the peaceful scene for some time before he spoke.

"I'm not altogether sure of that, my boy. Nothing seems to have been disturbed, there's no sign of a struggle, and more significantly, breakfast was over an hour ago. I suspect they may have left the train at one of the previous stops."

A sudden blast of cool air blew onto Mr. Goodfellow's face through a slightly open window to the side. He turned to look at it and smiled. It was propped open with Beatrice's carpetbag.

"Somehow they cottoned on to their pursuers, Edgar, and gave them the slip. Brave girls! And if I'm right, they should be on their way to the safety of Charlotte's home right now."

Mr. Goodfellow pulled Beatrice's bag out from the window ledge and tossed Charlotte's suitcase to Edgar. Mr. Goodfellow began to run and Edgar struggled once again to keep up. When they arrived back at the landing field they quickly strapped the two bags onto the machine, one at each wing, and pushed the contraption to the highest point of the hill. With Edgar in position, Mr. Goodfellow gave the machine a strong push and scrambled aboard. At first, the flying machine took a quick dip back to the earth, until Mr. Goodfellow grabbed at the controls and began to pedal with all his might. Before too long he had managed to gain sufficient lift again and they were on their way.

In one of his conversations with Beatrice over the last few days, Mr. Goodfellow had mentioned a passing interest in visiting Hartland Sparrow's ranch and spa one day. From Beatrice's description, he had a vague idea of its location, though he wished that he had made more specific inquiries. They could occasionally make out the terrain below as they headed north from the city: rocky cliffs and white surf, then deep green fields and meadows of bright wildflowers. The blanket of fog, however, was a persistent and annoying companion. Drops of dew glistened on the tips of their coats and dripped from their nose masks. Mr. Goodfellow tried to guide the craft around the fog but it was almost impossible to completely escape its clutches. As soon as he had successfully maneuvered their way past one bout of fog, another thick, swirling cloud closed in around them. The wetness tickled Edgar's face terribly and the urge to scratch was unbearable, but his fierce grip on the wooden frame was so tight, he couldn't even begin to move his furry fingers. Mr. Goodfellow had bigger concerns at the moment, though, as the continual dampness had started to soak into the light wooden frame of their aircraft. It soon began to swell and sag with the additional weight of the water. Despite Mr. Goodfellow's valiant efforts to maintain altitude, the controls were becoming more and more sluggish and they began to make a slow, unscheduled descent. The last thing Edgar could remember before impact, apart from Mr. Goodfellow's instructions to brace himself, was the lovely sight of hundreds of bright orange poppies spiraling up to meet them.

10

Fortune Favors

the Brave

"**A**AAHHH!" At the sound of this sudden yelp, Mr. Goodfellow immediately stopped talking and sat up. Sam, still beside him, was sitting upright, too, his back pushed against the pillow, his hands firmly clasped over his eyes. When he finally peeped through his fingers, he saw Mr. Goodfellow staring at him with grave concern. He smiled meekly and shrugged his shoulders.

"I'm sorry. I guess I got a bit carried away with the story."

He crawled back down again feeling a little embarrassed. With an air of melodrama, Mr. Goodfellow clutched his chest.

"Well, I suppose this proves that my old heart is still able to withstand loud and sudden noises," he joked. "I'll continue now if you promise not to scream like that again, my boy. It's a lucky thing your parents haven't charged in here yet."

"Sam! ... SAM!"

Mr. Goodfellow gasped and clutched his chest again. Sam's mother was calling from the bottom of the stairs.

"Hurry, Sam! I've lost track of the time. It's 1:15! We have to get a move on. Your Dad's almost dressed and you know how he grumbles when he has to wait."

Mr. Goodfellow rolled off the pillow with a thud and hurried toward his trunk. Sam could see him sorting through his suits. Sam sighed. His mother couldn't have picked a worse time to interrupt the story. It wasn't going to be easy to engage in espionage work at the university while Mr. Goodfellow and Edgar were still hurtling to the earth in their homemade flyer.

Ten minutes later, Sam was staring into the bathroom mirror. A rather miserable looking boy with a pale complexion and dark brown hair was staring back at him. Trapped in the confines of a crisp, white shirt, clip-on tartan tie, and brand new navy blazer, Sam pulled and tugged at the stiff collar. The bulky clip of the tie was pressing into the soft part of his neck just below his Adam's apple. To his great dismay, Sam had cultivated, over the past summer, an extensive new crop of freckles that covered both of his checks and the bridge of his nose. To make matters worse, he had also had to completely soak his head with water in an effort to flatten one obstinate tuft of hair that still seemed to stand to attention at the very center of his head. Mr. Goodfellow popped his head out of Sam's shirt pocket. He was wearing a white mouse suit this time, hoping that in the event of a mishap at the university, he could pass himself off as a rogue laboratory mouse on the lam. He pushed aside the lapel of Sam's navy blazer with a flourish.

"Are we ready yet, my boy? Oh, my! You look dashing. It reminds me of the time when Edgar and I..."

Just then, Sam's father tapped at the half-open door and popped his head into the room. Mr. Goodfellow dove back into the safety of Sam's pocket.

"Ready, Sam? Best let your mother in there now. We're running a bit late, you know." He leaned forward and whispered. "She wants to make just the right impression."

Sam's father turned and wandered off, muttering some-thing about renovating the downstairs bathroom.

Sam peered into his parent's room on his way to the stair-case. Dozens of discarded clothes lay strewn across the open suitcases on the floor. Sam's mother was scurrying back and forth, wearing one black shoe and one scarlet. Sam's father stood holding a different outfit in each hand.

"This one looks very nice, sweetheart," he offered hopefully.

"Oh, no! That's not appropriate at all for an afternoon function at an institution of learning," whispered Mr. Goodfellow, as he peeped out from behind the blazer again. "Tell them, Sam."

"Sshh!" said Sam, into his chest, walking as quickly as he could past his parent's door and down the stairs. He knew from experience that it was sometimes best not to get involved in these types of matters.

The car ride to the university seemed endless. Sam's father, a tireless fan of classic rock music, had popped his most recent acquisition—*Greatest Hits of 1972*—into the car's CD player, and turned the volume up to what Sam imagined must be a dangerously high level. His father had faithfully sent away for and received each disc offered in the '50s and '60s collections and Sam had already sat through each of these decades, year by long year. Thankfully, he had discovered that another use for his swimming earplugs was to drown out his father's music. He tended to carry them with him most of the time. On this particular trip, however, the incessant toe tapping from inside his shirt pocket wasn't allowing his earplugs to do their job. By the time they arrived at their destination, about a half-hour late, Sam was irritable.

The reception was being held at a courtyard nestled between

a number of old university buildings. Crowds of people milled about on the grass and along winding flagstone pathways, nibbling on hors d'oeuvres and sipping punch from little plastic cups. The main building, a large brick and stone structure, was covered in patches of thick, green ivy that cascaded from its roofline down to an impressive arched entranceway below. This building was home to the staff and administration offices, and also housed the Grand Reception Room, where an auction was to be held later that afternoon. Two long tables, decorated at each end with bunches of colorful balloons, had been set out on the lawn at the base of the front steps. One was manned by three of the university's administration clerks, who were busily handing out pens and name tag stickers. The other table held a pair of oversized punch bowls, one of cut glass and the other silver-plated. A ragged note (an apparent afterthought) had been taped to the silver bowl with the hastily scribbled message Adults Only, Please. This bulletin had appeared about ten minutes into the reception, but not before a number of the staff members and their families had stopped by for refreshment. A few parents could be seen now, happily pushing sleeping tots about the university grounds.

A troop of traveling performers had been hired to provide the afternoon's entertainment. There were strolling violinists, a juggler and magician, and games and pony rides for the children. In one corner of the courtyard, a gypsy fortune-teller's tent had been erected. Peggy Middleton grabbed her husband by the arm.

"Look, Trev! Madam Zorah: Fortunes Told to Young and Old. I've *always* wanted to have my fortune read. Come on, let's go in!"

Sam's father groaned. "You know I don't like that sort of thing, Peg." He shuddered. "It gives me the creeps."

"Oh, you're just being silly, Trevor. It's only for fun, right Sam? Will you go with me?"

"I guess so," said Sam, shrugging his shoulders. It was obvious that, fun or not, Sam's mother wasn't about to enter the tent alone.

Trevor Middleton rolled his eyes as his wife and son made their way over to consult Madam Zorah. "I'll be around here somewhere, I guess," he called after them.

Sam's mother pushed aside the beaded curtain that covered the entrance to the fortune teller's tent. A silver bell tinkled above their heads as they walked inside. It was dark in the tent, after being out in the bright sunlight. An old woman, Madam Zorah presumably, was hunched over a small round table in the center of the tent. One crooked candle, sitting on a rusty tin lid at the edge of the table, flickered in the darkness. A few strands of twisted gray hair fell across Madam Zorah's forehead. A pair of round gold earrings caught the candlelight as they dangled from her ears. Dressed in a long black skirt and shawl, the old gypsy beckoned them to sit in the chairs in front of her with the sweep of a slender, sinewy hand.

"Twenty," she said.

"I beg your pardon?" said Sam's mother.

"Twenty dollars."

"Oh, I see," said Sam's mother. She lifted her handbag onto her knee and began to look through her wallet. "I don't think I have enough," she whispered anxiously to Sam. She looked up at Madam Zorah. "Um... that does seem a trifle expensive for a reading, though I've not actually done this before and..."

"Two readings. Ten dollars each."

"Oh, dear, no... it's just for me actually. One reading please." Relieved, Sam's mother placed a ten dollar bill on top of the grubby tablecloth and pushed it towards Madam Zorah's open hand.

"Crystal ball or palm?"

"Ah...well. Let's see, now. The crystal ball looks very nice, doesn't it Sam?" Sam's mother was holding his hand so tightly, she wasn't sure if she'd be able to offer her palm anyway.

Madam Zorah leaned over the crystal ball and began to caress it with her hands. She glanced from time to time at Sam's mother.

"Is there anything special you wish to know from Madam Zorah?"

"Well, I was wondering...if we have done the right thing."

"You have come from far away?"

"Yes, we have actually," replied Sam's mother, a bit surprised.

"You have come to stay."

"Well, we hope so. Don't we, Sam?"

Sam shrugged his shoulders and grunted.

"Sam, please be nice," whispered his mother.

"The young one is not happy?" Madam Zorah was staring at Sam now.

"Our son's not taken to the move just yet, I'm afraid," replied Sam's mother. "I think he just needs a bit more time."

"Do not worry," said Madam Zorah, as she gazed into the ball again. "Your choice is good. The new life you are living will be successful for you."

"Oh, how wonderful! Wait until your Dad hears, Sam. What else does the crystal ball say?"

"Some other things." Madam Zorah waved her hands about as she reeled them off rather quickly. "I see big house, many guests, dogs..."

"Dogs?" asked Sam's mother. "That's peculiar. We don't have a dog. My husband suffers from allergies and..."

Sam's mother stopped talking. Madam Zorah didn't seem to be listening to her but staring with great fascination at Sam instead.

"I will read for the boy now?"

Sam's mother fingered her handbag nervously. "No, that's fine, thank you. We really should be getting back to my hus..."

"No charge," interrupted Madam Zorah.

The silver bell suddenly tinkled again as someone else pushed apart the long strands of beads at the tent door. It was Trevor Middleton. He squinted his eyes and looked inside.

"Peggy! Sam! Are you still in here? There's a frantic woman on the loose and she seems to be looking for us."

"Oh dear," said Sam's mother, rising from her chair. She thanked Madam Zorah and, still clutching Sam's hand, rushed from the tent.

Sam and his parents had barely reached the top of the steps to the main building when they were besieged by one Abigail Spender, administrative head of the Fine Arts Department. A bundle of energy in a flowered frock, she rushed forward with arms outstretched to greet them.

"Finally! You must be the Middletons! So wonderful that you could come today!" she gushed, quickly shepherding them through the entrance foyer and into the Grand Reception Room. "Please, you *must* let me introduce you to some of the distinguished members of our faculty!" This was clearly a part of her job that Abigail Spender took great delight in. In fact, she had been preparing for this moment all day long.

Ms. Spender had been up since the crack of dawn, primping and preening herself into a state of nervous exhaustion.

Hoping that her heart's desire would find the time in his busy schedule to attend the afternoon's event, she had spent hours at her bedroom mirror, fussing over her hairdo and makeup. Continual brushing of her light brown, wispy hair had caused it to take on a frizzed and fluffy look, so she had resorted to sweeping it into a nest-like structure at the top of her head. Satisfied with this achievement, she had then begun working her way down. She had never been happy with her eyes (pale gray with barely visible lashes and brows), and decided that now was the time to throw caution to the wind. With her black eyebrow pencil, she proceeded to encircle both eyes, completing the effect with a thick, black brow, giving her the overall appearance of a startled raccoon. Finally, the coup de resistance had been the gloriously pink rosebud print dress she'd draped herself in, so that from her transparent pink eyeglasses to her hot pink sandals, she was a rose-colored vision. Determined to make this a day to remember, Abigail Spender took one of Sam's parents in each arm, and began to grandly part the crowd.

Sam's father secretly dreaded these kinds of social occasions. He had somehow managed, over the years, to develop a mental block to cocktail party etiquette. No sooner had people been introduced to him than their names would instantly drift from his memory. He had come to rely on his wife to provide him with the appropriate information, whenever necessary. In times of desperation, he had even turned to Sam for assistance.

There was one gentleman in particular, however, who was about to make a lasting impression on all of them. Even at a considerable distance, he managed to stand out from the crowd. He was extremely tall and impeccably dressed. A rather unruly mop of sandy-colored hair, graying just a touch at the temples, crowned his head. At the tip of his long pointed nose, a pair of gold-framed glasses dangled magically. Surrounded by a group of admiring female colleagues, he was a shining example (in Ms. Spender's opinion especially) of what a distinguished academic should look like. As soon as Ms. Spender spotted him, she lunged across the floor to his side, dragging Sam's parents with her and scattering guests to and fro in their wake.

"Oh, Professor Mandrake. Toodle-oo! How marvelous to see you! You *must* let me introduce you to our new arrivals. They've just moved into our little community to open an art gallery that specializes in historical works. Isn't that wonderful? They'll be working with us on some very exciting new projects."

Abigail Spender's voice screeched through the room like nails on a chalkboard. Sam was sure he could see the professor's hand tighten around his cup of punch and his facial muscles twitch as he turned to greet her with a quick, steely smile. Ms. Spender extended her hand. The professor took it in his own and lifted her pink-polished fingertips to his lips.

"Always a pleasure, Ms. Spender. My, aren't you, uh, a vision this afternoon."

"Oh, Professor. You're too kind," she giggled back.

Abigail Spender stood silently floating on clouds of bliss until the professor continued.

"And who is it that you have with you, my dear Ms. Spender?"

Regaining her composure, Ms. Spender formally introduced Sam and the Middletons to the head of the archaeology department, Professor Avery Mandrake. A widower for the past few years, the professor was now one of the university's most eligible bachelors, and Ms. Spender seemed to be hopelessly smitten.

"Professor Mandrake is *such* a busy man. It's always a pleasant surprise when he is able to attend one of our little soirées!"

With Sam and his parents trapped at her side, Ms. Spender continued to natter on about Professor Mandrake's work at the university, oblivious to the barely polite interest returned to her. It did not take long, however, for Professor Mandrake to grow impatient with poor Ms. Spender's adoration. Soon he was gazing absently across the room while she prattled on, glancing back to her from time to time with a look of utter boredom. She, however, remained oblivious. Sam's parents shuffled uncomfortably. When Ms. Spender's conversation suddenly turned to the Middletons, however, and the location of their new gallery, the professor instantly perked up.

"The old Hawthorne place, is it? Well, a splendid location for an art gallery! Dripping with atmosphere and charm. I do hope it proves to be a most fruitful endeavor for you."

The professor sidled closer to Sam and his parents. Sam detected the faint odor of mothballs emanating from his clothes. He took a step back. The professor continued.

"I must admit, I was somewhat shocked when I heard of Professor Hawthorne's sudden departure. It's quite unprofessional. I can't imagine what got into the old man. I don't suppose you have a forwarding address for him?"

"The professor was well gone by the time we arrived," replied Sam's father.

"Nothing at all? A bit of mail, perhaps?" Professor Mandrake asked.

"I'm afraid not."

Professor Mandrake seemed very interested in Professor Hawthorne's whereabouts.

"We were very close colleagues, you know. I have fond memories of Professor Hawthorne. We shared many evenings of stimulating conversation. My office was right next to his, and with the natural overlap in our disciplines of history and archaeology, we would often talk late into the night about subjects that, I am quite sure, the average person wouldn't understand."

Professor Mandrake smiled again. This time, it was a cold and sly stretching of the lips that looked, to Sam at least, more like a grimace. That, along with a prominent gap between his two front teeth, gave the professor a distinctly reptilian appearance. Sam shuddered. Ms. Spender, giddy with thoughts of romance and a little too much fruit punch, giggled and touched the professor's arm lightly. She glanced across the room.

"Is that charming son of yours in attendance, Professor Mandrake?"

The professor, sensing an opportunity for escape, looked at Ms. Spender.

"Basil? Why, yes, indeed he is. I believe he is sampling some of the delightful fare at the buffet over there."

"Oh, wonderful!" trilled Ms. Spender. She leaned down and whispered to Sam. "Basil Mandrake would be a most suitable acquaintance for you, young man. Why don't you run along and introduce yourself?"

Sam looked across the room. Sampling the fare hardly described what the pudgy blond boy at the buffet table was doing. Holding a plate already piled with sandwiches, pieces of chicken, vegetables, and salads, the boy stood by the table, greedily stuffing into his mouth whatever remaining selections wouldn't fit onto his plate. Sam didn't like the look of the boy, but when his mother looked plaintively at him, he sighed and walked towards him. He was just about to say hello, when another smaller boy, his head tucked between the

covers of a very large book, bumped into him as he brushed past. The only part of the boy that Sam could see was a mop of curly black hair and the upper rim of a pair of thick, over-sized glasses.

"Sorry," the boy mumbled, slipping past.

"That's okay," said Sam.

Suddenly, Basil Mandrake stuck out a chunky black-booted foot and sent boy and book flying. Then Basil dropped a cel-ery stick to the floor.

Peeping above the rim of Sam's shirt pocket, Mr. Goodfellow let out a gasp as he watched the scene unfold. Trying to juggle his book as he stumbled, the boy fell headfirst onto the floor, then rolled over twice. He finally ended up flat on his back, his book trapped beneath him. His thick glasses had sailed through the air and landed in a bowl of shrimp dip. When everyone crowded about them, Basil reached down and picked the celery stick off the floor, claiming it as the reason for the boy's fall. Sam spun around to see if there was another witness to Basil's treachery, but he (and Mr. Goodfellow, of course) had been the only ones. Sam opened his mouth to protest when the unmistakably shrill voice of Abigail Spender shrieked across the room.

"Oh, dear!" she wailed, rushing over to observe the scene. "I do hope there's no serious injury."

A slightly built man and a buxom woman rushed out of the crowd and over to the boy. While Ms. Spender hovered nervously, they helped him to his feet and began to brush a thin layer of dust from his bottom.

"I'm okay, Mum," he whispered, his cheeks a bright red. "Dad, I'm fine, really."

It was clear to Sam that the boy was mortified. To Ms. Spender's relief, it appeared that the only injury had been to the boy's pride. Sam watched as he retreated across the room with his parents. An older girl who had been standing nearby browsing through a selection of antique books to be auctioned, retrieved the boy's book from the middle of the floor and joined them. The little group whispered amongst themselves until the father crept back to the buffet table and, as discreetly as possible, fished his son's glasses out of the shrimp dip.

Sam turned to stare pointedly at Basil Mandrake. Before turning to join his father at the opposite end of the room, Basil threw Sam a sly smirk. Sam followed his retreating figure, spurred by an equally outraged Mr. Goodfellow. When the boy reached his father, Sam was certain that he saw Avery Mandrake give his son a little wink.

Reluctantly, Sam went to stand next to his parents as they resumed their conversation with Professor Mandrake. Every now and then, he gave Basil an icy stare. There was something very strange about Avery Mandrake, and something down-right nasty about his son, too. Sam didn't trust either of them. His parents, however, seemed oblivious to the unpleasant undercurrents flowing between the boys. Sam's father was thrilled that he had remembered the professor's name without coaching. By the time their conversation had ended, Professor Mandrake had even managed to charm for himself and Basil a dinner invitation to the Middleton home on some future occasion. When it was time to finally move on, a reluctant Ms. Spender excused herself and the Middletons from the professor's side. She had left herself a grand total of ten minutes in which to whisk them around the room to meet the rest of the faculty before the start of the auction.

While his parents were busy with Ms. Spender, Sam found a quiet corner of the room to confer with Mr. Goodfellow.

"Well, that Professor Mandrake is very keen to know what's

become of our Professor Hawthorne, isn't he, my boy? We should keep an eye on him," said Mr. Goodfellow, peeping out from Sam's pocket. "Look! He's off to the buffet! Quick, take me over there, Sam! Now that I think of it, I am feeling a tad peckish myself, aren't you? I think you should probably give the shrimp dip a miss—but did you see the size of those figs?"

How Mr. Goodfellow could think of eating at a time like this was beyond Sam. All Sam could think about was having to deal with those horrible Mandrakes at his house, and how he was going to manage to slip out of the reception without being noticed. Mr. Goodfellow suggested they wait until the auction started—that way everyone would be preoccupied.

Sam wandered over to the buffet table, keeping a safe distance from Professor Mandrake, who was decorating his plate with an assortment of cheese and crackers. His mother rushed over to his side.

"Are you alright, dear? Having a nice time?"

"Yes, fine, Mum," said Sam, folding his arms across his chest. His mother looked up and sighed.

"Oh, goodness. Here she comes again."

Ms. Spender, waving a couple of auction paddles above her head, her nest of hair beginning to slide to one side, was hurrying across the floor towards them. The auction was about to start. She and her staff had been hard at work for the past few months canvassing local individuals and businesses. What they had managed to accumulate was an odd collection of items ranging from weekend trips and gift certificates to unidentifiable objects that would have probably been best left in someone's basement. All proceeds, however, were to benefit the university's Arts program, from the acquisition of new works for the on-site gallery to covering the costs of mounting and promoting future exhibitions. Everyone picked up their numbered paddles and took their seats in anticipation of the first bid.

"Will you be all right, dear?" said Sam's mother, before she was swept away again.

"Yes, Mum, fine. I think I'll try to find Professor Mandrake's son, Basil, okay?"

"That's sounds nice, dear, but don't wander too far away."

Sam walked back to his quiet corner of the room and looked into his shirt pocket where Mr. Goodfellow sat knee-deep in discarded date pits. He was busy brushing some cracker crumbs and bits of sticky fig from his coat when Sam poked a finger inside to remove the refuse.

"Thank you, my boy. It was beginning to get a bit tight in here. That's much better." He stretched himself and peered at the scene outside, wiping his mouth with a white handkerchief.

"Excellent! They're taking their seats, Sam. Our chance has come!"

Sam took one last look around the room, and slipped out the door. He found himself in a long, deserted hallway. His brand new sneakers, an additional item in his parent's moving bribe bag, squeaked noticeably as he made his way along the highly polished linoleum floor. At the end of the hall, he reached an intersection that had signs and arrows pointing in a number of directions. One pointed to the student cafeteria, one the sports gymnasium, another the administration services, and finally, one to the staff offices. Sam took a quick glance behind him and hurried down the appropriate hallway. There were dozens of doors, each bearing a black-lettered glass panel. The first one read "A. Spender—Department of Fine Arts," the second one, "S. Jaffrey—Department of Chemistry." There were a half dozen more doors before he reached "A.

Mandrake—Department of Archaeology." with "C. Hawthorne —Department of History" right next to it.

This was it! Sam had expected that the office doors would be locked, but Professor Hawthorne's door was strangely ajar. He tried a couple of the others, but they were all locked, including Professor Mandrake's. Sam touched the open door. It creaked ever so slightly as he gently pushed it with his fingertip. None of the offices had windows so, apart from the dim glow of the corridor light that filtered through the glass panel, it was dark inside. Sam pulled a thin penlight from his pocket and shone it around the room. The narrow beam of light hit a couple of cabinets, a rosewood credenza which held a beautiful globe of the ancient world, two swivel chairs, and another unmarked door at the side of the room. An even tinier beam of light, directed from the general direction of Sam's shirt pocket, also scoured the area. Sam trained his penlight on a large, oak desk in the middle of the room. Its surface was covered with stacks of notes, file folders, and books. Loose pieces of paper were lying in the seat of the padded leather chair with dozens more scattered on the floor beneath it.

"What a mess!" whispered Sam.

"Indeed!" replied Mr. Goodfellow.

As he leaned out of the pocket, Mr. Goodfellow directed Sam to sift through as many of the pages as he could. There were essays on Roman aqueducts and Greek military formations, notes on Egyptian burial rituals, Celtic marriage ceremonies, and Aboriginal rock painting.

"Interesting," said Mr. Goodfellow, as he perused each page, "but I don't think that this is what we're looking for. This ancient history is, well, ancient history, I'm afraid! What has captured the professor's fancy right now is anyone's guess."

167

Just then the sound of footsteps approached from down the hall.

"Someone's coming my boy!" whispered Mr. Goodfellow, quickly switching off his flashlight and popping his head back down into Sam's pocket.

The footsteps stopped just outside Professor Hawthorne's door. Sam switched off his penlight and held his breath. They could hear voices from the hallway.

"Are we supposed to clean in there, Al? There's stuff all over the place. Can't really expect us to clean around that, can they? He'll probably be back soon to straighten it up himself anyway, don't you think?"

"Your guess is as good as mine, Tom," said another voice. The first voice continued.

"Wonder where the old bird has flown to? I figured he was fused to that chair. Always seemed to be around, day and night, burning the midnight oil, you know. Nervous little guy too, always poking his head out the door to see who was about. He was friendly enough when he saw it was me, mind you. Offered me a cup of tea a couple of times. Seems funny not to see him here, although I gotta admit I was getting tired of those kooky sayings of his. I must have heard that 'cleanliness is next to godliness' one a million times! It's weird, too, eh? It's such a mess in there, and the guy was so fussy. Did ya see? Labels on everything."

"Yep," said the quieter man. "He was an odd bird, alright."

Sam could feel Mr. Goodfellow bristle in his pocket.

"Well, I never! Such disrespect! The man was, I mean *is*, a brilliant scholar. If they had any idea of the great thinking that had taken place within these four walls, the great mind that had toiled in that very chair! Hmph!"

Sam quickly placed his hand over his pocket to muffle Mr.

Goodfellow's speech. The little man was still mumbling away as Sam tiptoed to the far end of the office. He crouched down and wedged himself beneath the credenza and out of sight.

From their new location, Sam and Mr. Goodfellow could just barely make out the conversation from beyond the door.

"Speaking of tea, Al, I could really go for something like that right now. What do ya say? Coffee break?"

"That'll make the fourth one today, Tom. We'll be floating home!"

"Ah, come on, Al. I'll go get us a couple of chairs. You raid the machine this time."

There was a fair amount of clattering outside the door as Tom and Al secured their refreshments and made themselves comfortable. Mr. Goodfellow complained bitterly about the cleaning staff and their decision to park themselves in front of this very office.

Deciding to look on the positive side for a change, Sam arranged himself more comfortably on the floor and announced that now might be a good time to continue with Edgar's story.

"Tell the rest of the story now, my boy? I really don't think I could, under the circumstances."

"Oh, please!" implored Sam. "Maybe it'll help you calm down a bit."

"My nerves are quite alright, I assure you. I am simply frustrated. You must admit the events of the past few days have been enough to test anyone's temper." He studied Sam's face and then began to smile. "You're really keen on Edgar's adventures, aren't you? Very well. To the story it is! Where were we again? Oh, yes, the descent of the flying machine, wasn't it?"

Mr. Goodfellow settled himself down in Sam's pocket.

"I'll just make myself a little more comfortable. Can you hear me, my boy?"

"Yeah, no problem," replied Sam.

"Splendid. Off we go, then."

While the office cleaning crew took another long coffee break just outside the door, Sam, sitting cross-legged under Professor Hawthorne's rosewood credenza, awaited the fate of Edgar and his Uncle Jolly. He closed his eyes and returned to the scene of the da Vinci crash.

11

WHEN THE CAUSE IS
JUST, THE SMALL CONQUER
THE GREAT

The last few patches of dewy fog had floated inland now, beyond the coastal hills, to reveal a turquoise blue sky above. On the ground below, in a field of poppies, lay the crumpled remains of the miniature flying machine. Atop a mattress of beautiful, orange flowers, Mr. Goodfellow felt a troubling pressure on his face and chest. He labored to take each breath and slowly opened his eyes. He was greeted by pitch-blackness and was just beginning to panic when he realized it was because Edgar was lying on top of him. He raised his one free arm and prodded Edgar's behind a few times until he began to stir.

"I say, Edgar, are you able to move your arms and legs, my boy?"

"Yes, I think so, Uncle Jolly."

"Then, if you would be so kind, could you do so now? I believe I am in immediate peril of suffocation."

Edgar rolled off with a great thud. As he blew a few fur fibers past his teeth and into the air, Mr. Goodfellow struggled to his feet. There was a sudden, sharp pain at the base of his leg. Leaning onto Edgar's shoulder, he hobbled from the wreckage and sat down on a low, flat rock. He unbuttoned his mouse foot and rolled up a section of his suit to get a better look at his injury. Edgar winced. There was a large gash, just above the ankle in the soft fleshy part of his leg. Mr. Goodfellow directed Edgar to his trunk, which had rolled away from the flying machine and into a small ditch.

"Top drawer, right hand side, my boy," said Mr. Goodfellow, after Edgar managed to pull the trunk into an upright position.

Edgar found a small first aid kit, stocked with an abundant supply of gauze, bandages, and antiseptic, all clearly labeled in Uncle Jolly's neat handwriting. This was common territory to Edgar, who, in his relatively short existence, had gone through a lifetime's worth of first aid supplies. Tearing a small piece of gauze from the roll, he dabbed at his uncle's leg with the cool antiseptic liquid, then carefully wound the gauze round and round the leg. He secured it in place with a long strip of sticking plaster, rolling the suit leg down as far as it would go over the bulge of the bandage. Mr. Goodfellow then carefully slid his foot back into his mouse paw. Edgar wound a long piece of gauze two or three times around his ankle and fastened it with a tight knot.

They rested now, but only for a moment. It was already late afternoon and it was imperative they locate the Sparrow Ranch before dark. Edgar searched through the wreckage for an appropriate length of wood that Mr. Goodfellow could use as a walking stick. Beatrice and Charlotte's small bags were stacked inside the trunk, which Edgar insisted on pulling. Mr. Goodfellow was able to manage Edgar's suitcase and they continued their journey across the hills. With the guidance of the setting sun, they were able to make their way towards the northeast. The rather sketchy directions to the ranch that Mr.

Goodfellow remembered from Beatrice's conversations had led them in the right direction, but he wished again that they had a more detailed route to follow now that it was so late in the day.

"Watch your step, my boy, there appear to be a number of old gopher holes about," warned Mr. Goodfellow, as he maneuvered himself and his walking stick through the maze of deep, black holes that littered the ground.

He had no sooner said this, of course, when Edgar suddenly disappeared from view. He returned, moments later, flying through the air, having being violently ejected out of the hole. Handfuls of dirt sprayed up behind him. Baffled, Edgar staggered to his feet, brushing clouds of dust from his coat. Mr. Goodfellow tried to calm him down.

"This may have been a rather serendipitous encounter after all, my boy! I assumed these holes were abandoned, but apparently not. Do let me take care of this alone, Edgar. Gophers are easily unnerved, and on top of being reclusive they can also be occasionally unpleasant."

Mr. Goodfellow placed his face directly over the hole and shouted as loudly as possible (in a dialect familiar to the species).

"HELLO! I SAY...HELLOOOOOO!"

Another cloud of dirt burst out of the opening, followed by the large and rather menacing head of a gopher. Two prominent teeth and a pair of flashing eyes pierced through the mass of dirt-encrusted fur and crumpled whiskers. Edgar immediately jumped back. Wiping the dust from his eyes with the back of his arm, Mr. Goodfellow extended a friendly paw, but the creature did not respond.

"I do beg your pardon. My nephew and I are trying to locate the Sparrow Ranch and Spa."

There was still no response. Mr. Goodfellow tried again.

"It is most urgent that we speak with Hartland and Edwina Sparrow. Their granddaughter, Charlotte, may be in some danger, and..."

Specific mention of the Sparrow family seemed to strike a positive chord with the crusty gopher. Moving out slightly from the hole, and shifting his eyes from side to side, he pointed a trembling paw in the direction of the next hill. Then, he drew a map in the dirt with a broken twig. Edgar had never seen a gopher before. He noticed on closer study that his two front teeth were chipped and yellowing and clearly his toenails had not been attended to in some time.

"Well, thank you so very much. It was very kind of..." But before Mr. Goodfellow could properly thank him, the creature had disappeared down the hole again in a great cloud of dirt.

"He was very odd, wasn't he, Uncle Jolly?" said Edgar tactfully.

"They are, in general, quite a jumpy lot, my boy, but in my experience I have found them to be exceptionally intelligent and trustworthy."

The late afternoon sun had melted into dusk now. They trudged over the hills, as quickly as they could in light of Mr. Goodfellow's injury, in the direction provided by the gopher. They made their way past a number of small sheds and out-buildings, until the faint but welcoming glow of lights from a much bigger structure could be seen up ahead.

"If our gopher's directions were accurate, Edgar, and I don't doubt that they were, then those lights must be the Sparrow compound," said Mr. Goodfellow, pausing and pointing his walking stick into the air. When he hobbled on again, his voice took on a much more serious tone. "I do hope that Beatrice and Charlotte are both safely inside."

It was becoming difficult to see anything in the half-light, maneuvering as they were through fences, past lean-tos, boxes, barrels, and over the occasional pile of rocks. Edgar chattered to Mr. Goodfellow about the gopher, not paying particular attention to where he was going. Suddenly there was a bump followed by a gurgling sound.

"Uncle Jolly! Help!"

"Good gracious, my boy...what is it now?"

"I've fallen into something wet and sticky."

Mr. Goodfellow stepped in the direction of Edgar's pathetic cries. He had, it appeared, tripped headfirst into a large barrel of fermenting grapes. His furry paws gripped the wooden sides as Mr. Goodfellow reached out to assist him.

"Well, it looks as if we've reached the winemaking facility, my boy," said Mr. Goodfellow, sniffing delicately at the pungent grape smell wafting from Edgar.

Taking hold of one of Edgar's soggy paws he gave it a tug. Thankfully, the rest of Edgar soon followed behind. Edgar's suit had now become quite toxic. The unfortunate dunking had, if anything, enhanced the lingering odor of disinfectant and burnt fur. Mr. Goodfellow had to turn his nose away before he could speak again.

"I'm very sorry, Edgar, but that's it I'm afraid. The suit will have to go. Apart from the, well, aroma, I'm quite sure that you are also dangerously flammable. We haven't time to deal with it now, though. We must first attend to the situation at hand."

At that, he limped on towards the lights. Edgar took hold of the trunk handle again and shuffled along behind, looking down at his suit. His coat, now a rich cherry brown color, was beginning to dry in little spiked clumps. He couldn't wait to step out of it, especially before Charlotte laid her eyes (and nose) upon him. He looked up at the sky. Dark gray clouds had begun to blow in from the sea. It looked like rain and Edgar was sure he could hear thunder in the distance too.

They reached a carved wooden sign hanging from a nearby post. It had indeed been the lights of Sparrow Ranch that they had been making for all this time. A few steps later, they were relieved to find themselves off the dark hillsides and under the cover of a large front porch. Mr. Goodfellow gave the redwood door a forceful knock, and as he and Edgar waited for it to open, it began to drizzle. It was Hartland Sparrow who welcomed them inside, a powerful looking man whose movements were slow and labored. It immediately became apparent that Beatrice and Charlotte had not arrived, nor had they been heard from. Edwina, Hartland's wife, rushed to the door. At the sight of Mr. Goodfellow, the color drained from her face. She and Hartland had been expecting Beatrice and Charlotte any day now. When Mr. Goodfellow filled them in on the other more troubling aspects of the story, Edwina gasped and Hartland began to sway unsteadily on his feet.

Charlotte's baby brother, Porter, was playing happily in a playpen in the corner. He was blissfully unaware of the tense family drama that was unfolding before him and was understandably irritated when Edwina, fighting back a flood of tears, swept him into her arms and hugged him close. He pushed his chubby arms out as far as they would go and tried to wiggle free. Edwina held him even tighter.

"Oh, what has become of them?" she wailed.

Mr. Goodfellow feared that panic would soon engulf them all, until Edgar's small voice broke through.

"Who's that?" he cried pointing out the window to a figure, just visible through the steady rain, stumbling towards the house. Hartland pushed open the door and hobbled out-

176

side, returning moments later with a pale and dripping Charlotte clinging to his neck.

"Nana Beatrice pushed me away from them, Grandpa! Then she called those awful creatures to her and told me to run away. I ran and ran, as fast as I could!" Charlotte buried her face in Hartland's chest. "They were horrible things! I shouldn't have left her there, Grandpa, I shouldn't!" she sobbed.

Edwina, still clutching the baby, rushed to her granddaughter's side.

"You did the right thing, child. Your Grandpa and Mr. Goodfellow will take care of everything now."

Hartland tried to hide his growing concern as he glanced down at Mr. Goodfellow's bandaged leg and then his cane by the door.

Mr. Goodfellow stepped forward and began to speak quietly to Charlotte.

"Charlotte, think carefully now, my dear. Exactly where did you leave Beatrice?"

Charlotte, warm and safe in her grandfather's arms, had calmed down sufficiently to provide an accurate account of Beatrice's whereabouts. When The Fen had revealed themselves on the train, Beatrice and Charlotte had, as Mr. Goodfellow suspected, jumped out at an earlier stop to give them the slip. They had nearly made it as far as the Sparrow Ranch, but the Fen caught up to them, and they were suddenly cut off. Beatrice was apparently trapped at the edge of a bay, on a jagged strip of land that bordered the southernmost reaches of Hartland's fields.

Edgar had been listening carefully to Charlotte's story as he stood by the front door. He was also paying keen attention to the rolls of thunder in the distance. He shuffled over to his

177

suitcase and removed something from its interior. Then he turned, gently lifted the door latch, and crept out into the twilight. It was some time before anyone even noticed that he had disappeared.

"Edgar...Edgar?" Mr. Goodfellow's head spun around the room. "Where on earth has that boy gone?"

"You don't suppose..." began Edwina, her voice shaking, as she clutched her grandchildren to her.

Before she even had time to complete her sentence, Mr. Goodfellow was out the front door and halfway down the path. Not far behind him hobbled Hartland Sparrow, struggling into the arms and legs of his mouse suit.

It was quite dark and the rain had begun to fall with increasing strength. Though his mouse suit provided some protection from the rain's stinging blows, Edgar tried to stay under the canopy of grape leaves as he hurried through the storm. It was impossible, though, to escape the damp sea air that crept its way through his mouse suit to his pale, pink skin. By the time the ragged outline of the rocky cliffs came into view, Edgar was shivering from head to toe. Several times Edgar feared he would lose his nerve, but at each of those moments, the face of his father mysteriously filtered through the mist and beckoned him on.

In spite of the fading light, Edgar had little trouble finding Beatrice. The sinister presence of The Fen had become a powerful beacon. Edgar knew he was drawing nearer with every step. Sudden flashes of lightning illuminated his path, and Edgar carefully counted under his breath the seconds before each boom of thunder. Edgar became so engrossed in his counting that when he finally looked up he had nearly rushed straight into The Fen.

Dozens of the creatures had gathered, like a huge flock

of crows, at the edge of the cliff. A dark, swirling mass, they reeled round and round in the night air, their coal black cloaks flapping noisily in the wind. The revolting smell of mold and decay filled Edgar's nostrils as he crouched down and moved towards them. He was sure he remembered smelling this same horrible odor before—eighty-six floors above the city of New York, on the observation deck of the Empire State Building, just before the wind had carried it away. He covered the holes in his nose mask with one soggy paw. The unpleasant odor of his own wet mouse suit was nothing compared to The Fen. As he drew closer, he saw that the black swirling creatures were actually circling another figure. This figure was struggling valiantly within the sharp, twisted branches of an old grapevine. It was Beatrice.

"Leave her alone!" shouted Edgar, trying to control the tremor in his voice.

The Fen turned to stare into Edgar's eyes. Just for a second, within the dark recesses of their cloaks, Edgar could see the flash of their eyes and feel their cold, steel glare. They turned their backs on him but Edgar could still hear cruel, hissing laughter as they inched towards Beatrice.

"I said, leave her ALONE!" Edgar puffed out his chest and shouted even louder than before, but The Fen ignored him completely. He was too insignificant to interfere with their plans. What they didn't know, though, was that Edgar Goodfellow had a plan too.

"My name is Goodfellow and I'm on a mission!" he shouted again.

They turned slowly and looked at Edgar once again.

"Goodfellow?" he could hear one of them say in a deep crackling voice. "We know Goodfellows...Which are you?"

"I am Edgar Goodfellow, nephew of the great Jolly and... and son of Filbert!" he cried out.

They began to move towards him.

"It isn't often we get this close to a Goodfellow," croaked another. "Your kind have been a thorn in our sides for far too long. You're nothing but a puny boy. What is your mission?"

Edgar took a deep breath, and backed up to the edge of the cliff. There was nothing below but razor-sharp rocks and the pounding waves of the sea.

"Come closer, if you dare, and I will tell you!" said Edgar.

"Edgar, my boy, no!" shouted Mr. Goodfellow. He and Hartland rushed out from a row of vines towards him.

Edgar waved at his uncle to keep back. The dark shapes crept nearer, trapping him at the edge of the cliff. If he could control his trembling for a moment longer, he would be able to carry out the last step of his plan. There was only an inch or two of ground between Edgar and the churning mass of rocks and water below, and there was no pause now between the cracks of thunder and flashes of lightning. The storm was directly overhead. The Fen edged closer to Edgar. He could hear their evil whispers and feel their chilling breath upon his neck. Then, reaching into his mouse suit, he drew out the metal staple that had clamped his tail to his suit that day in Central Park. He held it over the cliff's edge. Then he looked straight up into the swirling clouds overhead and, with all of his might and in the name of everything good and pure, Edgar Goodfellow prayed for the biggest accident of his life.

There was a sudden, strange silence. The Fen took the opportunity to lunge at Edgar. At the same time, a deafening *CRACK* filled the air! A huge ball of white lightning lit up the night sky. Edgar was instantly catapulted into a pile of nearby grape leaves as the lightning arced toward the staple in his hand. The Fen, who only seconds before had lunged at him, shrieked and scattered into the night. Edgar crawled back to the cliff's edge and peered over. It was too dark to see anything in the churning surf below. What had befallen The Fen was unclear, but the element of surprise had definitely worked in Edgar's favor. Mr. Goodfellow rushed to his side and pulled him up from the ground. They were rid of the evil creatures, at least for now.

"An act of astonishing bravery, but terribly foolish, my boy! You've got those devils on the run! I think it would be most prudent of us to leave this place as quickly as possible, Edgar. The Fen hate to be disturbed from their evil work. Your rather explosive behavior has probably riled them to distraction. If they get their second wind and return, I fear we may all be in the soup!"

They rushed over to Beatrice's side and freed her from the tanglehold of twisted grapevines. When she finally stood free, she turned to Mr. Goodfellow and clung to him as if she would never let go. The four of them then raced through the rows of vines, back to the safety of the ranch. Luckily, The Fen did not return after the electrical explosion, but Mr. Goodfellow warned his group to keep a vigilant watch nevertheless. Beatrice vowed that she would never allow those diabolical creatures to get as close to her again. She would now happily take all the advice that Jolly had to offer.

Weary from their encounters, Beatrice, Edgar, and Mr. Goodfellow decided to spend the next few weeks recuperating at the Sparrow Ranch. The rest of the world would have to wait. Beatrice took this time to have long talks with her cousin. It wasn't often that they had the opportunity. The stirrings in Europe were never far from Beatrice's thoughts now.

She didn't know how long it would be before she and Edwina would see each other again.

Mr. Goodfellow and Hartland had become fast friends. Mr. Goodfellow even convinced him to include a proverb in the next Sparrow Spa brochure—now to be known as the Soaring Sparrow Spa and Vineyard Tour. "A change is often as good as a rest—let Soaring Sparrow make your nest," it read. Edgar even painted a beautiful landscape of the ranch for the brochure's cover.

Edgar and his Uncle Jolly also spent a great deal of time getting to know each other better. Long walks through the Sparrow vineyard created the perfect atmosphere for renewal and reflection. They talked of many things, but the greatest gift that Mr. Goodfellow was able to bestow upon his nephew were his memories of Edgar's father, Filbert. These were wonderful tales that only a younger brother could tell and Edgar knew he would treasure them for a lifetime. Day after day the two could be seen walking under the warm sun, through rows of towering vines, sagging with giant orbs of sweet, round fruit. On one of their daily walks, Edgar felt compelled to broach a subject that had been troubling him for some time.

"For a while now, Uncle Jolly, well, sometimes anyway, I think I can see my Dad. Most of the time it's when I'm feeling sad about something. Mum says it's because of all the pictures of him she keeps around the house, but..."

Mr. Goodfellow stepped in. "She's probably right, my boy. I think of him often, too, and I swear that I can see him from time to time. I'm not one to believe in ghosts, though. Just wishful thinking, I've always thought."

Dear Filbert, Mr. Goodfellow thought to himself. He smiled affectionately at Edgar.

"Your father was a very special soul, and a memory worth

treasuring. You have a great deal to be proud of." He gave his nephew a hug as Edgar nodded his head.

"It doesn't upset you, does it my boy? Seeing him, I mean?"

"No, Uncle Jolly. It makes me feel safe, really." Edgar looked down at the ground, as they continued their walk. "But, it's as if he's trying to say something to me. Then, before I can make it out, he fades away. It's been happening a lot more lately, too. On the night with The Fen it was as if he was actually there, trying to talk to me and help me."

Mr. Goodfellow felt an odd tickling sensation run down his spine. How extraordinary, he thought. He'd had the very same experience himself. It was what Edgar said next though that hit him like a bolt from out of the blue.

"The strangest thing about it, though, Uncle Jolly, is that we don't have any photos of Dad with hair. Dad's bald in all our pictures, so why do I always see him with hair? And with a beard, too?"

Another shiver, with a particularly electrical force, snaked its way from Mr. Goodfellow's neck all the way down to the tip of his tailbone. He and Edgar were having the exact same vision of Filbert! Could these be ghostly warnings or supernatural visitations? He did not want to alarm Edgar any more than necessary. His young nephew was exhausted after their recent adventures, but this development must surely be significant. He decided to keep this confusing information to himself for the time being, until he could determine what it meant.

It was on one of their afternoon walks, later that same week, when Mr. Goodfellow made a decision and turned to his nephew.

"Well, Edgar, I think the time for rejuvenating ourselves is over. We should be thinking about returning home now." Mr.

Goodfellow gave Edgar an affectionate squeeze. "All our sweetest hours fly fastest, don't they, my boy?"

Edgar nodded his head sadly. He wished with all of his heart that this special time didn't have to end.

The day for goodbyes came much too soon for each of them. Edgar's heroic actions on the cliff, and the fact that he looked particularly handsome in Mr. Goodfellow's formal attire, was suddenly making a favorable impression on Charlotte. She actually felt quite sad to see him preparing for departure.

When it came time to leave, Mr. Goodfellow handed Edgar his blue suitcase and asked him to open it. Edgar turned the case on its side, snapped open the locks and lifted the lid. Sitting on top of a great pile of mismatched paws was Mr. Goodfellow's beloved paintbox. Edgar gasped.

"But Uncle Jolly, your paints—you can't give them away!"

"I can, my boy, and I have. Sometimes you feel in your heart when you've made the right decision. These paints are yours to treasure now and you have earned them. You looked fear square in the face, Edgar. I'm very proud of you. We all owe you a debt of gratitude that I very much doubt any of us will ever be able to repay."

He stopped for a moment while he rummaged around in his inside pocket.

"But, perhaps there is one other thing that I can do for you."

Mr. Goodfellow crouched down and gently slapped the side of Edgar's suitcase with his hand. When Edgar leaned down to take a look, there was another sticker on his suitcase's surface: big and bright and red. The others beside it paled in comparison. It said, "Home, Sweet Home." Edgar couldn't believe his eyes. When he looked up again, Mr. Goodfellow was smiling. Edgar threw his arms around his uncle and hugged him close. Mr. Goodfellow happily returned the embrace and whispered into Edgar's ear.

"We're going home, Edgar. I hope these travels will always mean something to you. And you know, my boy, I think I've learned a valuable lesson, too. We all have a part to play in this world, don't we? Happy, indeed, is the man who can find his own special role before it's too late."

After Edwina and Beatrice had dried their tears, after Porter had been sufficiently bounced and tickled and cuddled, and after everyone else had embraced and exchanged their hopes and promises, it was time to leave the haven of Soaring Sparrow. Hartland, Edwina, and little Porter waved from the front porch as Charlotte accompanied Mr. Goodfellow, Beatrice, and Edgar to the edge of the vineyard. They wanted to take one last walk in the luscious fields, hoping this sweet memory would sustain them through whatever trials the future had in store. It was a truly magical place, caressed by soft mists and sea winds, with its rocky cliffs and gently rolling hills. Beatrice could only hope that her own little coastal refuge might one day be as captivating.

12

EVERY PICTURE TELLS
A STORY

"That's it! That's it!" cried Sam, as Mr. Goodfellow ended his story. "That's where the photograph in the album was taken! The one with the two fuzzy blobs. The one with you and Edgar together! The bright blue sky and green fields. It was in Hartland Sparrow's vineyards, wasn't it?"

"Why, yes, my boy, I believe it was." Mr. Goodfellow had a faraway look in his eyes.

"Did you take any other pictures?" asked Sam.

"Let me see, yes, I believe we did. I had discovered, quite by accident, my old camera in the bottom drawer of my trunk, just the day before. There were two shots left. I believe young Charlotte may have taken the snap of Edgar and myself."

"You said two shots—what about the other one? Is it in the album?" asked Sam.

Mr. Goodfellow gazed about him absently.

"No, no, my boy, it's not in the album."

Reaching beneath his mouse suit to the inside pocket of his blue checked shirt, Mr. Goodfellow pulled out a little white handkerchief. It had purple flowers embroidered at the corners and had been folded into a neat square. He carefully unwrapped the handkerchief, corner by corner, revealing a creased and much-handled photograph within. He looked at it closely, slowly running his finger around its dog-eared edges, before handing it to Sam.

"Edgar took this one, I believe."

He must have, thought Sam to himself. There was a big black thumb smudge completely blocking the bottom right side of the picture. Luckily, the blur had missed the two figures at the center, although the photographer had managed to clip off the tips of their mouse ears. It was, of course, Beatrice and Mr. Goodfellow, standing together, arm in arm. Sam noticed that the picture had a sweet, flowery scent about it.

Mr. Goodfellow took the photograph back and slowly wrapped it in the little white handkerchief. He slipped it inside his shirt pocket, and patted it affectionately before he zipped up his suit.

"I have some wonderful memories, Sam. The remembrance of a life well spent is sweet."

When he looked down into his face, Sam noticed that Mr. Goodfellow's dark twinkling eyes had tiny pools of water in each corner.

"That was quite a remarkable summer, indeed," Mr. Goodfellow mumbled quietly.

"But what happened next? What happened to everyone?" Sam demanded. "What about Beatrice? Did she follow her dream? Did she make a difference? You have to tell me that!"

Mr. Goodfellow lifted his head.

"Yes, Sam, indeed she did, and with great flourish, too, I might add. All in all, you could say that it was her finest hour!" he continued. He wiped his eyes with the back of his paw and they began to twinkle playfully again. "I did hear tell, though, that by the end of her mission, she had cultivated quite an appetite for cigars. But that, my boy, is another story."

"And Charlotte?"

"She and Porter remained at Sparrow Ranch with Hartland and Edwina until their parents returned from South America a few months later. Let's see... Charlotte would be apprenticing now and young Porter must be almost five. My, how time flies!"

Sam remembered what Mr. Goodfellow had said about how the end of Edgar's story had never been written.

"Mr. Goodfellow?" Sam asked slowly. "What happened to Edgar?"

Mr. Goodfellow looked up at Sam sadly. He had known as he was telling Edgar's story that he would face this question at the end.

"I don't know, Sam."

"What do you mean?"

"After we returned to England at the end of the summer, Edgar and I bid farewell to dear Beatrice. She was anxious to get on with her work. Edgar had grown quite fond of her, and I, well... as always it was very difficult for me to say a proper goodbye. Edgar and I made our way to my flat for the night. The next day we planned to travel to Great Uncle Cyrus' house where we would be meeting with the rest of the family again. We would have to tell them, of course, that the apprenticing had not gone quite according to plan. I encouraged Edgar to tell them that he believed he would be better suited to pursue another role in life. He was naturally apprehensive about this, but I told him to have faith. I armed myself with a portfolio of his artwork and stories of his remarkable abilities to engage young ones. I, for one, have felt for a number of years that the education and cultural nurturing of young Sage could do with a substantial overhaul. I have often dreamed of starting a progressive academy of some sort, where our young people could discover more about the world and be exposed to the contributions of all the great Sage before them. And as far as running the school, Edgar would be a perfect candidate to groom for the job. When I tucked him into bed that night I reminded him of an important adage. 'Know thyself, Edgar Goodfellow, and to thine own self be true.' I never dreamed that might be the last thing I would say to him or the last time I might ever see him."

The tears were streaming liberally from Mr. Goodfellow's eyes now. As he continued, he attempted to stem the flow with a soggy hanky.

"When I awoke the next morning, Edgar was gone. At first I thought that he'd had an attack of nerves and that he would turn up some time later. I postponed the meeting with the family and waited at home. A few days passed and I began to grow concerned. Edgar would not have let me worry so. By the end of the week, I was heartsick. I could delay no longer. I had to inform the family that Edgar was gone, spirited away from us just like his father. And just like his father, there were no clues to his fate. It was quite unbearable. The two people that meant the most to me in the world had disappeared. And my sister-in-law, Hazel—well, I can't begin to tell you what she has gone through all these years. I can't imagine how she has managed to cope with the loss of both her husband and her son. It is a tragedy that no one should have to bear."

"Did you try to find Edgar?" asked Sam, quietly.

"Of course, my boy, but to no avail, I'm afraid. There were no clues and no trail to follow. It was as if he had vanished into thin air."

Mr. Goodfellow closed his eyes and sighed. Telling Edgar's

story to Sam had been a memory-laden journey for him. Thoughts of Edgar and Filbert and how much he missed them both filled his mind. He thought, too, of Beatrice and the ocean of years that lay between them. One of his collected proverbs came to mind and it was true indeed: "all the treasures of the earth could not bring back one lost moment." How he wished with all his heart that he could turn back the clock.

Sam didn't know what to say. He felt he knew Edgar so well that it was as if he, too, had suddenly lost his dearest friend.

13

A Good Cause
Makes a Stout Heart
and a Strong Arm

There was a sudden flurry of activity outside Professor Hawthorne's office door. Metal chair legs scratched against the hallway floor. Voices grew louder, then gradually faded into the distance. As the cleaning crew wandered down the hall and around another corner, Mr. Goodfellow pulled himself out of his melancholy and tugged at Sam's shirt. He suggested they finish up quickly and be on their way too.

Sam crawled out from under the credenza. Turning their flashlights on again, they were about to direct their attention to another pile of papers on top of the professor's desk, when the sound of more footsteps made them freeze in their tracks. A nearby door was unlocked and opened. Sam quickly turned off his light and tried very hard not to breathe.

"It really is getting a bit too busy around here for my liking. Perhaps it would be prudent to cut short our visit for now, my boy," whispered Mr. Goodfellow.

Sam agreed and tiptoed towards the door. All was quiet and still. Just as Sam was about to slip back out into the corridor, he heard the creak of another door opening somewhere behind him. Suddenly someone grabbed him by the collar of his Nana blazer and pulled him away from the door. Sam's clip-on tie dug deeply into his neck as he struggled to take a breath. Thrashing about in the dark, Sam's heart was pounding. Inside his pocket, the heart of Mr. Goodfellow was pounding even harder. And in that tangle of arms and hands and twisted clothes, Sam could make out the distinct and overwhelming stench of mothballs. As he swung his arms about in an attempt to free himself, the collar and lapel of his brand new navy blazer suddenly tore loose. He was free at last! He pushed open the door, raced down the hall and out the nearest exit into the near blinding light of the afternoon sun. Footsteps pounded behind him.

Sam scrambled down a grassy embankment and onto the courtyard lawn. There was only a handful of people wandering about now. Most of the crowd had settled inside for the auction. Sam's eyes darted one way and then another, in a desperate attempt to find a hiding spot. He finally settled on the bright red and gold stripes of Madam Zorah's tent. Racing across the last stretch of lawn, Sam slipped through the beaded curtain and into the dark interior. He slumped down on one of the chairs in front of the table, breathless and shaking.

"You have come back to me, I see. For your fortune, no?"

"Aaahh!" Sam screamed. His eyes had not yet adjusted to the dim lighting and the sound of Madam Zorah's voice seemed to come from nowhere.

"Do not be frightened, young one. Give me your hand," she said.

"No!" cried Sam. Then, "Um...I mean okay."

"Good," said Madam Zorah. "I hoped you would return."

Sam stared at the flickering candle reflected in the old

gypsy's eyes. The dying light danced down Madam Zorah's wrinkled forehead and across her hollowed cheeks and thin ruby lips. Suddenly she reached across the table and grabbed one of Sam's hands, holding it with her long bony fingers. Sam struggled to free himself from her icy grasp, but he was trapped. She turned his palm up and pulled it closer to her.

"Let me see what the lines say about you."

Sam licked his lips nervously. Madam Zorah stared intently at his palm.

"Lifeline is very long. Strong, too, I see."

Whew! thought Sam. At least he wasn't going to be murdered at the reception.

"You are a determined young man. You will be successful in your work, but I do not see what your work will be. Soon you must make a decision. It will be a very important decision—very difficult." Madam Zorah slowly drew a long yellow nail across Sam's palm. "Such a decision is unusual for one so young."

Then she dropped Sam's hand and looked straight into his eyes.

"Aha! It is as I thought when you came with your mother. There is something strange about you. I see strange visions, too—the stars and planets, journeys of many years, lines and circles. Fields of grain? I cannot explain. What do these things mean to you, child?"

"I don't know, said Sam nervously. "I don't know what they mean."

Madam Zorah continued. "There is something protecting you, but great evil follows you too. It is an evil as old as time."

Sam swallowed with difficulty, turning to look toward the beaded curtain. Madame Zorah grabbed his hand again and pulled it closer.

"Something else, child. I sense an ancient life force in you. It is very powerful," she continued. "What do I see now? Two souls?" She looked at him suspiciously.

"Oops," whispered Sam. Mr. Goodfellow began to squirm inside his pocket. Madam Zorah was good, he thought.

"I think I have to go," said Sam. "My parents must be looking for me."

"No, please!" pleaded Madame Zorah. "Stay with me, child. There is more!" Madam Zorah reached out once again with her long yellow fingernails.

"No! I really have to go!" Sam stood up quickly knocking his wooden chair to the ground and bumping the table with his knee. The candle tottered for a moment then fell to the floor, sizzling in the oozing wax as a thin wisp of gray smoke rose into the air. The old gypsy rose from her chair too. Then she lifted her hands to cup the sides of her head. Even in the dim light of the tent's interior, Sam could see a strange expression on her face.

"Wait! There are three souls now! Three!" She stared at Sam with wide, frightened eyes. Her hands were trembling and her body began to sway back and forth. "I feel badly," she said thickly, "I must speak with my husband. Wait for me here, child!" Madam Zorah brushed past him and out through the beaded curtain.

"Sam?" Mr. Goodfellow whispered from the shirt pocket. "Is she gone, my boy?"

"Yes. She didn't look very well."

"Hardly surprising, really. It must have come as quite a shock to the poor lady to sense the presence of two souls before her. I am at a loss to explain, however, what on earth she meant about three..."

"Uncle Jolly?"

"Yes, Sam?" said Mr. Goodfellow, thinking how nice it was that the boy felt close enough to him to call him uncle.

"Uh, I didn't say anything," said Sam.

"Are you sure? I distinctly heard...Oh, never mind." Mr. Goodfellow sighed. "Perhaps I shouldn't have gone on so about Edgar the way I did, my boy. I fear I am to be plagued now." Mr. Goodfellow tapped the side of his head. "Is there no end to the torment? First it was that incessant humming noise. Now that it has finally subsided, my mind has resorted to playing even crueler tricks on me, Sam. I thought I heard..."

"Uncle Jolly, is...is that *you*?"

Sam and Mr. Goodfellow froze. Sam hadn't said a word.

"Edgar?" Mr. Goodfellow shouted frantically. "Edgar? It can't be! Is that you?" Mr. Goodfellow began to scramble out of Sam's pocket.

"Down here, Uncle Jolly. By the table leg." Sam knelt down on the ground and lifted up the tablecloth to peer beneath. Tucked away in the shadows was a small figure.

"Quickly, Sam! Help me down!"

Oblivious to danger in his excitement, Mr. Goodfellow had already swung one furry leg and the greater portion of his backside out of the shirt pocket and was dangling precariously over the edge. Sam scooped him up and set him gently on the ground.

"Edgar! Edgar!" Mr. Goodfellow raced under the table. The smaller figure, dressed in a dark-colored mouse suit, slipped out from behind a table leg, and threw itself into Mr. Goodfellow's outstretched arms.

Tears trickled out from under Mr. Goodfellow's face mask. He pulled the mask off over his head and let it drop to the ground. He lifted Edgar's face mask up, too, and set it on top of his head.

"Let me look at you, my dear boy! I feared I would never see you again. But in all those years, I never gave up hope. Never...not once! What on earth are you doing here, Edgar? Where have you been?"

"I was passing by the tent when I heard Madam Zorah's reading. I couldn't believe what she was saying so I slipped under the canvas to hear the rest. You see, she was giving the boy the exact same fortune that I was given by a fortune teller mouse just yesterday, word for word!" Edgar had lowered his voice to barely a whisper and Sam strained to hear.

"Who is that boy, Uncle Jolly? And why were you in his pocket? I didn't think we were supposed to..."

"It's alright, Edgar. It's a bit of a long story, but I found myself in a most awkward predicament. I owe a great deal to this boy. His name is Sam. Say hello, Edgar."

"Well, I don't know. I've never actually spoken to..."

"Go ahead, Edgar. Sam is quite special. You'll see."

Edgar shuffled forward, wiping his tears away with a furry sleeve.

"Hello," he said shyly.

"Hi," said Sam, feeling odd. It was strange to be meeting Edgar for the first time. He knew so much about him already.

Mr. Goodfellow couldn't resist giving his nephew another bear hug.

"I still can't believe it's you, dear boy! Where in creation have you been?"

"Traveling in secret with the gypsies, Uncle Jolly. Madam Zorah and her husband and the others," explained Edgar. "I live with the mice that follow them."

"All these years, Edgar? All this time? But why?"

"I had to, Uncle Jolly. I had to keep moving." Edgar looked around nervously. "I have to keep moving, even now. I may already have put you in danger. The longer I stay here with you, the greater the danger is. I don't think I should say anymore about it. But when I heard your voice, I just had to see you. Please, Uncle Jolly, let me go now!"

Edgar started to pull away, but Mr. Goodfellow struggled to hold him still. He had waited sixty-five years to find his nephew and he wasn't about to let him go now without a fight.

"What are you talking about, Edgar? What has happened to you? Why did you run away?"

Edgar buried his head in his uncle's shoulder.

"It's too awful, Uncle Jolly. Too awful!"

"Whatever it is, Edgar, you must tell me about it."

Edgar lifted his head.

"I've done a terrible thing, Uncle Jolly, and they have vowed to hunt me down."

"Who have, Edgar?" asked Mr. Goodfellow, bracing himself. "Is it...The Fen?"

Sam felt icy fingers creep along his spine.

Edgar nodded.

"Remember that night, at the edge of the Sparrow vineyards, when the lightning hit my suit and there was that explosion? Well, one of The Fen fell from the cliffs and perished on the rocks below. He was very important in the Fen world, a creature of great evil influence. His name was Feral."

The color drained from Mr. Goodfellow's face.

"How do you know this, Edgar?"

"Well, after the other Fen reported Feral's death, his family vowed to seek revenge. They came to me the night we arrived back at your flat. There was a horrible creature, the brother of Feral, called..."

"Shrike," finished Mr. Goodfellow.

"Yes," cried Edgar. "How did you know?"

"I've had many encounters with The Fen through the centuries, Edgar, and I have made it my business to know. The work of Feral and Shrike Fen is quite legendary." When he looked at Sam and Edgar, Mr. Goodfellow's face was pale and drawn. "I am quite sure that both of you would recognize the names of the scoundrels and villains they have inspired."

"Shrike and his followers began to trail us when we left America that summer," Edgar continued. "When they finally found me, Shrike decided to make a bit of a sport of it. That night, he granted me a head start, but only if I left at that very moment. I couldn't take anything with me, and I didn't even have time to write a note. If I hadn't gone, Shrike said he would kill me, and you too, Uncle Jolly! I couldn't contact any Sage. There was no other way, Uncle Jolly. I had to play Shrike's game. I had to run and I've been running ever since! I've been so worried about everyone. Is my Mum...?"

"She's fine, Edgar. You poor boy! If only you had come to me, Edgar! I could have helped you." Mr. Goodfellow buried his head in his hands.

"I couldn't take that chance, Uncle Jolly. I remembered everything you tried to teach me that summer, though. I've tried to keep one step ahead of them this whole time. I never let my guard down. It was very lonely at first. Then I met a band of traveling mice. When they learned of my plight, they insisted on taking me in, and I have been with them ever since. Madam Zorah and the rest of the gypsies are always on the move, and the gypsy mice and I are never far behind. The mice have been very kind to me, Uncle Jolly. They know all about The Fen and have protected me all these years. I owe them my life. I have tried to repay their kindness too. I've painted their wooden caravans, and entertained the younger mice..."

"Still at it, I see, Edgar." Mr. Goodfellow couldn't help but smile at this.

"Yes, Uncle Jolly. I guess so."

"But what kind of a life can that be, Edgar? Never able to settle down, never free from worry, and never seeing your own family?"

Edgar smiled sadly.

"I would give anything to come home, Uncle Jolly. But knowing that you and Mum are safe will keep me going and..."

"No Edgar! You have been courageous long enough. You cannot shoulder this alone any longer, my boy! I was at those cliffs too, Edgar. And so were Beatrice and Hartland Sparrow. If they knew of this terrible burden that you had been forced to bear all these years, they would be heartsick. I am going to help you Edgar, and that's the end of it!"

"But it was me, Uncle Jolly! I did it! I attracted the lightning. It was me that caused the explosion." Edgar tried to pull away. "I wish I had never called out to you! They are going to try to destroy us all now, Uncle Jolly, and it's my fault!"

"Let them come, Edgar. Let Shrike Fen and his revolting henchmen do their worst. I will remain by your side. We'll make a formidable team, Edgar, the two of us."

"No!" cried Sam.

Mr. Goodfellow and Edgar swung their heads to look up at the boy they had all but forgotten about in their emotional discussion.

"It will be the three of us," finished Sam.

Edgar looked intently at Sam. He thought of the reason he had been drawn into the fortune teller's tent in the first place.

"The two identical readings, Uncle Jolly. Sam's from Madam Zorah and the one the gypsy mouse gave to me. What do they mean?"

"I'm not entirely sure, Edgar. It's a most curious phenomenon. Something I pray we'll have time to investigate later. You are coming with us now, Edgar, back to Sam's. It's the old Hawthorne house."

"Hawthorne!" cried Edgar. "The same Hawthorne that..."

"Oh dear! I had almost forgotten. There is quite a lot to fill you in on I'm afraid, Edgar. Yes, it's the same Hawthorne case your father worked on. The files have been reactivated, my boy, and given to me. The problem is that the current assignee, Professor Cedric Hawthorne, has vanished. I have enlisted Sam here to help me find him. I've also been hoping, Edgar, that if I could manage to locate the professor, I might also find out what happened to your dear father. I think that about covers it, doesn't it Sam?"

"Except for the Mandrakes," said Sam after a moment.

Mr. Goodfellow rolled his eyes and took another deep breath.

"Oh yes, how could I forget. The Mandrakes, Professor Avery—a colleague of Professor Hawthorne's—and his son Basil, a most unpleasant pair, have shown quite an interest in the activities and whereabouts of our professor. Sam and I suspect that they may be up to no good. There now. Any questions, Edgar?"

Edgar, who had been silent for the last few minutes, suddenly looked up. There was a single tear on his cheek.

"I still see him, you know, Uncle Jolly. A lot more lately, too."

"Your dad?" asked Sam.

Edgar nodded.

"I do too, Edgar," said Mr. Goodfellow. "It has always given me hope. The hope that I might find both of you. One day we'll discover what it's all about. I promise."

"Sshh!" whispered Sam. "Did you hear that?"

"It's Madam Zorah and her husband, Gregor!" said Edgar.

"Sam! Let's get out of the tent, my boy! Quickly!" Mr. Goodfellow grabbed Edgar by the arm. Sam picked them both up in his hand and ran to the back of the tent. Lifting the tent flap as high as he could, he fell to his knees and shuffled under the canvas to the grass on the other side. He pulled his shirt pocket wide open.

"I hope you have some garments with larger compartments, Sam," complained Mr. Goodfellow, as he and Edgar squeezed themselves inside. "I suggest we make our way back to the auction, now. You have been absent for far too long."

Sam dashed across the courtyard and bolted up the stone steps of the main building.

"I never had a chance to say goodbye to the gypsy mice, Uncle Jolly," cried Edgar, as he bounced up and down in Sam's pocket. "Or even tell them where I was going! They've been so wonderful to me, and there was one in particular that I..."

"We'll find a way to get word to them, Edgar," interrupted Mr. Goodfellow. "Don't worry. We'll send them a message through the mouse post."

Once he had safely made his way through the main doors, Sam slowed down to a more reasonable speed. Mr. Goodfellow, who by now was growing accustomed to pocket travel, lifted Edgar into an upright position. Mr. Goodfellow suggested a bit of fresh air on the terrace might be beneficial.

Sam casually meandered along a row of empty chairs at the back of the room and out through the big French doors to the stone porch. He stood at the railing and took a few deep breaths. He felt much better now that he was outside and away from Madame Zorah and the professor's office. A variety of birds were flitting about two wire feeders hanging from a nearby pine tree. Out of the corner of his eye, he spotted a large, beautiful beetle ambling its way across the flagstone floor. It was a striking iridescent green and it shimmered in the late afternoon light. It was quite unlike any beetle Sam had ever seen before.

"Wow! Take a look at that!" he whispered.

"Hmm...that *is* a nice one, Sam," said Mr. Goodfellow, as he leaned out of the pocket to take a look. This pleasant distraction would be good for all of them, he thought. He blew some fur out of his mouth as Edgar squeezed beside him to take a look too.

Sam pulled his magnifying glass from around his neck and got down on his hands and knees to take a closer look. He was peering at the unusual specimen when the toe of a large black boot suddenly appeared in his line of vision, followed by an unpleasant crunching sound. Sam looked up into the round, pudgy face of Basil Mandrake. Dropping his magnifying glass to the ground, Sam jumped up, his hands balled into fists at his side.

"You did that on purpose! You, you, MURDERER!"

There was another sly smile on Basil's face. He looked down at the ground and lifted his boot. The lovely green beetle had been squashed flat.

"Oh, my. I'm so sorry. Was that a friend of yours, Stan?"

"That's SAM!"

"Whatever. It was just an accident," replied Basil smugly. He pushed his big, round face closer to Sam's. "When you're as puny as that, it's easy to get squished, isn't it?"

Sam could feel his heart pounding. He stuck out his chin, and stepped towards Basil.

"The bigger you are, the harder you fall!" said Sam quietly.

Just then, Sam felt a firm hand on his shoulder.

"Come on now, boys. I'm sure we can sort all of this out," said Sam's father calmly.

The conniving look on Basil's face suddenly vanished and he became the model of respect and conciliation. He even extended his meaty hand in friendship. Sam gritted his teeth, then shook hands in return.

"What was *that* all about? And what happened to your blazer?" asked his father, once Basil had walked away. But Sam was angry that another chance to thwart Basil's cruelty had escaped him and he turned away without answering. One day someone was going to have to teach Basil Mandrake a lesson.

As Sam walked from the terrace, he noticed two figures standing at the side of the stone railing. It was the boy who had been tripped by Basil's boot and the older girl. As Basil walked past them, he raised his eyebrows and then opened his mouth in a wide, exaggerated yawn. Sam could see the boy clench his fists at his sides and the girl glare at his retreating figure. It was obvious that this had not been their first encounter with Basil Mandrake. When Sam passed by, a moment later, the girl smiled at him and the boy gave him a covert wave.

The ride home from the auction was distinctly cooler than their arrival, especially after Sam's mother discovered the damage to the Nana blazer. For once, Sam was thankful for *The Sounds of the '70s*.

Sam's father insisted on picking up a jumbo order of Mr. Flounder fish and chips on the way home. After Sam had wolfed down his portion (including the small plate of fruit and low fat cheese his mother always felt compelled to place in front of him), he stood up from the table, stretched his arms above his head, and yawned.

"I think I'm going to go to bed now," he announced.

"You must be kidding, Sam," said his father, "it's only 7:30. Are you really that tired?"

His mother placed a hand on his forehead.

"I hope you're not coming down with something, dear."

"I'm fine, Mum, really. Early to bed, early to rise, will make me healthy, wealthy and wise..." Sam's words trailed off as he walked down the hall and up the stairs.

His parents were confused. Where on earth were those proverbs coming from?

14

WITHOUT A FRIEND THE
WORLD IS A WILDERNESS

S am raced up the stairs into his room, quickly shutting the door behind him. He pulled Mr. Goodfellow and Edgar out of his shirt pocket and set them on the floor. Edgar took a good look around the room.

"There's not much in here, is there, Uncle Jolly?" said Edgar suppressing a shudder. "It's a bit of a creepy old place."

Sam looked at Edgar admiringly. Here, at last, was someone who saw things the way he did.

"It's not *that* bad, Edgar," said Mr. Goodfellow, rubbing the small of his back. "Anyway, Sam and his parents have just moved in. I believe their things haven't been delivered yet."

Edgar didn't seem the worse for wear after the ride in Sam's pocket, but Mr. Goodfellow was bent into rather an odd shape. Spending the last few hours in such close quarters had taken its toll on him.

"I seem to have developed a bit of a backache, boys. I'm not built to travel like a sardine. If you would be so kind..."

Sam knelt down and with Edgar's able assistance helped Mr. Goodfellow to straighten up. Then Sam reached into his pants pocket, pulled out a balled paper napkin, and unwrapped it on the floor. With Edgar peering hopefully from behind his shoulder, Mr. Goodfellow looked over the contents. Hmm...a nice slice of Gouda, some toast crusts, three luscious looking raspberries, and, thankfully, two delightfully plump and crispy chips, complete with salt and malt vinegar. Excellent, Mr. Goodfellow thought. He glanced at Sam from time to time as he and Edgar nibbled contentedly at their feast.

"Well, apart from our blessed reunion with Edgar, that affair at the university did not work out quite the way I was hoping. If we hadn't been so rudely interrupted in the professor's office, we may have found what we were looking for. Perhaps there's another way for us to get to the bottom of this."

He dabbed at his moustache with a corner of the white paper napkin, then continued.

"My guess is that the professor must be on the run to have left his office in such disarray. You heard what that janitor said—the professor never left his things in a mess. Unless, of course, someone else had already been through his office.... In any event, I have a feeling that someone, somewhere, must know his whereabouts."

He munched on absently.

"We'll have to keep a close watch on that Avery Mandrake too. A most disagreeable, and I dare say, dangerous man."

Sam couldn't agree more, and it wasn't just the pungent aroma of mothballs surrounding Mandrake that made him disagreeable.

When he was quite full of cheese, toast, raspberries, and chips, Mr. Goodfellow stood up and stretched his arms high above his head. He chattered on about having a few more kinks to work out, then lay upon the floor, patting his tummy and closing his eyes.

Edgar was still finishing off his last bit of chip. A drop of malt vinegar dribbled down his chin. He looked up at Sam, who was sitting next to him, and smiled nervously.

"I really don't want to be a bother to anyone, Sam. If I don't keep moving, The Fen will track me down. I do hope that Uncle Jolly has done the right thing insisting that I stay here with you."

"It didn't look to me like he was going to have it any other way," said Sam, smiling back.

"I suppose not," said Edgar resignedly. "My uncle can be *very* persistent. I think it's one of the things that I admire the most about him. Do you know that one time when we were in a desperate situation, Uncle Jolly actually built..."

"A flying machine!" interrupted Sam. "I know. He told me all about your summer together, Edgar. I feel I know you already."

"Really?" said Edgar, studying Sam's face. "Well, the strange thing is, I feel like I know you too. What do you make of it? And what about our fortunes?"

Sam shook his head.

"Blast! Is there to be no rest for me?" Mr. Goodfellow sat up suddenly and looked around.

"Sorry, Uncle Jolly," whispered Edgar. "We'll try and be a bit more quiet."

"No, it's not you two. I find the sound of your voices chattering away to be quite pleasant, actually. It's that confounded noise again. It's driving me mad!"

"You mean that humming sound?" asked Edgar.

"Good heavens, Edgar! You can hear it too? Thank goodness! I was beginning to believe I was either losing my mind or developing a chronic ear condition."

"I just thought someone had left a machine on or something, Uncle Jolly."

"No, we've been over that already, Edgar. Sam's furniture and belongings have not arrived yet. There's nothing of that sort in the house, is there Sam?"

"No, not until Monday," said Sam. "*I* can't hear anything, you know. Is that impor...?"

"There, you see Edgar," said Mr. Goodfellow, adamantly. "The house things aren't even arriving until tomorrow." He poked a finger inside each ear and wandered around the room. "I really hope we can find out where it's coming from."

"Tomorrow's Monday?" cried Sam suddenly.

"What was that, my boy?" asked Mr. Goodfellow, taking his fingers out of his ears. "You look as if the very weight of the world was upon you."

"I can't believe I forgot!" Sam cried. "I have to start school tomorrow! New kids, new teacher, new everything. It's going to be terrible!"

The afternoon's expedition to the university and the discovery of Edgar had distracted Sam from the horror of having to start at a new school, with no friends. He sat cross-legged on the floor, cradling his head in his hands.

Mr. Goodfellow trotted forward with a look of genuine concern.

"Nonsense, my boy! Just think of it as another grand adventure. Tomorrow is fresh fields and pastures new, I say! Isn't that right, Edgar?"

"Well, actually, Uncle Jolly, I was never that fond of school, as you know. I think that's why I've wanted to do something a bit different."

"Edgar! Please!" said Mr. Goodfellow, nodding his head in Sam's direction. "I'm trying to offer encouragement here!"

Sam rolled over on to his side, shaking his head. Mr. Goodfellow's words of advice didn't seem to be working and

Edgar wasn't being in the least bit helpful. Mr. Goodfellow gave Sam's toe a tap and tried again.

"Footprints in the sands of time are not made by lying down, Sam!"

Sam, still lying sideways upon the floor let out a loud sigh.

Oh dear, thought Mr. Goodfellow—this was some of his best material. The situation at hand called for a different approach.

"You know, Sam, until I discover the whereabouts of Professor Hawthorne, I'm afraid I'm more or less stuck here, too. So, I'll tell you what. If you like, I'll accompany you to school in the morning. A trouble shared, is a trouble halved, remember?" He paused, then looked at Edgar. "On second thought, Sam, you gave me hope and companionship when I truly needed it. Perhaps you and Edgar can do the same for each other now."

Sam raised his head and looked at the little man, then at Edgar.

"You'd do that for me, really?"

Edgar nodded. "If you want me to, Sam. It would be an interesting excursion, I think."

"There, it's settled," said Mr. Goodfellow. "And now I recommend a good night's sleep if you're going to make a suitable impression tomorrow. Agreed?"

"I guess so," said Sam. He was already beginning to feel better as he shuffled into his sleeping bag.

Mr. Goodfellow returned to his trunk, opened up the third drawer, and proceeded with his nighttime routine. Then, rummaging around at the back of the drawer, he produced a second folded cot.

"Do you remember this, Edgar?"

Edgar, in the midst of removing his mouse feet, looked over in astonishment.

"My cot! You've been carrying it around with you all this time, Uncle Jolly?"

"Of course, Edgar. I suppose it started off as a bit of a super-stition. I always felt that if I kept it with me, I could somehow keep alive the hope of finding you one day. It's a good job I hung on to it, isn't it?"

Edgar nodded his head as he struggled furiously with the button at his neck. Mr. Goodfellow walked over to offer assis-tance. Sam raised his head from his pillow and leaned back on his elbows to watch.

"Careful, Edgar, you're going to rip something there!" cried Mr. Goodfellow. "My goodness, that button is going to cut off your circulation. Do stop struggling!"

Edgar dropped his arms obediently and Mr. Goodfellow continued his attempts to extricate him from his suit.

"This is a familiar scene, isn't it Edgar? You always did have problems with your suits. And this one is a bit of a tight fit, to say the least. You've certainly grown since 1936."

"Yes, Uncle Jolly," said Edgar proudly. "Three whole millimeters."

"Indeed! And your neck has grown too! You have the Goodfellow neck, my boy. Just like your father. I, of course, have inherited the more slender physique from the Troutbrook side of the family." He lifted his chin up to reveal his rather scrawny neck before returning to his task. "I've been meaning to ask you about this suit Edgar. It looks familiar— even with all this dirt on it."

"Sixty-five years worth of dirt, actually, Uncle Jolly."

Mr. Goodfellow examined the faded black fur more closely. Under the layers of grime, there was hardly a spot that hadn't been glued or pinned or patched.

"Good heavens! It's the formal, isn't it? Have you been wearing it all this time, then?"

"I had to. It was all I had. I'm sorry, Uncle Jolly. I've made rather a mess of it."

"Understandably, my boy. But, it just won't do anymore, Edgar." He walked around to view the suit from behind. "This white mark down your backside, Edgar, where did that come from?"

"It was during one of my caravan painting projects. I backed into a panel that hadn't quite dried and..."

"Well, it makes you look like a skunk, Edgar! We can't possibly allow you to go out like this anymore. If someone should happen upon you they will think they have discovered an extremely rare species. If you think The Fen are relentless then you haven't met with any members of the scientific community. No, I'm afraid that suit just won't do at all!" Mr. Goodfellow turned back to his trunk and began to sort through the row of hanging suits.

"Here we go. I think this one might fit rather well. It always was a bit loose around the neck for my liking." Mr. Goodfellow was holding up a white suit with large black and brown spots.

"It's a bit loud, isn't it?" complained Edgar.

"Nonsense, Edgar. I remember when these were all the rage. Take it, my boy. Please."

Edgar looked up at Sam with an expression of despair. Sam looked back sympathetically.

Edgar stepped out of the old black suit for the last time slowly. They had been through a lot together. It was hard to say goodbye.

"I bet if Beatrice were here she would be able to make it lovely again, wouldn't she, Uncle Jolly?" said Edgar.

"Um...yes, Edgar. I imagine she would." At the mention of Beatrice's name, Mr. Goodfellow dove back into his row of suits. He popped his head out after a while. "I've been meaning to sort this mess out for ages, you know. No time like the present! I'll see you both in the morning, then."

Sam looked quizzically at Edgar, who shrugged his shoulders and began to fluff up the pillow on his cot. Sam slid back down into his sleeping bag and closed his eyes.

When he was certain that Sam and Edgar were in bed, Mr. Goodfellow opened the second drawer of his trunk to retrieve his pen and journal. Drowsy but still awake, Sam listened to the tapping of his pen, longing to know what the little man was writing. Mr. Goodfellow seemed to be making a particularly lengthy entry this evening. By the time the tapping had stopped and the little flashlight had been extinguished, Sam was fast asleep.

When Mr. Goodfellow finally settled down on the thin mattress of his cot, his mind was still contemplating his latest journal entry. He lay awake in the dark room, worrying over Edgar and The Fen, and Sam and Professor Hawthorne. He was sure that something strange was happening, and that it was more than coincidence that was drawing them together.

15

YOU NEVER KNOW WHAT
YOU CAN DO UNTIL YOU TRY

The next morning Sam stood by the front door waiting for the schoolbus to take him to his first day at Elm Street Elementary. His mum handed him his lunchbag.

"Sorry about all this mess, dear. It'll feel more like home when the furniture arrives later this morning. Then we can all get back to normal, I hope." She paused and looked into her son's eyes. "Are you sure you don't want me to drive you to school, dear? It is your first day, after all, and I think your Dad can handle the movers. You can take the bus tomorrow."

"No, Mum. It's all right... really. Thanks anyway."

She gave him a kiss on the top of his head. "Are you sure?"

"Positive," he said.

The yellow bus pulled up alongside the curb at the corner and honked its horn.

"It's here!" he cried. He walked out the door and down the porch steps. This time he held his hand against his shirt pocket as he walked, so as not to jostle the passenger within.

He stepped onto the bus, feeling awkward as he passed the rows of staring strangers. He found an empty seat near the back and quickly sat down. A short time later, the school bus stopped in front of a huge concrete building. Elm Street Elementary was twice as big as his old school. There was a paved playground to one side with monkey bars and slides. Beyond that was a green soccer field surrounded by an oval running track. Sam followed the other kids past the playground and through the wide double doors into the school. He eventually found his way to the principal's office. The secretary there led him to Ms. Stemple's fifth grade class and then turned and walked back down the hallway. Sam stood on his toes and peered through the glass window into the room. It was full of kids. And these kids had been there for a whole week of school already. He hesitated at the door until he felt a stirring inside his shirt pocket.

"Go on, Sam," whispered a quiet voice. "Like Uncle Jolly would say, it's always the first step that's the most difficult."

Sam swallowed, then opened the door and walked in. Ms. Stemple seemed very tall as she smiled down at him.

"We have a new student with us today, class. This is Samuel."

Everyone in the class turned to look at him. Sam could feel the full gaze of twenty-one pairs of eyes. Then, from a desk at the very front of the room, somebody snorted. It was Basil Mandrake. Sam's blood immediately started pounding through his veins. He sat down at the nearest empty desk, midway down the second row, and lowered his head. From inside his shirt pocket, another pair of much smaller and friendlier eyes were twinkling up at him. Sam suddenly felt much better.

Ms. Stemple picked up a long wooden pointer. She reached above the blackboard and pulled down on a long, looped string, unfurling a huge map of the world.

"As I trust you will recall class, in our first geography lesson last week, we were discussing the continent of Africa." Ms. Stemple tapped her pointer against the map.

Sam groaned. "Oh, no...I'm terrible at geography."

"Actually, it was one of the few subjects I was rather good at," whispered Edgar. "I think it had something to do with hearing all about Uncle Jolly's travels." Ms. Stemple's voice grew shrill. "Can anyone tell me the name of the large island off Africa's East Coast?"

A sudden silence fell across the room.

Sam heard Edgar's voice from his pocket. "Madagascar... mad...a...gas...car."

Sam raised his hand.

"Yes, Samuel?" said Ms. Stemple.

"Uh...Madagascar?"

"That's correct. Now, does anyone know what is at the bottom tip of Africa?"

"The Cape of Good Hope!"

"Yes, Samuel?"

"Um...The Cape of Good Hope?"

"Very good, Samuel. Well class, we seem to have a geography scholar with us!"

The little voice in his pocket sounded quite excited now. "You see, Sam, we've made an impression already!"

But Sam was not so sure. Later, as the class filed out for recess, he noticed the other kids eyeing him suspiciously. When they reached the playground, the students broke apart and formed various groups. In one of them, five or six kids leaned in toward one another and whispered excitedly—they were centered round Basil Mandrake. Every now and then they turned to stare and laugh in Sam's direction. He stood alone in the playground, his hands stuffed into his pockets, kicking at the sand with the toe of one sneaker.

Edgar spoke up again. "Of course, Sam, I don't think that Uncle Jolly would condone me giving you answers but..."

Sam interrupted, "I think maybe we overdid it."

Edgar popped his head out and looked around. "Oh...I see what you mean. I'm sorry, Sam. Leave this to me."

He pointed a paw towards another group of Sam's class-mates clustered around the school's front steps.

"Just walk over there, and I'll do the rest," said Edgar, as he shuffled back down into Sam's shirt pocket.

Sam rolled his eyes and reluctantly made his way toward the group. On arrival, Edgar suddenly popped his head out of Sam's pocket again.

"Wow!" said one of the boys. "You've got a mouse!"

"Yeah," said Sam nervously, not quite sure what Edgar was about to do. He reached into his pocket and gently lifted him out. Edgar's white spotted suit gleamed in the morning sunlight.

"Oh, he's so cute! What's his name?" asked one little girl with short blond pigtails.

"Uh...it's...um...Edgar," said Sam slowly.

"Does he do any tricks?"

Sam stammered. "Uh, well...I don't..."

Just then, Edgar leapt from Sam's hand onto one of the concrete steps.

First he took a long, low bow, then he performed a somer-sault, four push-ups, two cartwheels and a pirouette—he fin-ished off with a perfectly straight handstand.

Then he jumped into Sam's trouser cuff, raced up his leg and dove back into his shirt pocket. The other children stood gaping with their mouths wide open.

"Wow, how did you get him to do that?"

Sam shrugged and smiled.

"Well, it took a lot of practice, but he's kind of a smart little guy."

The admiring gasps from the kids surrounding Sam soon sucked Basil Mandrake's gang away from his side and over to the school's front steps. Basil remained in the playground, casually peering over at them to see what was going on.

The school bell suddenly rang signaling the end of recess. As everyone began to walk back inside, Sam noticed a familiar figure, half-hidden behind a book, perched on the corner of the bottom step. It was the boy from the university reception, the one Basil Mandrake sent flying in front of the buffet table.

"Who's that?" Sam asked the blonde pigtailed girl.

"Oh, that's Fletcher Jaffrey," she replied, "he's a bookworm. He doesn't talk much. He just reads *all* the time."

For the rest of the morning, Sam decided to tone down his (and Edgar's) academic expertise. Ms. Stemple kept looking hopefully in his direction whenever she asked the class a question, but Sam decided that for now, silence was golden.

When the twelve o'clock bell rang, Sam followed the others to the lunchroom. A few kids looked up from their tables and smiled at him. Some even said "Hey, Sam, how's the mouse?" There were a few empty spots at the rows of long tables, but Sam, encouraged by the gentle prodding of a black and white spotted paw in his pocket, walked to the last table by the wall. He sat down opposite the bookworm.

"Hello, I'm Sam."

Curls of black hair, followed by thick-rimmed spectacles appeared over the top of the book.

"I'm Fletcher," the boy responded.

There was a long pause as the two boys looked at one another. Sam drummed his fingers on top of the table.

"I'm going to be a great scientist one day. Maybe even an entomologist," said Sam. "You know, study bugs."

Fletcher nodded his head. Sam leaned across the table.

"What are you reading?"

"It's a book by Carl Sagan, you know, the astronomer? I'm going to be an astronaut."

"Oh," said Sam. "I just finished this book on the life cycle of the Surinam cave cockroach." He stood up for a moment and pulled a rolled paperback out of his back pocket. He laid it on the table and tried to flatten it out with the palm of his hand.

"Really?" said Fletcher. "I'd like to read that sometime."

Sam shrugged. "Maybe we could trade?"

"Sure," said Fletcher, with a similar shrug.

They exchanged books across the table and grinned at each other.

"What do you have for lunch?" asked Sam, as he unwrapped his egg roll and airline snacks.

"Pizza," said Fletcher, looking with interest at Sam's food. "Homemade. With extra cheese."

"Wow," said Sam. "Homemade..."

When Sam returned home later that day, an enormous white moving van was parked in the driveway. Boxes and furniture were slowly being unpacked by three men wearing matching blue overalls. Sam slipped through the front door, stepping over crates and boxes, and bumped into his parents. "How was your first day at school, Sam?" they asked. When Sam replied with a casual "It was okay," his parents beamed at one another. This was even better than they had dared hope.

Sam raced up the stairs two at a time and gently unloaded Edgar from his pocket before he grabbed his pillow from the floor and leapt onto the boxspring and mattress that had been assembled against one of the walls.

Mr. Goodfellow, who had spent the better part of the day sorting through the contents of his trunk and keeping well out of the way of the movers, peeped cautiously from behind the bookcase before venturing forth.

"A successful day, I hope?" he inquired.

"We've made a friend, already!" said Sam triumphantly.

"Indeed!" said Mr. Goodfellow.

"Sam met a boy from the university, Uncle Jolly," said Edgar.

"Really? That wouldn't be young Basil's victim from the buffet table, would it?"

"Yeah—his name's Fletcher, and he's going to be an astronaut! He's learning everything he can about space already!"

"Well, that's wonderful, Sam. The journey of a million miles begins with a single step, doesn't it? Now then, aren't you in the habit of getting some sort of after school snack?" Mr. Goodfellow asked, patting his stomach in anticipation.

Sam obliged, returning some time later with a plate of partially crumbled chocolate chip cookies and a glass of milk. After devouring his share, Mr. Goodfellow felt sufficiently refreshed to continue with the conversation. He was just about to go over the events of his own day, when there was an unexpected knock at the door. Sam, Edgar, and Mr. Goodfellow froze.

"Sam, are you in there?"

"Yes, Dad, just a minute!"

Sam leapt into action, quickly hiding all evidence of The Sage as Edgar and Mr. Goodfellow ran to the shelter of the old bookcase. When Sam had Mr. Goodfellow's all clear, he opened the door slightly. His father peered into the room.

"Everything alright, son?"

"Yeah sure, Dad. What do you want?"

"Well, your mum's just popping out to the store, so dinner won't be for an hour or two."

Sam opened the door a little wider. His father was holding a cardboard box.

"I put this away for you so it wouldn't get mixed up with anything else. I thought it might make you feel more at home," he said hopefully. "Last thing on the truck, first thing off I guess! You almost forgot this stuff! If it wasn't for your old dad here, you'd have left all this behind."

"Oh, thanks, Dad."

Sam reached out and took the box.

His father hesitated. "You know, son, it isn't always easy to make changes. It's going to be all right, though. You just wait and see, I'm sure of it."

"I know, Dad. I think so, too."

"You do? Really?"

"Really, Dad."

"Well, alright, then. I'll leave you to it."

Trevor Middleton could barely contain his grin as he closed his son's bedroom door. Sam could hear him humming to himself as he dashed down the stairs to tell his wife this latest bulletin.

Sam carried the box to the middle of the room and laid it down on the floor. From the time he was quite young, he had made a point of storing certain things on top of the built-in bookshelves in his old room. He had kept these things for so long now, he'd all but forgotten what he'd put up there. The move had been such a hurried affair, that it wasn't until his father's last minute inspection of the house that the items on top of the bookshelf had been discovered. Sam's father had grabbed an empty cardboard box, tossed everything inside, taped it up and marked it TOP SHELF—SAM, before throwing it into the moving van.

Sam leaned over that box, picking away at the masking tape until he could pry the two top flaps apart with his fingers. He pulled it open with a pop and stared inside. There didn't appear to be anything particularly valuable in there. Then he began to lift a few things out.

Edgar, who had climbed onto Sam's knee to get a closer look at the items coming out of the box, let out a gasp.

Sitting on the floor, next to the cardboard box, was a bright yellow yo-yo, a glass jar of glistening red candies, a box of watercolors, half a dozen hand-painted landscapes, a small pewter statue of the Empire State Building, and an old program from "The Inventions of Leonardo" exhibition at the museum. There was also an assortment of postcards from a variety of places: the vineyards of northern California, the Manhattan skyline, the *Queen Mary* in her berth at Long Beach, the tranquil English countryside.

Sam stared at all the things that had meant so much to him over the years.

"I remember this," he said, picking up one of the postcards. "My uncle David had this huge collection of postcards. Every time we visited him, he'd let me pick one to keep." He ran his finger over one of the watercolor paintings. "I think I did this last summer."

"It's very good, you know, my boy. You have quite a talent," Mr. Goodfellow remarked, smiling.

Sam looked up. Those words sounded familiar. Mr. Goodfellow had a strange look in his dark twinkling eyes. Edgar looked utterly confused.

"Do you know what this means, Sam?" asked Mr. Goodfellow. "Do you, Edgar?"

"Well...I'm not sure, but..." Sam spoke quietly. He picked each item up and held it in his hands before he turned to Edgar. "My stuff looks like it could be your stuff."

Edgar shook his head slowly from side to side.

"No, Sam," said Mr. Goodfellow quietly. "These are your things."

The little man hopped down from Sam's knee and scrambled over to his trunk, returning with his old journal.

"It's just as I suspected, my boys. I couldn't believe it at first. I had been hoping to do some more investigating as soon as I was able to contact The Sage Council, just to be certain, but now, with all of this...."

He gazed at the candies, paintings and postcards on the floor, cradling his journal in his arms.

"It must be true," he said.

"What's true?" asked Sam.

"What did you write in there?" asked Edgar.

"Just the musings of an old man...or so, I thought." Mr. Goodfellow held the book up to Sam and Edgar. "Here, lads, I think you should have a look at this."

Sam reached for the journal, placing it squarely on his knee so that Edgar could read from it as well. Then he pulled his magnifying glass from around his neck and bent over the opened pages. Mr. Goodfellow stretched to indicate the entry for September 13th, the day that he and Sam had arrived at the Hawthorne house.

"I believe it starts right here."

> *A most dreadful turn of events, indeed! I have decided to lodge a complaint at the highest level. I have arrived at the Hawthorne house to find it has been abandoned by the professor (and all the resi-*

*dent mice) and is now occupied by a family of three.
And I have been apprehended by the youngest member of the aforementioned family! Fortunately, he
has turned out to be a decent boy. There was something most familiar about him and I was so put out
by the events of the day, I confided my mission to
him. Whether or not I was right to do this will be
discussed at length (I am sure) at some future council meeting. I am hoping the young lad will be of
assistance. I began to tell him my nephew Edgar's
story—since he reminded me so much of him.*

*I will end my entry now for today. Curse this
cursive writing! I am not only exhausted but
afflicted now with a hand cramp. Thankfully, I
have convinced the lad to rest too. He is anxious to
continue with Edgar's story, but we both need more
than a few winks first. I cannot help but feel that
there is something very special about this boy.
Perhaps the dawn of a new day will shed some
light.*

Sam's hands were trembling as he and Edgar looked at one another. Sam turned the page to read Mr. Goodfellow's next entry.

September 14th
*A most eventful morning. The enchantment Sam
feels for Edgar's story grows. Each time we begin, he
falls deeper into it. I am beginning to form a rather
interesting theory. It is so farfetched, however, that I
will refrain from putting it to paper, at least for the
time being. I must sign off now.*

Sam looked at Mr. Goodfellow again before he turned to the final page of writing. Edgar, his eyes transfixed on the journal, listened intently as Sam began to read again.

> *By the will of the fates, I have been reunited with dear Edgar once again, after all these years! It was soon after I finished telling Sam the story of Edgar's summer adventures. Sam was transfixed. His deep involvement in the tale cannot be entirely attributed to my storytelling alone. I believe that he is somehow drawn to Edgar himself. When Sam and Edgar met for the first time this afternoon, there was an unmistakable charge in the air. It was as if destiny had deliberately thrown them together. It can be only one thing. If I am right, if this is indeed the Sacred Seal and if the Seal is still between the two of them, then something is terribly wrong. How this could be is beyond my understanding. The Seal should have been dissolved years ago. I will not rest until I find out how this has happened, for both of their sakes.*

This was the final entry. Sam closed the journal and looked at Mr. Goodfellow. Edgar, quite overcome by all he had heard, stared absently at the closed cover of the journal.

"What does it mean?" asked Sam. "I don't understand."

"It's crystal clear to me now," answered Mr. Goodfellow. "At some time in your life, Sam, you were to have been one of Edgar's assignments, a gifted one. However, because Edgar never finished his apprenticeship, he should never have been assigned any cases. Somewhere along the way, a mistake was made, or more correctly, two mistakes. Not only were you assigned to Edgar before his graduation, but after he had gone missing, you should have been reassigned to someone else. Reassignment itself is not unheard of, as you know, as was the case with Filbert's disappearance. But your situation, my boy, is the result of a ghastly error."

Sam looked at the floor.

"But why did I save all of those things?"

"It's quite simple, really. The fact that you and Edgar were to work together one day was never erased. It is the Sacred Seal, my boy. That's how it works. It's like *déjà vu*."

"What's that?" asked Sam.

"Déjà vu is the feeling people get when they think they have done something or been somewhere before, even though they're experiencing it for the first time. Or perhaps you feel you already know someone, even though you are just meeting them for the first time. The experiences of Edgar's life have touched your heart and live there now. All of those things that you saved—you knew they were special. They were special to Edgar, too. The fact that you put on mismatched socks this morning did not escape my attention either, my boy," said Mr. Goodfellow.

Sam looked down at one black ankle and one dark blue one.

"Rats, I've done it again!"

"Me too," said Edgar, pulling open the tops of his mouse feet and looking down at one white sock and one brown one.

"Somehow, Sam," continued Mr. Goodfellow, "you have fallen through the cracks. On a positive note, though, you were to have been the assignment of young Edgar here, a Goodfellow no less. A most auspicious destiny indeed! However, because of this colossal blunder, you seem to have been overlooked—your future as a gifted one is in jeopardy.

Well, I can promise you that I will not stand idle on this!"

Edgar, who had been sitting quietly on Sam's knee, his chin cradled in his hands, looked up suddenly.

"It's my fault, Uncle Jolly! If I had only finished my apprenticeship it would never have turned out this way!"

"There's no sense blaming yourself, Edgar. A mistake was made and it's as simple as that. None of this should have happened to Sam, regardless of what happened to you. You followed your heart all those years ago—no one can fault you for that."

He tried his best to comfort Edgar, but by the pained look on his face, Mr. Goodfellow could see that the boy felt responsible.

"All I can do right now, lads, is to promise you both that I will do everything in my power to resolve this situation, as soon as I am able. I will put this problem before the Sage Governing Council at the first possible opportunity. I trust that once the Sage elders investigate the matter thoroughly, they will reach a fair and equitable solution."

Mr. Goodfellow's words of encouragement did little to make either Sam or Edgar feel any better. It had been a bittersweet revelation for Sam to learn that he was a gifted one, destined to become a great scientist—but what did it matter when he'd been forgotten? If it was true that this kind of mistake had never happened before in the history of The Sage, maybe there would be no way to resolve it.

Edgar, feeling equally hopeless, retreated to his cot. These last two days had taken him from the heights of joy back down to the depths of despair. He could use some time on his own. When Sam brought offerings from dinner later that evening, Edgar could not be tempted. And when Mr. Goodfellow saw him refuse food, he understood just how badly Edgar felt.

16

A Friend in Need Is a Friend Indeed

Over the next week or so, Sam continued to attend his new school. School, at least, was a convenient distraction from thoughts of the Sacred Seal. Mr. Goodfellow took the time to consider how best to present this problem to the Sage Governing Council. He was hopeful, too, that some kind of clue to Professor Hawthorne's whereabouts would eventually present itself, and that the house mice would soon return and share any information they had regarding the professor's disappearance.

Edgar was inconsolable for the first day or two, but with Mr. Goodfellow's prodding, he eventually agreed to accompany Sam to school on a few occasions. When Edgar was with Sam he was able to put aside his worries about The Fen and the Sacred Seal and enjoy himself for a while.

In the meantime, Sam's friendship with Fletcher Jaffrey progressed in leaps and bounds. Sam became the only other person (next to Fletcher's immediate family) to learn about his secret desire—to be the first man on Mars. To look at him, a boy half the size of his classmates with glasses one-quarter-inch thick, one might have found this prospect ridiculous. But

Sam, an accomplished dreamer in his own right, thought it was excellent. In no time at all, Sam and Fletcher were spending afternoons at each other's houses after school.

Both Sam's and Fletcher's parents were delighted to see their sons become fast friends. Fletcher found the Middleton house, despite the scattered furnishings and stacks of unopened cardboard boxes, to be a quiet, peaceful oasis. It was worlds away from the frantic condition of his own home. Sam, on the other hand, loved the hubbub at the Jaffrey house. There was always a great deal of noise, clutter, and laughter, due in large part to the fact that the Jaffreys were active in the Boxer Rescue program. In addition to their own two dogs, Gilbert and Sullivan, there were usually at least a half dozen other boisterous dogs in attendance as well, awaiting adoption. Sam found this arrangement to be great fun, especially at mealtimes. An invitation to dine at Fletcher's was an event not to be missed.

The Jaffreys' was the only kitchen that Sam had ever seen with two stoves. Pots and pans bubbled and steamed on all eight elements. Under the skilled direction of Fletcher's parents, each meal was a triumph of converging cultures. Leonora, Fletcher's opera singing mother, presided over her soups and pastas as if she were giving a command performance. Fletcher's father, Sanjid, the chemistry professor, measured and stirred his curries and vindaloo sauces as though he were following an intricate chemical formula. The results were always breathtaking. Tureens of minestrone and casseroles of lasagna sat in concert with platters of shrimp masala and plates of tandoori chicken. In the center of the table, there was always a huge basket of bread—crusty rolls and roti, paninis and poppadums. Somehow, it all seemed to fit together. Fletcher, who'd grown up with this gourmet abundance, always seemed to be content to dine on peanut butter and jelly sandwiches at Sam's, however. Fletcher and Sam had not only found friendship, they had found refuge, too.

Professor Jaffrey had called their eldest child, a daughter, India, in honor of the country of his birth. When their son arrived, three years later, it was Leonora's turn. She named him Fletcher, after Fletcher Christian, her favorite naval character, who had led the mutiny on the infamous ship *Bounty*.

India was an unusual girl. Tall and willowy with long, black hair and deep brown, piercing eyes, she was a straight-A student and, like her brother, a voracious reader. Most of her time seemed to be spent speeding through a vast number of historical romances. The pink and purple paperbacks could be found in every room of the house. Sam wasn't sure if he had ever seen her without her nose buried in one of her books. The only thing that could pry her attention away from them was the announcement that a trip to the local bakery was at hand. After each weekly excursion there, the Jaffreys would return with a fresh assortment of goodies: cupcakes, danishes, cookies, and tarts. India liked only one thing—gingerbread. If there was none to be had, she would look so forlorn, the baker felt compelled to apologize to her.

It was during the second week of Sam and Fletcher's friendship when Fletcher's mother announced some very upsetting news.

Sam had been busily eating his dinner. He had no trouble with the pasta courses, having more or less existed on take-out pizza and tinned spaghetti for the better part of his life. The highly spiced dishes, however, presented more of a challenge. Sam had tried to force them down, but halfway through the meal he discovered that the dogs, who had taken up temporary residence under the table, would eagerly eat anything his own stomach couldn't handle.

"We're so delighted that your parents have invited us over for dinner this Sunday, Sam. We're really looking forward to it!" announced Fletcher's mother.

"Oh," said Sam, a little puzzled. "I didn't know you were coming. But that's great!"

"She just called about an hour ago," continued Leonora. "I understand it was a bit of an impulse. I expect she'll tell you about it when you get home."

"Perhaps we should bring something along, my dear?" suggested Fletcher's father, looking up for a moment from his dinner.

"I did make the gesture, Sanjid, but I think Peggy wants to tackle it herself," Leonora replied, turning to Sam. "I do hope she and your father don't run themselves ragged trying to get the house ready. I suggested she give herself more time before starting to entertain, but apparently Professor Mandrake had popped by to inquire about the progress of their art gallery and more or less invited himself to dinner. I should have warned her about that man. He can be quite persuasive."

Fletcher's father made an unpleasant face at the mention of Avery Mandrake's name.

"Are you feeling alright, Sam?" asked Fletcher's mother. "Sometimes these spices can be a little overwhelming for the uninitiated."

"Uh . . . no. I'm okay," mumbled Sam.

When they had been excused from the table, Sam followed Fletcher up the stairs to his room.

"Hey, Sam, you didn't look too good when my mom mentioned Professor Mandrake. Do you know him?"

"Yeah," said Sam, "and I don't like him."

"Neither do I! He's a creep! And Basil's just as bad! How come you don't like him? How do you know him?"

Over the next hour, Sam told Fletcher as much of Professor Hawthorne's story as he felt he could, without revealing the existence of the Goodfellows. When he mentioned the Hawthorne scroll, Fletcher, surprisingly, already knew all about it.

The ancient relic that had been in the Hawthorne family for decades was a bit of a local legend. Over the years, tales of strange goings-on at the professor's house, rumors about his mysterious experiments, and the odd behavior of the original owner of the scroll, Elijah Hawthorne, had kept generations of town gossips very busy.

Sam told Fletcher about "accidentally" stumbling into Professor Hawthorne's office at the university on the day of the auction and that he was sure Professor Mandrake had almost caught him there. He told Fletcher that he was also sure the reason Professor Hawthorne had left in such a hurry was because he was actually in some kind of danger. And he was willing to bet that somehow Professor Mandrake was involved.

"I knew there was something weird about Mandrake!" exclaimed Fletcher. "Even my father hates him—and they work together! I don't think Mandrake ever liked the fact that my dad and Professor Hawthorne were friends."

"Your dad was a friend of the professor's?" asked Sam.

"Yeah. He used to come over for dinner all the time. He was nice enough, but he was always kind of nervous. I didn't really listen to them talk, but I did hear them mention Mandrake a lot. My dad was really upset when Professor Hawthorne left. He never even said goodbye to us, you know."

"Really?" said Sam. "So what else do you know about Professor Mandrake?"

Fletcher went on to describe how both Avery and Basil Mandrake had been a continual source of irritation ever since Fletcher's father had joined the Chemistry Department four years earlier.

Professor Sanjid Jaffrey was one of the few faculty members who had never succumbed to the Mandrake charm. In fact, the two had clashed over university policy and procedure on a number of occasions. And Basil was clearly no better than his father. Fletcher had been teased, taunted, and bullied for four long years. Last year, Fletcher had been glued to a lunchroom chair, had his shoelaces tied together, been locked in a stall in the boy's washroom (twice), and spent a whole day with an embarrassing note taped to his back, all in the final week of school. If Sam needed help outwitting the Mandrakes, then Fletcher was going to do everything in his power to assist him.

"What are you going to do, Sam?"

"I don't know yet, Fletcher, but I have a feeling that Professor Mandrake is looking to find more than dinner at my place on Sunday. We'll have to find a way to stop him from snooping around," said Sam.

17

NEVER COUNT YOUR CHICKENS...

When Sam returned home from the Jaffreys' that night, he immediately ran up the stairs, after shouting a hurried "Hi Mum, I'm home!" He shut his bedroom door behind him, dropped to his knees, and called out softly, "Edgar? Mr. Goodfellow? Are you there?"

When his two friends appeared, Sam told them both all about his conversation with Fletcher. Mr. Goodfellow was intrigued by the news that Professor Hawthorne had been good friends with Fletcher's father. "Whenever one door closes, another one opens," he said. At the news of the impending dinner party, and the way in which Professor Mandrake had wrangled his invitation, Mr. Goodfellow let out a long whistle.

"Well, that's interesting, isn't it boys? We'll have to be very careful on Sunday—I have a feeling that something is not quite right with Professor Mandrake. You'll have your work cut out for you, Sam."

"Fletcher's going to help me," Sam replied.

"Excellent, my boy. He seems a faithful lad. Just remember that you mustn't reveal our existence to him, Sam."

To both Sam and Fletcher's relief, it turned out that Basil Mandrake was not going to attend the dinner on Sunday night. Only two days earlier, Basil's fencing team had made it to the final round of a regional tournament. He would be far away competing on Sunday and that suited Sam just fine. By now, the guest list for dinner had expanded anyway. When Abigail Spender "heard" that her beloved professor would be dining with the Middletons (he had circled the date and jotted down the details in red ink on his desktop calendar), she had immediately telephoned Sam's mother and hinted openly for an invitation as well. Sam's mother, after being more or less forced to invite Ms. Spender, then decided that more might be merrier and had invited Mrs. Stanwyck, the real estate agent, too.

Sam's parents had worked frantically to get the house in order for their first dinner party. Before long the old Hawthorne place began to resemble a home. Sam tackled his own room, too, setting up his microscope and computer and sticking up his posters. His mother salvaged Professor Hawthorne's old bookcase, which was dusted off and polished up. Sam's father repaired the broken bottom shelf. The book that had been trapped underneath it was also saved and it was soon sitting in between two of Sam's favorite books: a paperback copy of *The Martian Chronicles* and a crayoned edition of *The Fairy Caravan*.

By the time Sunday rolled around, the head count for dinner remained at ten—four Jaffreys, three Middletons, one Mandrake, a Stanwyck, and a Spender. Sam, Edgar, and Mr. Goodfellow had been in a state all week preparing for the Mandrake invasion, hoping that their search of the house had not overlooked something that Professor Mandrake might find.

At precisely 5:00 in the afternoon (after Sam had been called to help set the table), a band of twenty mice—the ones who had been so rudely expelled by the exterminators on the day of Sam's arrival—decided to return to their home in the Hawthorne house. They entered through a crack in the foundation and into the basement where they had decided to establish their new camp. Once inside the house, though, one of the elder mice became convinced that he could detect the presence of a Sage. He had been proud, as he frequently mentioned, to assist one of the Bluebottle Sage in an assignment only the year before. Considering himself a veteran now, he thought he might be of assistance and was determined to seek them out. The mice were extremely nervous that there might be some lingering effects from the exterminators, but holding their paws over their snouts, they made their way to the upstairs floors via their old mouse tunnels. Upon reaching Sam's room, however, they realized that the exit hole there had been sealed shut. They tapped politely at first, then, unable to hold their breath any longer, began to pound quite violently. Edgar and Mr. Goodfellow heard them and soon came to their rescue.

With the aid of a pen and a nail file, Edgar and Mr. Goodfellow began to stab away at the barrier in earnest. When they finally broke through, twenty mice tumbled out from behind the wall and onto Sam's floor. Convinced that they had inhaled some poisoned air through their ordeal, Edgar and Mr. Goodfellow were unable to calm them down until Mr. Goodfellow searched through his trunk and found a number of old handkerchiefs, bandanas, and scarves that he and Edgar helped them fashion into makeshift gas masks. In light of the distress that they had just endured, not to mention their recent exile, Mr. Goodfellow decided not to enforce the "no trinket" rule on this occasion.

Despite their displacement from the Hawthorne house, the

mice had not let their food acquisition activities in the community fall off. A particularly lovely cheese shop had just opened up on a corner of the street directly behind Sam's house. While Edgar and Mr. Goodfellow became acquainted with the mice, three of their party, masks in place, immediately made their way back outside through the basement exit hole. They returned a short while later with armloads of truffles, assorted flatbreads, exotic cheeses, pickled walnuts, and brandied fruits. Ever mindful of their tendency toward excess, however, Mr. Goodfellow was careful to limit the mice's consumption of the last item.

When Sam had finished helping his parents downstairs, he returned to a very bizarre scene in his bedroom. One side of the floor was littered with plastic wood fragments, a crooked nail file, a blunted pen, and a layer of fine dust. In the middle of this mess sat Edgar and Mr. Goodfellow. Their mouths full of pickled walnut, they were surrounded by a troop of feasting mice, some of whom were wearing bandanas, and looking like tiny, furry bandits.

"Hey, what's going on?" whispered Sam, locking the door behind him. "I've only been gone for forty-five minutes!"

Edgar quickly swallowed his last piece of walnut and wiped his chin on the scarf of the little mouse sitting next to him.

"Edgar!" Mr. Goodfellow admonished. "Manners!"

"Sorry, Uncle Jolly."

"I'm terribly sorry for the mess, Sam, but as you can see we've had a spot of trouble here," explained Mr. Goodfellow. "These poor souls have chosen tonight of all nights to return to their home, and Edgar and I have been helping them settle in."

"Settle in?" cried Sam, slumping to the floor. "No way! Mandrake's going to be here any minute!"

"It's quite all right, my boy," said Mr. Goodfellow. "I have explained everything to the mice already. They want to help. This old chap here has even had some previous experience assisting The Sage."

A gray-whiskered mouse, wearing a red and white spotted scarf across his nose, lifted his paw in acknowledgment.

"Well, if you say so," mumbled Sam, feeling foolish as he waved back at the mouse.

"Don't be alarmed, my boy! It may actually be quite fortuitous that they have happened along!" yelled Mr. Goodfellow.

"Why are you shouting, Uncle Jolly?"

"It's that noise again, Edgar! I swear it's gotten worse! I can hardly hear myself think anymore! Isn't it bothering you?"

"Well, it is a little, Uncle Jolly, but I've been using these for a while," said Edgar, pulling a tiny ball of pinkish goo out of each ear. "Sam gave me some putty to play with and I think they make pretty good earplugs."

"Well! I wish you had thought to share that brilliant idea with me, Edgar!" Mr. Goodfellow said, walking towards the mouse hole.

"I've made some extras, Uncle Jolly. I'll fetch you a pair. They really do help to deaden the noise." Edgar scampered under the bookcase.

"Hmm. That's interesting. The noise is distinctly louder over here, Edgar," Mr. Goodfellow called from across the room. "There was far too much hammering and squeaking going on when we were breaking through the mouse hole for us to notice, I expect." He listened at the jagged opening for a moment, then popped his head inside.

"Aaahh!" cried Mr. Goodfellow, as he jumped back from the hole and landed on the floor with a bump.

"Rollo!" cried Edgar. He sprang up and rushed over to the

mouse hole. The head of a smallish black mouse was peeping out. Edgar grabbed the creature by the arms, pulled him through the opening and enveloped him in a tremendous hug.

"No, don't worry anyone, I'm perfectly alright," said Mr. Goodfellow dryly, as he picked himself up from the floor and brushed the dust from his coat. "And who might this young fellow be, Edgar?"

"It's my dear friend, Rollo, Uncle Jolly! He's one of the gypsy mice I've been living with."

Rollo squeaked excitedly into Edgar's ear.

"He's been looking all over for me. He was worried that The Fen had finally tracked me down. He's been searching the local mouse communities to see if anyone knew anything. When he saw some mice at the back of the cheese shop squeaking about a Sage, he followed them here."

Sam, who had been watching the proceedings with fascination, shuffled over to Edgar.

"His name is Rollo? I didn't know that any of the mice had names," Sam whispered, not wishing to offend the black mouse.

"Of course they have names!" Edgar whispered back. "Names they call each other, that is. I was never able to get my tongue around his proper mouse name, though. It's very long and has this high-pitched squeal at the end that always makes my lips feel funny. We agreed that I would call him Rollo."

"Oh," said Sam.

"Rollo doesn't really like the wandering life, you know," continued Edgar. "He's always dreamed of staying in one place and putting down roots. I suppose that's why we became friends. We're both in the same boat, you see. Rollo and his family have *always* followed the gypsy caravans. It's a tradition. And I, of course, have had no choice but to follow tradition, too.

Rollo looked over at Mr. Goodfellow and then squeaked something else into Edgar's ear.

"He's very sorry that he alarmed you, Uncle Jolly."

"That's quite alright, Rollo," said Mr. Goodfellow. "My reactions wouldn't be so exaggerated, I'm sure, if I could find some relief from this blasted noise."

There was more squeaking from Rollo.

"Uncle Jolly, Rollo says the noise is much louder farther inside the tunnels."

"Really? How extraordinary! The other mice don't seem to be affected by these sounds. Nor is Sam."

"Well, Rollo *is* kind of different, I suppose, Uncle Jolly. He's a gypsy mouse, after all, and he and his family have been following Madam Zorah and her family his whole life. Maybe he picked up some kind of psychic vibrations. I guess he's learned a thing or two living with the gypsies. Actually, it was Rollo who read my fortune."

"*The* fortune?" asked Sam. "The one that was the same as mine?"

Edgar nodded.

Mr. Goodfellow, who was rubbing his chin distractedly, suddenly brightened.

"That's it Edgar! It must be something mystical, with an energy that can only be detected by those who operate on a metaphysical plane. Its power is so great that it can disturb the delicate inner balance of those sensitive to these kind of fluctuations. Like you and me, Edgar. And apparently young Rollo here, too!"

"What, Uncle Jolly? What?"

"The scroll, dear boy! The Hawthorne scroll! It was

rumored to possess strange powers—it must still be here in the house after all! And out of its case, too, I'll wager!"

Mr. Goodfellow rushed towards the mouse hole again, with Edgar, Rollo, and the rest of the mice at his heels.

"Where are you going?" cried Sam.

"Mounting a search for the scroll, of course, my boy."

"Now?" Sam looked anxiously at his wristwatch. "It's almost six o'clock! Mandrake will be here any minute!"

"All the more reason to locate it immediately, Sam," explained Mr. Goodfellow. He turned around. The old gray-whiskered mouse was tapping his shoulder.

"Yes, what is it my dear fellow?" asked Mr. Goodfellow. He looked at Edgar. "I expect the mice would like to assist us—"

The old mouse tapped and squeaked furiously.

"Good heavens, what is it?" asked Mr. Goodfellow, as the mouse squeaked into his ear.

"What?" replied Mr. Goodfellow, as the mouse continued at length. "Really? Well, yes, that could be it!"

"Quickly, Edgar! Follow me!" Mr. Goodfellow cried and they scrambled through the hole together. "The mice think they know where the scroll is!"

Sam, unable to fit much more than his nose beyond the opening in the baseboard had, of course, been left behind as Edgar, Mr. Goodfellow, and the entire troop of mice disappeared through the mouse hole. Holding his ear to the opening, Sam could hear the faint sound of Mr. Goodfellow's voice drifting back through the tunnel.

"Apparently the mice discovered a long narrow tube some time ago," shouted Mr. Goodfellow, "although I am not clear if it was before or after Professor Hawthorne vacated the house. Inside this tube was the scroll—and they say that it is quite beautiful. Apparently the scroll is now on display in their communal meeting hall. They report that it gives off a soft, reddish glow, and a warm, soothing heat. Edgar—it *must* be the scroll!" Mr. Goodfellow's voice began to grow faint. "Not only is the scroll beautiful, Edgar, and you *know* how mice appreciate beauty, but it has been most functional, too, especially during the cooler weather. Of course, they had no idea what it was that they had! I have explained to our old mouse friend that it is, in fact, an extremely ancient and powerful relic. The poor old fellow feels quite dreadful about keeping it. We must return it to its protective case, Edgar. I believe it may be the only way to douse its effects and contain the power..."

Mr. Goodfellow's voice faded away until Sam was left in silence. As he sat cross-legged on the wooden floor, he considered how strange his life had become in just two short weeks. He wondered if it could possibly get any stranger. Then the doorbell rang.

Sam sprang to his feet and flew to the window. A yellow car was parked in the driveway. Sam pushed his face flat against the windowpane and twisted his neck to the side in a desperate attempt to see who might be standing at the front door. When that didn't work, Sam fiddled with the rusty latch, then pushed the window halfway up and stuck his head through. All he could make out was a large, pink bow perched atop a mountain of light brown frizzy hair. Abigail Spender!

"Whew!" said Sam, pulling his head back into the room. As he ran back to the mouse hole, he prayed that Mandrake would be late.

Pressing his ear against the opening in the wall again, Sam waited as the minutes ticked past. Each moment seemed like an eternity. Finally, a pitter-pattering sound began to float through the tunnel. They were back! Hopefully they had found the scroll and secured it.

Sam pushed his face up to the hole and peered into the darkness. Something sharp hit the end of his nose and he quickly pulled back. The scroll, shimmering as it caught the last few rays of fading sunlight, began to inch its way through the mouse hole and into Sam's room. When about half of it had made its way in, all movement suddenly ceased. Sam could hear Mr. Goodfellow shouting through the wall and a great deal of squeaking too. Mr. Goodfellow's head suddenly popped into the room, above the top of the scroll.

"Sam, the nail file! Quickly!"

Sam picked the nail file up from the pile of dust and handed it over. Clutching it under his arm, Mr. Goodfellow shuffled backwards and disappeared once again behind the wall. Sam could hear more shouting and squeaking, and then the sounds of tapping and filing.

The scroll began to move again, very slowly at first, stopping for a brief moment before it finally popped out of the hole. It was about a foot long and, before coming to rest, it rolled a short distance across the floor, glistening like a precious jewel. Mr. Goodfellow, Edgar, and the mice tumbled out after it, still discussing whose fault it was that the scroll had become stuck midway through the mouse hole. Leaning their backs against the wall, Edgar took several deep breaths while Mr. Goodfellow mopped his brow with his hanky. It had been a Herculean task to keep everyone organized and focused during the procedure.

The scroll, which had been lying quite still since rolling to a stop on the floor, suddenly began to twitch. A slow ripple undulated along its length as it began to unfurl itself. Line upon line of strange symbols and script, set upon a radiant background of warm glowing silver, were revealed.

"It's absolutely magnificent, isn't it, Sam?" shouted Mr.

Goodfellow, holding his paws over his mouse ears to drown out what was now an almost painful high-pitched whining noise.

"These earplugs of yours can't drown out the noise at this close proximity, Edgar!" he shouted.

But Edgar, who had retreated to a safer distance from the scroll with Rollo, the gypsy mouse, had his paws clamped too tightly over his ears to hear Mr. Goodfellow's comment.

Sam, still unaffected by the scroll's deafening emissions, had leaned forward to inspect it more closely. Its beauty was mesmerizing. Sam was fascinated by the lines and circles that seemed to dance across its sparkling surface. He could see that the scroll was only paper thin, but as he looked into it, it could have been as deep as the ocean. The sound of the doorbell ringing again broke his trance.

"Oh great! Someone else is here!" Sam cried, tapping at Mr. Goodfellow's furry arm. "We can't keep the scroll in my room!"

Mr. Goodfellow conferred with the elder mice for a moment, before he announced, "We're in a spot of trouble, I'm afraid. Usually the scroll is kept in a protective case, but it's nowhere to be found. The younger mice, I'm told, may have apprehended it for use as some kind of play apparatus. The problem is, none of the little tykes can remember where they left it."

"But what are we going to do? Mandrake is probably already here!" cried Sam.

"It's quite alright, my boy. The mice are off to search for it right now."

"But what are we going to do with the scroll in the meantime? We can't leave it here!" wailed Sam. He was wringing his hands and hopping from foot to foot.

"Considering the difficulty we just encountered getting it out, I'm not keen on shoving it back into the mouse tunnel, Sam. It could get damaged," said Mr. Goodfellow. "I suggest we roll it up and hide it somewhere until the mice can locate the case." He looked around the room. "What about your laundry hamper? I don't think Mandrake is going sift through your dirty clothes, even for the scroll. And your poor mother, frazzled as she is, is unlikely to pop a load into the washer now, either. Might you have a rubber band, my boy?"

It didn't look like Sam was going to have much choice in the matter. He walked over to his desk, took a rubber band out of the top drawer, and brought it back to Edgar and Mr. Goodfellow.

"Why did Professor Hawthorne leave the scroll here, Mr. Goodfellow? Why wouldn't he have taken it with him?" asked Sam.

"I asked myself the very same question, my boy. I suspect the professor thought it was safer to leave it in the house. It sat here, undiscovered, for 120 years, after all. Have you noticed the paneling on the wall over there?"

Mr. Goodfellow trotted across the room and pointed to a section of the wall to the left of Sam's closet door.

"Right here, lads. See?"

Sam knelt down and ran his finger slowly along the seam that Mr. Goodfellow was pointing to with his paw. The color of the wood paneling on either side of the seam was identical, except for a slight difference in texture.

"Quite a remarkable match, isn't it, Sam? Hardly notice-able to the unsuspecting eye. My theory is that our Professor Hawthorne undertook some home renovations at one point and discovered the scroll in the recesses behind the wall. He probably decided to leave it there on purpose—actually a very intelligent thing to do! After all, whoever is looking for the scroll would never imagine that the professor would leave it behind and then sell the house! All he would have to do would be to return at a later date, gain access to the house, and reclaim the scroll! Quite brilliant, really. Of course, it's also possible that he did intend to take the scroll with him, but the mice had already spirited it away. Maybe by then the house had already been sold and the professor had no option but to leave without it. Anything is possible, really."

"So, wherever Professor Hawthorne is, he may not even know what has happened to the scroll, Uncle Jolly?"

"Indeed, Edgar, that is entirely possible. If so, then the poor old soul must be frantic with worry. All the more reason to find him and help him."

Sam, Edgar, and Mr. Goodfellow returned to the scroll and gazed down at it.

"I have seen countless relics in my time, lads—the written testaments of many great civilizations. This one, however, is quite unlike anything I have encountered before. What type of material do you think this is, Edgar?" pondered Mr. Goodfellow, as he ran his paw along the top edge of the scroll. "It has the strength and appearance of metal, but you can crumple it easily and it springs right back again, flat and smooth, when you let it go. Look!"

Mr. Goodfellow folded one of the scroll's corners over. When he let go, it sprang back to its original shape. There wasn't a line or wrinkle to be seen on its smooth shimmering surface.

"It projects a wonderful warmth, too," he said, rubbing his paws together. "And the script is fascinating. Quite unique. The pictograms, too. Hmm, there is something familiar about those pictograms. Where have I seen them before?"

Mr. Goodfellow's musings were interrupted by a knock on Sam's bedroom door.

"Sam! It's me, Fletcher. Open the door!"

Sam's eyes flew wide open, and Edgar and Mr. Goodfellow sprang up and immediately began to gather their things together.

"Um...just a second, Fletcher! I'll be right there!"

Sam rolled the scroll up tightly and wrapped the rubber band around it. He ran over to the laundry hamper and pushed it down through the pile of dirty clothes as far as he could.

"SAM! OPEN THE DOOR!"

"Sam!" whispered Mr. Goodfellow urgently. "We'll have to leave you now. Edgar and I will join the search for the scroll tube in the tunnels. Will you be alright?"

"Yeah, I'll be fine," he said, "but what about Mandrake?"

"Trust Fletcher to help you if you need assistance. Above all, my boy, don't let Mandrake get that scroll!"

"Okay, I won't. See you later."

Edgar and Mr. Goodfellow ran through the mouse hole and disappeared behind the wall. Sam turned to unlock his door.

Fletcher pushed his way in.

"What were you doing, Sam? I just saw Mandrake getting out of his car. He's got Basil with him!"

"Basil? Oh *great*!" sighed Sam. "I can't watch Basil and Professor Mandrake at the same time—you've got to help me, Fletch!"

"For sure Sam, anything," said Fletcher.

"Fletcher," said Sam, as they walked into the hallway and he turned to close the bedroom door behind them, "I've found the scroll."

"What? No way! The Hawthorne scroll? You mean it's been in the house all this time? Where was it—let me see it!"

"It was behind the wall in my room."

"How did you...?"

"I'll tell you later, Fletch. It's a long story. Right now we've got to keep the Mandrakes out of my room—that's where I've hidden it.

"Alright, but what does it look like?" asked Fletcher.

"It's really beautiful, kind of glowing red and silver, and it's covered in weird letters and stuff. I bet you Professor Hawthorne is the only person who could figure out what they mean—that is, if we ever find out where he is."

As Sam and Fletcher made their way downstairs, the sound of loud barking could be heard from the front hall.

"What's that?" asked Sam.

"Oh, that's Brunhilda." Fletcher had to shout to be heard over the dog's barking.

"Brunhilda? Isn't she supposed to have her puppies any day now?"

"Yeah, she's way overdue. My mom didn't want to leave her alone tonight. I hope your parents won't mind."

The horrified look on Sam's mother's face as she stood in the front hall gaping at the pregnant, barking dog suggested otherwise. Brunhilda, however, seemed to be having a marvelous time greeting the next guest at the door by wiping her slobbery jowls across his pant leg.

"Oh, Professor Mandrake! I'm terribly sorry! Let me help you clean that up." Sam's mother rushed forward, pushing Brunhilda out of the way.

"TREVOR! In the hallway, dear. PLEASE!"

Sam's father, the rest of the Jaffrey family, and Abigail Spender rushed into the entrance hall. While Fletcher's father took a firm hold of Brunhilda's collar, Sam's father hovered over a very agitated Professor Mandrake.

"Frightfully sorry, old man," offered Sanjid Jaffrey. "That's what boxers are like—it's those massive jowls of theirs."

"Yes," said Professor Mandrake coldly. "Quite." He patted at his pants with a disgusted look on his face.

Ms. Spender suddenly leaped forward holding a wad of white Kleenex in her hand and leaned down to wipe the dog drool from Professor Mandrake's clothes. She "tut-tutted" in sympathy. Professor Mandrake brushed both Ms. Spender and her assembly of tissues aside. Sam's father, sneezing violently, grabbed at one of them as it floated to the floor. Ms. Spender tottered precariously on her high heels and blinked repeatedly at the professor.

"Please don't bother, Ms. Spender. I actually love dogs. There's nothing like the happy, playful greeting of a loyal canine. There, there, now, old fellow," said Professor Mandrake as he gingerly patted the top of Brunhilda's head.

Brunhilda let out a low growl.

"We'd better just pop her in the kitchen, Sanjid," Fletcher's mother said.

"In the kitchen? Don't you think she would be happier upstairs?" Sam's mother asked hopefully.

"No, no. She just loves kitchens, dear. That's where she feels most at home. She'll be no trouble at all and that way we can keep an eye on her through dinner, too."

Fletcher's mother whispered to her husband as they led Brunhilda towards the kitchen.

"Loves dogs my foot, Sanjid! He can't tell a female from a male, even when she's about to pup any day! And he calls himself an academic!"

"My dear lady," said Professor Mandrake, turning to Sam's

mother and taking her by the elbow. "I do hope it's not an imposition, but I've brought Basil along with me after all." He looked behind him for a moment, then popped his head back out the front door.

"BASIL! GET OUT OF THE CAR!"

Professor Mandrake turned around again and smiled sweetly. When Basil appeared on the front step, his father pulled him inside by his sleeve.

"You see, there was an unfortunate incident at the fencing trials this afternoon. Basil here seems to have inadvertently run through one of the judges with his epée."

"Oh my!" gasped Ms. Spender.

"Fortunately, it was little more than a scratch," continued Professor Mandrake. "I understand the man should be out of the hospital in just a few days. However, Basil has been disqualified from the rest of the tournament as a result—most unfair really. It's been quite a blow to him."

Basil sighed and ran his chunky fingers through his short, spiky blond hair. Then he clasped his hands tightly in front of him, and tried to look as dejected as he possibly could. He gazed at the floor.

"The poor boy," said Ms. Spender.

"I told the officials that they should have checked the equipment more vigorously. It's not Basil's fault the safety tip of his sword came off," said Professor Mandrake, patting his son on the back. "But accidents do happen, I suppose. I thought a night out in the company of his school chums would be the perfect thing to take his mind off his woes."

Basil raised his head and stared directly at Sam and Fletcher. A sly smirk crept across his face.

"Well, of course, Professor Mandrake, we're so pleased Basil could join us," said Sam's mother, thankful that she'd had the foresight to pop an extra Cornish hen in the roasting pan. "Sam, why don't you take Basil and Fletcher up to your room."

"NO!" cried Sam and Fletcher in unison.

"Sam, don't be rude!"

"But Mum, my room is a real mess. Don't worry, we'll find something else to do with Basil, right Fletcher?"

Fletcher stared straight ahead and nodded mechanically.

The doorbell rang yet again.

As Professor Mandrake was closest to the door, he gallantly welcomed the final guest inside. A forty-ish woman with frost-tipped auburn hair and a floor length mink coat swept through the doorway. A waft of French perfume floated in behind her. It was Mrs. Stanwyck, the real estate lady. Called "Tippy" by her friends, Mrs. Stanwyck was a flamboyant divorcée known about town for her flaming red sports car and expensive taste. By the look on Professor Mandrake's face, she was the most gorgeous creature he had ever laid eyes on. After they'd been introduced, it was obvious that Mrs. Stanwyck was thinking exactly the same thing of the professor. When she offered to clean the remaining doggy drool off his trouser leg, he made not a word of protest. Ms. Spender stood off to the side, forgotten, but plotting her revenge.

The guests soon installed themselves in the living room and nibbled on the cheese and cracker tray that Trevor Middleton carried in from the kitchen. Wedged between Abigail Spender and Tippy Stanwyck, on a loveseat meant for two, Professor Mandrake preferred to remain oblivious to the venomous looks between the two ladies. He opened his mouth wide as Tippy slipped a morsel of cheese between his teeth.

In the meantime, Sam and Fletcher decided to check on

the mother-to-be in the kitchen. Basil trailed behind them. Leashed to a table leg and resting quietly in her portable dog bed, Brunhilda's tail thumped a happy response to the company, at first. Sam and Fletcher tickled her behind her ears and gently stroked her back.

"How come your dog's so fat, Jaffrey? Don't your folks know they're supposed to feed you more than the dog?" Basil poked his fingers into Brunhilda's stomach causing her to let out a yelp of pain.

Basil continued to prod and slap until Brunhilda began to emit a series of low, unmistakable growls. Sam caught Fletcher's eye. When Basil had tired of tormenting Brunhilda, he wandered out of the kitchen. Sam and Fletcher followed.

"That's it! Basil's gone too far this time!" whispered Sam. "I think we're gonna have to fight fire with fire." "What?" asked Fletcher. "You know, give Basil a dose of his own medicine." "Huh?" "Teach him a lesson, Fletch!" "Ohhh. Right, Sam."

Basil suggested a game of hide and seek in the upstairs rooms. Sam and Fletcher quickly lured him into the main floor den instead, next to the living room. A dartboard, Ping-Pong table, and shuffleboard game had been recently unpacked and set up there. Basil scanned the room and smiled slyly. The possibilities were endless. Basil couldn't wait to have his way with his intended victims.

"So are you ready for some fun, Basil?" asked Sam, as he slowly closed the door behind them.

From the muffled whoops and hollers that could be heard through the door over the next half an hour, it appeared to the adults sitting in the next room that the boys were thoroughly enjoying their games. At one point, Sam slipped outside and raced up the stairs, returning a few moments later with a small box.

When Sam's mother called everyone for supper about ten minutes later, Basil marched into the dining room wearing a crooked Band-Aid across his nose, another on his forehead and one at the back of his neck. He immediately went to sit next to his father. Unfortunately, the two chairs on either side of Avery Mandrake had already been claimed. Basil had no choice but to squeeze between India and Leonora Jaffrey. He slumped into his chair—anything would be better than sitting next to Sam or Fletcher.

"What have you done to yourself, Basil?" asked his father. "I don't recall you arriving with so many wounds."

Basil glared across the table at his opponents.

"The nose one was my fault actually, Professor Mandrake," said Sam apologetically. "I lost control of my paddle during Ping-Pong."

"I think the one on his forehead was yours too, Sam."

"Oh, yeah, thanks Fletcher. That was my shuffleboard pole, wasn't it? Yours was the dart in the back of the neck."

Sam's father sent him a stern look from across the table. Luckily, his mother arrived just then with the soup course. Sam decided that now would be a good time to jump up and help her serve.

While his mother held the tureen, Sam began to ladle the soup into everyone's bowl. When he reached Basil, however, the soup ladle suddenly flew from his hand and landed right in the middle of Basil's soup plate. Orangey-red liquid immediately sprayed a thick line up his shirt and partway up his left nostril. Even Sam's mother, who was not inclined to suspect her son of unpleasant behavior, shot him a cold glance. Sam looked over at Fletcher and raised his eyebrows. Fletcher quickly covered his face with his napkin but the muffled sound of snorting could still be heard. At least Brunhilda had been avenged. Ms. Spender produced a wad of white Kleenex again and gave it, this time, to Basil.

With the soup course out of the way, Sam's mother returned to the kitchen to take another look at her main course. She removed a roasting pan from the oven, that held eleven deliciously plump Cornish hens and sat it on top of the stove. The hens were a rich and golden brown. She smiled with satisfaction as she walked back into the dining room to clear the soup plates.

When she returned again, a mere six minutes later, Brunhilda was ominously poised over the array of now slightly mangled hens like a giant brown vulture. Her stumpy tail was wagging delightedly.

"Brunhilda, no! You bad, bad dog!" Sam's mother rushed forward and began swatting at the dog's backside with a tea towel. Brunhilda, quite offended, retreated to her bed under the kitchen table and curled into a very small ball. She turned her head to the wall with a pitiful sigh. Peggy Middleton looked down at the dog sympathetically. She noticed that her water dish had been overturned, and wondered briefly how that had happened. But now was no time for idle speculation—there was a dinner to save and no time to lose.

Peggy Middleton swept into the dining room just a few minutes later holding the first two dinner plates. They were a lovely sight to behold—a stuffed Cornish hen was in the center of each plate, surrounded by a medley of braised vegetables. The mashed butternut squash had been artfully drizzled over each hen. Everyone admired the arrangements.

"What an interesting poultry dish," remarked Ms. Spender. "The presentation is quite unique. The stuffing is exquisite, Peggy."

"Yes, it's wonderful," agreed Leonora Jaffrey.

"Is it a requirement of the recipe that both of the wing portions be removed?" asked Professor Mandrake dryly as he picked over his hen. "No, wait a moment. I stand corrected. This chap does seem to have *one* wing."

Peggy Middleton was eternally grateful to Sanjid Jaffrey that he chose that very moment to change the subject.

"How are the new plans for the gallery going, Trevor?"

"Well, they've all been drawn up," Sam's father replied. "The next step is to start on the renovations."

Dinner progressed smoothly as everyone discussed the Middleton's future gallery. Then Professor Mandrake decided to steer the conversation in another direction.

"I was hoping you'd be kind enough to give us a tour of this magnificent old house after dinner, Trevor."

Sam's eyes instantly sought out Fletcher's from across the table.

"Why Avery, I would have thought that you knew this place inside out already," replied Fletcher's father, a playful sparkle in his eye. "I was under the impression that you and Cedric Hawthorne dined together quite frequently."

"Ahh...well...yes. That's true," replied Professor Mandrake, uncomfortably. "But the dear old professor was a dreadful cook, you see. We usually dined out."

"How odd. I'd heard that cooking was rather a hobby of his," continued Fletcher's father. "He studied at the Cordon Bleu one summer..."

"I have to go to the bathroom!" Basil announced suddenly, pushing his chair back from the table.

"Yes, of course dear," said Sam's mother. "It's right upstairs. Not the first bathroom, though. That one needs some plumbing repairs, I'm afraid. Just go to the end of the hall and turn right. It's the second door on your left."

"I'll show you where it is!" Sam announced.

"I'll come with you!" Fletcher chimed.

Basil glared at them.

"Well, since you seem to be finished your dinner," Sam's father said, "why don't you run along and play. You can have some dessert later."

Basil, with a disgruntled look on his face, turned to leave the table only to suddenly stumble as he took a step.

"DAD!" Basil yelled as he fell to the ground.

"Why, your shoelaces are tied together Basil," said Professor Mandrake, peering under the tablecloth.

Sam's father glared at his son again.

"Way to go, Fletcher!" Sam whispered into his friend's ear.

"Hey, I thought you did that!" Fletcher whispered back.

Sam was perplexed. He looked around the table, and his eyes fell upon India Jaffrey, her head bowed innocently towards the table. She was sitting next to Basil. When she felt Sam's gaze, she lifted her head and winked.

18

COURAGE IN DANGER IS
HALF THE BATTLE

Sam and Fletcher took the stairs two by two after Basil. "Why don't you guys act like beetles and bug off!" growled Basil as he opened the bathroom door.

"We're just going to wait for you," said Sam smiling. Fletcher nodded.

"Don't bother!" Basil snarled as he slammed the bathroom door behind him.

Sam stepped back from the door, dragging Fletcher with him by the sleeve. "I think I'd better check on the scroll, Fletcher," he whispered into his ear.

"What, now?" Fletcher whispered back. "What if he comes out and starts snooping around?"

"Uh, I know! We can lock him in the bathroom! He'll think the door's stuck or something. Just until I get back. Then we'll let him out and take him down to the den again. Now we just gotta lock the door with something."

Sam opened the linen closet next to the bathroom and began to rummage around inside. Finally, he pulled out a roll of leftover picture wire. He wound it around the bathroom doorknob several times, pulling it as tight as he could. Then he wound the other end around the knob on the door across the hall.

"That should hold him for awhile. You'd better keep guard though, Fletch. Just in case. And whatever happens, don't let him near my room! I'll be back in a minute! Okay?"

"Okay Sam, whatever you say," Fletcher whispered, staring determinedly at the bathroom door as he listened to the gurgling toilet.

Sam was already halfway down the hallway to his bedroom. He was anxious to know how the Goodfellows had fared with the missing scroll case.

Only a few minutes earlier, just as Basil had tumbled to the floor when his shoelaces had been tied together, Edgar and Mr. Goodfellow had returned to Sam's room from their search in the mouse tunnels. It had not been easy scurrying through the miles of dark passages and it was good to finally rest and breathe fresh air again. Better suited to the world behind the walls, the mice had insisted on pressing on with the search while Edgar and Mr. Goodfellow checked on the scroll.

As they entered Sam's room, Mr. Goodfellow was sure he heard what sounded distinctly like a whimper.

"Edgar, did you hear that noise?" He scurried across the room, stopping to listen at the wall that separated Sam's room from his parent's master bedroom.

"It sounds as if someone is in distress. Wait here, my boy. Keep your eye on the scroll. I'll be back shortly."

Mr. Goodfellow glanced at the closed bedroom door, then ran over to his trunk. He removed his mountain climbing gear and rushed to the door. First he scrambled up to the top of the bookcase, just opposite the doorknob. Then attaching a grappling hook to the end of his climbing wire, he threw the wire over the doorknob. It took him only a few tries.

When he pulled on the wire, the hook caught against the bottom of the doorknob. As Mr. Goodfellow tugged, the doorknob began to move.

"Edgar," he called out, "would you be so good as to open the door, my boy?"

Edgar rushed over and pulled the door open by grasping the lower edge in his paws and pulling it towards him. When it was open by just an inch, Mr. Goodfellow loosened the wire. Then he let it drop. The wire and hook fell softly to the ground. Edgar gathered it up as Mr. Goodfellow climbed down the bookcase.

Another whimper could be heard coming from down the hallway.

"Just put these back in my trunk, Edgar. I'll be as fast as I can." He patted Edgar on the shoulder, then with a quick look up and down the dimly lit hallway, dashed off in the direction of the master bedroom. When he returned a few moments later, he was obviously very excited.

"There's a large dog in need of immediate assistance, Edgar! She has collapsed and, if I'm not mistaken, she is about to give birth any second! I'm afraid I'm going to have to leave you, my boy, while I try to provide as much comfort as I can to the poor animal. Someone's got to watch over her!"

"What do you want me to do, Uncle Jolly? Shall I come and help?"

"No, Edgar, I think one of us will be enough for the suffering creature. You must guard the scroll with your life while I'm gone. I will return as soon as I am able!" He turned away then, scampering out of Sam's room and back down the hallway.

Edgar, alone in Sam's room, leaned down to make some minor adjustments to his suit. The inner lining of his left

263

mouse foot had bunched up during the hectic case search. When he had rearranged the material, he made his way over to the laundry hamper. An odd scuffling sound from Sam's open window drew his attention upwards. Edgar stopped and looked up. The white lace curtain was fluttering and a peculiar odor seemed to be blowing into the room. Edgar wrinkled his nose, then froze. He knew that horrible, moldy smell—it was the smell of The Fen! Suddenly, a black billowing shadow floated down from the windowsill. The creature landed with a sickening thud on the wooden floor in front of him.

Edgar stood paralyzed with fear, his heart thumping madly against his ribs. The Fen had caught up with him at last.

"What's this?" the shadow hissed at him. "The sickly scent of a Sage? And a familiar one, too."

The moonlight outside suddenly chose this very moment to illuminate the room. Edgar swayed unsteadily on his feet. It was Shrike Fen. For just a second, a shaft of moonlight penetrated the shadows that surrounded his black hooded cloak. Edgar gasped as Shrike turned his sharp-featured face towards him and sneered. A thin layer of translucent, sickly white skin covered his long bony nose and chin. The top of his head was round and shiny. Long, white, skeletal fingers grasped the sides of his cloak as Shrike wrapped himself deeper inside it. The Fen began to cackle gleefully.

"Well, well, well. I do believe it's Edgar Goodfellow. How delightful! I was quite torn when I was called away to my new assignment—after all, I had nearly caught up with you! I was looking forward to picking up your trail again, though, and now you've dropped right into my lap! How very convenient!"

Edgar breathed in a lungful of putrid Fen air. He had no choice but to confront his fate. And he couldn't let The Fen find the scroll.

"You don't scare me, Shrike Fen! I'm not running away from you any longer! My uncle Jolly was just saying..."

"What's that? Don't tell me that the great Jolly Goodfellow is here, too? What Fennish luck!" he chortled.

Edgar clamped his mouth shut—but it was too late. He wished he'd thought not to mention his Uncle Jolly.

"Well, that makes things more interesting, doesn't it? Come to think of it, I was feeling something far beyond anything you could have produced. It's a most unusual energy—it can't be Sage alone. But, Jolly Goodfellow indeed! How delicious! I've been looking for him even longer than I've been hunting for you! However, I'll have to deal with him later. It's you first, Edgar, and then the great Jolly. He will be the icing on my cake!" Shrike hissed. "Let's just have some fun first, shall we?"

Edgar's feet were trembling in his mouse shoes. His only hope was to remain strong and focused or all would be lost.

Shrike Fen began to close in on Edgar. With every step, the smell of decay became stronger and more pungent. Each time Shrike hissed, Edgar felt a cold, slimy spray land upon his face.

"What a coincidence. It just so happens that I, too, have my nephew with me. Did you know that my brother had a child?"

Edgar shook his head.

"His name is Bogg. He is apprenticing with his Uncle Shrike. You see, his father is no longer with us. My brother Feral was one of the greatest of our kind—perhaps you remember him?"

Edgar gulped.

"Come, Bogg. Why don't you show your Uncle Shrike how much you've learned."

A smaller figure crept out of the shadows towards Edgar. It

began to circle around him in great, sweeping arcs. Edgar tried very hard to keep his eye on Bogg, but all the spinning was beginning to make him feel quite dizzy. As he whirled around, faster and faster, Bogg's black cloak fluttered open several times to reveal the same white, bony features of his uncle. Bogg's head, however, was covered in little tufts of dirty, matted hair. Bogg began to poke and jab at Edgar's mouse suit with the razor-sharp tips of his long, white nails.

"Excellent, Bogg! You're mesmerizing him. Just a bit longer, then Uncle Shrike will put this pathetic little Sage out of his misery."

"You'll have to finish me off first! And I'm a lot bigger than he is!"

Sam's voice echoed across the room from the open doorway.

There was a shriek of surprise from Shrike Fen. Bogg stopped twirling and ran to his uncle's side. Edgar fell to his knees, scratched and bleeding.

"A human! It's impossible!" snarled Shrike.

"Leave him alone!" cried Sam.

"My, my, you don't think you can protect that miserable Sage, do you? You may have surprised me for a second, human, but you cannot hope to defeat me. I have many powerful weapons at my disposal."

"Sam! You've got to get out of here!" Edgar cried. "The Fen are pure evil, they have ways of twisting your thoughts. I've seen it happen Sam! You've got to go! Now—while you still can!" Edgar's voice trembled as he looked pleadingly at Sam.

"I'm not going to leave you, Edgar!" Sam cried. "And I'm not afraid—I won't let them hurt you!"

Shrike Fen began to inch closer to Sam. He spread his black cloak out and then fluttered awkwardly up the bookcase, shelf by shelf, to the top. There he perched at the edge of the shadows like a gargoyle.

"Watch and learn, young Bogg!" he hissed. "Uncle Shrike is going to show you how it's done." He began to talk in a slow, slithery whisper, "Let's see now, Sam, what is it that you want most in this world? Power? Riches? Fame, perhaps? Or the life of this miserable Sage? I can spare him, if you want it badly enough."

"Don't listen to him, Sam!" Edgar shouted. "He's trying to trick you! You've got to get away before it's too late!"

"I can't leave you, Edgar! I won't!"

Shrike's words began to echo in Sam's head. Strange visions flooded through his mind. A swirling black pit seemed to be sucking up all of his thoughts. He felt his head getting heavy and his eyelids drooping. He leaned against the side of the bookcase, then slid down to the floor.

"Edgar," Sam whispered, holding his head in his hands and fluttering his eyelids. "What's happening to me? I can't think. I'm falling asleep!"

"Sam, don't fall asleep! You mustn't. He'll have you then. Think, Sam, think of something good, before it's too late. Think of Uncle Jolly!"

With Bogg circling round him again, Edgar, too weak to stand, looked at his friend in desperation.

Staring directly into each other's eyes, Sam and Edgar began to concentrate. They thought only of kindness and sacrifice, loyalty and love, until every negative, fearful, envious, jealous, vengeful thing had been emptied from their minds.

Shrike Fen began to sway atop the bookcase.

"What kind of mind trickery is this?" he snarled.

Sam strained to keep his thoughts focused.

"That pitiful little Sage can't help you! I have you just

where I want, human! And I have defeated far bigger prey than you!"

The relentless barrage of Shrike's words began to break through Sam's valiant attempts to concentrate. He could feel his thoughts slowly slipping.

"Fool!" croaked Shrike. "Your mind tricks won't protect you forever! You'll be mine in the end. Why, I might even have you eliminate this annoying Sage for me. Now wouldn't that make a fine end to our little game, Bogg?"

Shrieking with excitement, Bogg once again began to twirl around Edgar, stabbing him repeatedly with his jagged nails. Edgar covered his head with his arms, rolled onto his side and curled into a ball, in a desperate attempt to avoid Bogg's vicious thrusts. Trickles of blood ran from his face and into his mouse paws.

"You know something, Bogg," Shrike Fen cried out, fluttering his cloak about him. "I'm getting rather bored with this game. Besides, our assignment awaits! Let's finish these two off!"

"Sam?...Sam? You're going to listen to me now, aren't you?"

The slippery sound of Shrike's words slithered into Sam's mind. Sam could now feel the full force of The Fen's evil thoughts. A terrible pounding began to drum at his temples, as his own thoughts began to slip further away.

"You can still save your wretched friend, Sam," hissed Shrike, "if that's what you really want. You're very tired, aren't you? Give up the fight, human. It will be easier for you if you come to me willingly."

"No!" Sam struggled to control his thoughts. "Never!"

"Have it your way then, fool!" With a bloodcurdling scream, Shrike swirled his black cloak around him and edged down the bookcase until he was perched directly beside Sam.

Cold, slimy ooze dripped into Sam's ear when Shrike Fen hopped upon his shoulder and stretched out his cloak.

Sam felt a creeping blackness begin to spread through his mind. His head began to throb horribly. He had to fight to stay focused. He channeled his thoughts and concentrated on the things that meant the most to him—the love of his parents, his friendship with Mr. Goodfellow, the bond he shared with Edgar. The pain began to lessen. Somehow, Sam knew this might be his only chance. With his last ounce of strength, Sam lifted his head from his chest, though it felt as though a thousand arrows were piercing his brain, and called out.

"Edgar! Our only chance is to fight them with our hearts, fight with me Edgar—concentrate on what is true!"

Sam's pleading must have had some effect, because Edgar's still figure stirred. Bogg suddenly stopped his maddening circles and stepped back. With all the strength he had left, Edgar clenched his fists, raised himself up on his elbows and turned to look at Sam. Their gazes locked and held.

Shrike felt a surge of energy that sent him flying backwards off Sam's shoulder and directly into the side of the bookcase. He fell with a thump to the floor.

"Mind games and trickery!" he shrieked, picking himself up. "You will not master me!"

Oblivious to the life-and-death events taking place in Sam's room, Mr. Goodfellow, wiping his coat with a white handkerchief, slipped into the dark room.

"Ah, there you are!" he said, squinting at Sam against the bookcase. "I've just delivered four lovely puppies! There was a bit of a medical emergency with the last pup, but I administered mouth to muzzle resuscitation just in time and I think he's going to pull through. Sam? Is everything all right, my boy? Where is Edgar? He lifted his nose mask and sniffed the air. "What's going…good heavens! FEN!" Mr. Goodfellow's handkerchief floated to the ground. "How could I have missed your hideous presence? Something must be interfering with my instincts."

"Yes, and we both know what that would be, don't we? Another power source!" screamed Shrike. "Just as I suspected! And you know all about it, don't you, Sage?"

As Shrike shrieked at him, Mr. Goodfellow began to edge slowly into the room. His eyes adjusted to the gloom and he could see Edgar lying in a heap on the floor beneath the window. Bogg was standing only inches from him.

"What have you done to these boys, Shrike? If you've harmed even a hair on their heads, you'll rue the day!"

Temporarily freed from the onslaught of Shrike's evil thoughts, Sam groaned and put his hands up to his head. He rubbed his throbbing temples. Bogg slunk back into the shadows under the windowsill. Mr. Goodfellow raced across the room to his nephew's side. He took Edgar into his arms, trying desperately to lift him to his feet.

"Not so fast, Goodfellow!" hissed Shrike, loping across the room towards them. "The game's not over yet. I'd say we're only just beginning. I'd nearly finished with your nephew and that pathetic human until you barged in—Ugh! And that smell—you smell as bad as those revolting animals! Dogs! Despicable, loyal creatures. I'd rid the world of them if I only had the chance!"

"Don't come any closer, Shrike Fen!" Mr. Goodfellow cried, holding up one hand as he struggled to hold Edgar upright with the other.

"Why not, Goodfellow? It's all over for you now. Nothing can stop me," he cackled again, rubbing his long white fingers together.

As Shrike and Bogg began to close in on Mr. Goodfellow,

their collective chortling drowned out the sound of the door as it was pushed farther open. The hulking shape of Brunhilda staggered in.

Brunhilda clearly sensed evil in the room. Her ears flattened against her head and the short hair along her spine stood straight up. Her eyes locked on Shrike Fen and a low growl rose from her throat.

"What is that wretched animal doing?" Shrike screamed before he leapt into the shadows surrounding Bogg. "Bogg, attack!"

Bogg, however, didn't move.

"You attack, Uncle Shrike. I'll stay here and protect you," Bogg responded.

"The creature's instincts are right on target—she doesn't like you, Shrike Fen," said Mr. Goodfellow.

"Ridiculous!" Shrike cried. "That miserable dog won't get in my way! I've waited sixty-five years for this moment. Come, Bogg!" he hissed, rattling his cloak around him again. "It is time to avenge your father!"

Shrike Fen slipped out of the shadows and stood in front of Edgar and Mr. Goodfellow. "No more games, Bogg. I've grown weary of games." He lifted one side of his black cloak and pointed a bony finger across the room. "Drag the little Sage over there, Bogg, and finish him off. I'll take care of the great Jolly Goodfellow myself!"

"Edgar, dear boy. You've got to get up!" Mr. Goodfellow implored, shaking him gently. Bogg drew nearer.

Sam shook his head back and forth to rid himself of the last vestiges of Shrike's mindhold. Then he crawled into a kneeling position and tried to call out Edgar's name. There was no time to spare, and if he didn't do something now, it would be too late for them all. Sam stared intently ahead of him. The last time he and Edgar had joined thoughts, they had knocked Shrike off his perch. But this would be their last chance.

"Edgar!" Sam croaked. "You've got to look at me." Sam stared across the dimly lit room. "Think of your father, Edgar," Sam implored breathlessly. "Remember? Think of him now, Edgar. I'll help you!"

"Yes, Sam, by Jove, you've got it! Edgar—think of your father, dear boy!" Mr. Goodfellow cried. He and Edgar turned toward Sam and their eyes locked together.

Sam concentrated on all the wonderful things The Sage had taught him, and Edgar and Mr. Goodfellow thought of Filbert.

"Bogg, don't you see what they are doing? They're creating a shield of good energy! We've got to stop them!" Shrike cried out. "We must interrupt their channeling!"

"Uncle Shrike, I...I can't move!" Bogg wailed.

Still holding Edgar against him, Mr. Goodfellow suddenly felt him straighten up on his own. As Edgar, Sam, and Mr. Goodfellow continued to stare at one another, a spark flared between them. It began to grow into a small ball of white light, then a larger one. The growing light glowed and pulsated and sparks began to shoot from its center. It flew from one corner of the room to the other, bouncing off the walls, and finally swooping down over the heads of The Fen. A shower of sparks suddenly sprayed out from the light as it danced across the room. Bogg and Shrike flapped at the flames that sprung up from their black cloaks. Shrieking and hissing, they cowered in frustration and pain.

The spinning light finally came to rest. It hovered in the center of the room where it began to swell to an enormous size, filling the entire space between the ceiling and floor. At its glowing center, surrounded by a thousand sparks, a

shape began to materialize. Edgar, Sam, and Mr. Goodfellow, their mouth gaping open, stared in awe as the face of Filbert Goodfellow, Edgar's beloved father, appeared in front of them.

"What's this?" sneered Shrike, staring at the vision before him. "What have your puny minds thought up now? Another feeble trick, Sage?"

Mr. Goodfellow gazed into the face of his dear brother. "No, Shrike. It's no trick. Our puny minds, as you call them, have summoned a force that you could never hope to defeat. It is the force of love. I believe the balance of power has just shifted our way, Fen!"

"Never! It's nothing but lies!"

Bogg, terrified by the looming vision above him, began to whimper.

"Stop sniveling, Bogg!" Shrike snarled. "We must defeat them!"

"But Uncle Shrike," he cried, drawing his cloak close around him and crumpling to the floor, "I can't think anymore. I..."

Filbert's filmy vision floated in the air between them. It appeared to be looking directly at Edgar. A powerful energy seemed to fill the room.

Hissing, Shrike and Bogg crept backwards toward the window.

"It's no use—these sickening, syrupy thoughts are too strong!" Shrike yelled, beating his cowled head with two bony fists. He fell to the ground and crawled over to Bogg and, grabbing him by the back of his cloak, dragged him toward the window. In one final burst of strength, Shrike swept onto the windowsill with Bogg in his grasp.

"You may have won this battle Sage," he hissed, "but I am

not through with you yet. I will hunt you down! Mark my words! Next time you will not be so lucky!"

Brunhilda suddenly moved forward toward the window.

"Stay back, you stupid beast!" Shrike hissed.

Brunhilda walked up to the windowsill and pulled her lips back to reveal two glistening rows of sharp, white teeth. Her lips quivered as she snarled at Shrike. An eerie, gurgling sound seemed to rise from deep within her. The powerful muscles in her chest rippled and twitched.

Pushing Bogg out the window, Shrike turned back to taunt her.

"Idiotic creature!" he sneered. "If I had more time, I'd drown those miserable puppies of yours."

Brunhilda lunged.

At that very moment, in the living room below, Leonora Jaffrey was in the midst of performing a selection from Bizet's *Carmen*, with India as her accompanist at the piano. Just as she reached, and held, a particularly piercing high note, Shrike Fen let out a bloodcurdling shriek from the room directly above.

Shrike struggled to loosen himself from Brunhilda's powerful jaws, twisting and flapping in every direction. Sam crawled over to Edgar and Mr. Goodfellow, grimacing at the sound of Shrike's hideous screams. They stared in shocked silence as The Fen continued to fight within Brunhilda's enormous jaws. She swung her massive neck back and forth. Streams of saliva flew across the room.

Downstairs, Rollo the gypsy mouse had taken a wrong turn in one of the wall tunnels and gotten terribly lost. He scurried out of a very tiny hole in the living room's baseboard and, terrified by the assembly of humans in front of him, made a mad dash to another hole he spied across the

room. He scrambled over Leonora's Jaffrey's shiny black pumps along the way. Leonora froze when she felt something scurry across her feet, then she let out a bloodcurdling shriek. At first, no one was certain if her high-pitched squeals were supposed to be part of the singing, until the word "Mouse!" became obvious between her shrieking. When Ms. Spender and Mrs. Stanwyck added their own high-pitched squeals to Leonora's, it became apparent that something was seriously amiss.

"I'll sue those exterminators!" Mrs. Stanwyck screamed, holding her skirt and standing in the middle of the sofa.

"You never told us that the house had a rodent problem!" Peggy Middleton shouted back from the top of a wing-backed chair.

Startled by all the loud noise, India had jumped up suddenly from the piano and stumbled into Professor Mandrake. His glass of Madeira wine tipped forward and emptied its contents down his light brown trousers and onto his beige suede shoes. The muscles at the sides of his face began to twitch violently.

"What an absolutely *delightful* way to end the evening, my dear," he sneered sarcastically.

Back in the bedroom, Sam's hands were still clamped tightly over his ears as Shrike Fen screamed and twisted in Brunhilda's locked jaws. Suddenly all fell silent. Brunhilda gave her head a great toss, as she appeared to gulp something down. Then she shook her entire body, starting from her head and moving down to the tip of her stubby tail. She turned around and trotted out of the room and back to her puppies.

Sam, Edgar, and Mr. Goodfellow looked at each other in wonder, then at the windowsill and the curtain blowing beside it. The bright, white light and the image of Filbert

Goodfellow had vanished. Only the three of them remained. In all of the noise and excitement, none of them had noticed when Filbert's vision had faded away. Sam poked his head out through the open window and peered into the bushes below, but it was too dark to see anything but a few broken branches. When he turned around again, Edgar and Mr. Goodfellow were staring into the empty space at the center of the room where the haunting face of Filbert had loomed only moments before. It was some time later before any of them could talk of what had transpired.

"Are you alright, Edgar?" Sam looked at his friend with concern.

Edgar smiled back at him. "Yes, Sam, I'm fine now. If it hadn't been for my Dad..." Edgar's voice trailed off.

"We certainly have a lot to thank dear Filbert for," Mr. Goodfellow continued, patting Edgar on the back. "This has been a most extraordinary day. You two lads have a great deal to be proud of. But Sam, how long have you been up here, my boy? You had better get back downstairs at once!"

"Yikes!" Sam gasped. "I left Fletcher with Basil!" He leapt to his feet and rushed down the hallway, praying that Fletcher was all right. He didn't know how long it had been since he'd left him guarding the bathroom door.

"A minute, Sam! You said you'd be back in a minute! Where the heck have you been? Basil's going crazy in there! We've got to let him out!" Fletcher stood by the bathroom door. He was clinging to the wire that was holding the door shut so hard, his fingers and knuckles had turned white. Basil was rattling the doorknob and thumping wildly on the bathroom door.

"I'm really sorry, Fletcher. There was an emergency I had to take care of—I'll tell you about it later."

"Had to take care of? What could be more important than this?"

"Uhhh...it's Brunhilda, Fletch. She's had her puppies." Sam grabbed Fletcher's arm.

"What? No way!"

"Yeah, just now. Four of them. I had to help her."

"COOL!" exclaimed Fletcher.

The thumping on the bathroom door suddenly stopped.

"Hey! Is somebody out there? GET ME OUT OF HERE!" screamed Basil.

Sam and Fletcher stared at the door. Then Sam motioned for Fletcher to hold onto the bathroom doorknob. He began to carefully untie the wire.

After he had shoved the wire into his pocket, Sam began to rattle the knob.

"Basil?" he called out. "Are you in there?"

"YEAH! I'M IN HERE!" Basil yelled back. "CAN'T YOU HEAR ME? OPEN THE DOOR, YOU IDIOTS! I'M STUCK!"

"BASIL, DO YOU REALLY THINK YOU SHOULD TALK TO US LIKE THAT WHEN YOU CAN'T GET OUT? I THINK YOU SHOULD APOLOGIZE!" Fletcher shouted back, smiling slyly at Sam.

Basil was silent. Then they heard a very soft "Sorry."

"What was that, Basil? I didn't quite hear you," Fletcher said. Sam had to clamp a hand over his mouth to stop him from laughing out loud.

"I said sorry, okay? Now open the door! I'm claustrophobic, you know!" Basil yelled.

Sam rattled the doorknob for effect, then let go. Basil, who had been pulling from the other side, suddenly tumbled backward as the door swung open. He struggled to his feet then staggered out into the hallway.

"What's going on? What took you guys so long?" he snarled.

"It's this old doorknob, Basil. It gets stuck sometimes," explained Sam apologetically, as he continued to fiddle with it.

"We were playing around on Sam's computer. We figured you'd gone back downstairs," said Fletcher.

"Fletcher was the one who heard you, when he came here to go to the bathroom," added Sam. "If it wasn't for him, we might never have found you."

Fletcher smiled and then slipped past Basil into the bathroom. Basil glared at Sam then turned and marched down the hallway toward the stairs.

19

ACCIDENTS CAN HAPPEN
EVEN IN THE BEST RUN
FAMILIES

T revor Middleton rushed frantically about the living
room. His attempts to calm everyone down were
proving useless. Peggy Middleton's eyes had filled
with tears. Ms. Spender had run into the hallway looking for
her coat, quickly excusing herself for the evening. Where
there was one mouse, she reasoned, there were bound to be
two, or three, or...she just couldn't bear to think about it.

Mrs. Stanwyck left soon after Ms. Spender. Her exit elicited
a sad sigh from Professor Mandrake. He sat on the sofa with a
floral print tea towel, attempting to mop up the red wine that
had left a large purple stain on his pants. His investigation of
the Hawthorne premises had apparently been thwarted. After
the rodent incident, a house tour seemed unlikely. Somewhere
in the back of his mind, it occurred to him that he hadn't seen
his son in quite some time. The evening had proven to be a
total disaster.

Leonora, still unnerved at the thought of little mouse paws
running across her new black pumps, was beginning to
develop a headache. Her immediate concern, however, was
Peggy Middleton. Peggy sat forlornly at one end of the

loveseat, dabbing her swollen eyes with a limp tissue. Leonora sat down next to her and tried to provide some comfort, but Sam's mother was inconsolable.

"Perhaps it would be best if we left now, too, dear. Give you some time alone," offered Leonora, as she motioned her husband toward the kitchen to retrieve the dog.

"We must be off, as well, I'm afraid," Professor Mandrake announced dryly, pulling his damp trouser legs away from his shins as he stood up. He glanced with annoyance toward the staircase in the front hallway. "What *are* those boys up to?"

A concerted effort to find Basil was soon mounted. The remaining guests gathered in the hallway, and just as Trevor Middleton was about the head up the stairs, Basil suddenly appeared on the upper landing.

"What's wrong with you *now*, Basil? Where on earth have you been? How many times have I told you that I do not like to be kept waiting?" the professor inquired.

Basil trailed sullenly down the stairs, his fat lower lip clamped between his teeth. He complained bitterly that he had been trapped in the bathroom and had been shouting and pounding on the door, for at least half an hour.

Trevor Middleton glared in the direction of the stairs.

"SAM!" he called sternly.

Sanjid Jaffrey suddenly rushed through from the kitchen with Brunhilda's leash dangling in his hand. The ensuing panic was soon dispelled by Sam's calls from upstairs.

"Brunhilda's had her puppies!"

"Right in the middle of Mr. and Mrs. Middleton's bed!" added Fletcher.

Sam's mother began to sway. Leonora put a bracing arm around her.

"There, there, Peggy. I know a wonderful dry cleaner in town. He works miracles! We'll call him first thing in the morning, dear, right after we call the wildlife removal people."

Sam's mother laid her head on Leonora Jaffrey's ample shoulder and sobbed.

Professor Mandrake quickly said his goodbyes, hastily buttoned a still whining Basil into his coat, and dragged him out to the car.

The Middletons and Jaffreys climbed the stairs to the master bedroom. Brunhilda lay upon the soiled and rumpled four-poster bed, licking and nuzzling her little ones. Leonora and India squealed over the four brown, squirming puppies. Even Sam's mother could not refuse them a tiny smile.

"I'll find...something to put them...in," offered Sam's father, stifling a sneeze.

Scratching at his hives, Trevor Middleton wandered down the hall towards the linen closet. He soon returned with a cardboard box and an old bath towel.

The Jaffreys quickly bundled the puppies into the box and then gathered the rest of their things. Just as they were saying their goodbyes, Brunhilda suddenly began to cough and choke. Leonora rushed to her aid, prized her jowls open and pushed a hand deep into the dog's throat.

"What have you got in there, dear?" said Leonora, fishing around while the animal continued to splutter.

When it appeared that more extensive measures were required, Leonora threw her arms around Brunhilda's chest and performed a canine version of the Heimlich maneuver. Finally, something shot out of her mouth and flew across the floor. Leonora, still on her hands and knees, crawled over to take a look.

"Brunhilda! What's this thing?" she said, picking up the

dislodged object from the floor and holding it up to the light. "It looks like a chicken bone."

Sam's mother began to sway again.

"And what's this little piece of black cloth?" Leonora continued. "Oh, Peggy! I do hope she hasn't gotten into anything valuable upstairs. They're absolutely lovely dogs, you know, but they do have a tendency to chew things. Naughty Brunhilda!"

As the Jaffreys finally trooped out the front door, Sam caught Fletcher by the arm.

"Thanks, Fletch," he whispered. "I couldn't have done it without you. Call me tomorrow, okay?"

Fletcher nodded and slipped outside.

Sam stood at the door for a moment, watching and waving as the Jaffreys drove away. His mother, her white knuckles gripping the banister, was already making her way to one of the upstairs guestrooms for a much-needed rest.

When Sam turned around again his father was standing right in front of him, arms folded tightly across his chest. He was rhythmically tapping one foot, and he was not smiling.

Sam grinned nervously.

"Uh, I'd better get back upstairs, Dad. I think Fletcher and I left the computer on in my room and the volume's *way* up. It might bother Mum."

Sam's father opened his mouth to reply, but instead suddenly emitted one last seismic sneeze. Sam took the opportunity to squeeze past him and bounded up the stairs. Once Trevor Middleton had recovered, he shook his head and then walked slowly into the kitchen to face the dirty dishes.

Upstairs, into Sam's room, Mr. Goodfellow had removed Edgar's mouse suit and was carefully examining his injuries. The more serious ones were to his head and legs. When Sam slipped back into his room, Mr. Goodfellow asked him to retrieve his first aid kit from the trunk.

Carefully opening the blue drawers with a fingernail, Sam searched with his magnifying glass until he found a white box marked with a red cross. He carried it over.

Edgar sat quietly, wincing every now and then as Mr. Goodfellow tended to the cuts and slashes on his head with antiseptic. Fen wounds, even the smallest ones, had a tendency to become infected quickly. Mr. Goodfellow wasn't about to take any chances.

Sitting on the floor next to his friends, Sam asked why The Fen despised animals so much.

"Animals are pure spirits, Sam," replied Mr. Goodfellow, "they are inherently good creatures. That is why The Fen hate them so, and why it is our duty to protect them. And quite often, as you have seen for yourself, they protect us, too. They have no human faults, such as envy, spite, ego, or cruelty. In fact, they are wise and old spirits. They return to the earth over and over in their journey through time, and they always return as a different kind of animal—as whales, or gophers, or mice, or monkeys."

"Even insects?" asked Sam.

"Of course."

"And birds and fish too?"

"Yes, Sam, all animals. All, that is, but man. Man has received a different journey in life. It is one that is fraught with many puzzling questions and temptations."

Mr. Goodfellow placed a bandage over the last cut on Edgar's forehead.

"Is that comfortable, Edgar?"

Edgar, too exhausted to make conversation, nodded his head and offered a brave smile.

"So, remember Sam," continued Mr. Goodfellow, patting Edgar gently on the shoulder, "when you pick up one of Brunhilda's puppies, you may, in fact, be holding something that is many thousands of years old."

Mr. Goodfellow looked down at his suit.

"I'm afraid that this suit of mine needs a thorough cleaning," he said, reaching to unzip it. "In my effort to deliver soothing words of comfort to Brunhilda in her time of need, I seem to have picked up a considerable amount of drool. I would appreciate it if you would find me something else to wear from my trunk, Sam. I think I may require a clean shirt and trousers, too. There's a good lad."

Sam shuffled over to the trunk again while Mr. Goodfellow removed his soggy suit.

Without his mouse suit on, Mr. Goodfellow suddenly felt the chill in the air through his damp shirt. He quickly slipped it off and stifled a shiver.

"Thank you, my boy," said Mr. Goodfellow reaching for the clothes and mouse suit that Sam held out to him. When he bent over to remove his trousers, Sam gasped. Two bony bumps protruded from either side of Mr. Goodfellow's back.

"There's no need for concern, my boy," Mr. Goodfellow said, responding to Sam's gasp as he turned his head around. "We all have these things. Don't we, Edgar?"

Edgar nodded.

"No one is quite sure what they are," continued Mr. Goodfellow. "They're generally regarded as an evolutionary relic from our past; a useless appendage, rather like an appendix or a sixth toe."

Sam couldn't help but feel there was something strangely familiar about the knobby protuberances. They reminded him of the remains of a small bird he'd found once. Sam had wanted to keep it intact but, when he lifted it from the soil, the tiny wings had broken loose, leaving an odd-looking skeleton with two bony knobs on its back.

Mr. Goodfellow chattered on.

"Personally, I have always imagined there's more to it than the sixth toe theory. My brother Filbert was quite interested in this mystery. He engaged in some rather intriguing speculations."

Suddenly a loud squeak from the mouse hole interrupted their conversation. Sam rushed over to the hole and pushed his face against the opening.

"Something is going on in there! I think they might have found the scroll case, Mr. Goodfellow!" he cried.

"I certainly hope so, my boy! Let's get the scroll inside it as quickly as possible. Even with these putty plugs, I don't believe my old ears can take much more noise!"

Mr. Goodfellow donned his clean clothes and suit and rushed through the mouse hole to help the mice push the silver-colored tube out. It clattered to the floor and rolled towards Edgar. Rollo leapt out of the mouse hole behind it. He held a round silver disc under one arm. The old gray-whiskered mouse followed soon after, holding an identical disc. Mr. Goodfellow and the rest of the mice tumbled out of the hole behind him.

Sam dashed across his room and dove headfirst into the laundry hamper. Soon dirty clothes were flying around the room as he dug for the scroll. He resurfaced seconds later with the scroll grasped firmly in his hand. Everyone met in the center of the room, where Mr. Goodfellow had taken charge of the re-tubing operation.

Edgar climbed into the tube to direct the scroll as it was pushed inside.

"Uncle Jolly! There's some yellow paper in here. I think it's one of those sticky notes. There's writing on it."

"A note, Edgar? What does it say?"

"Just some scribbles, Uncle Jolly. Dates and a flight number, I think. And train times, too."

"Bring it over and let's have a look, Edgar."

Mr. Goodfellow brushed past the crowd of mice that had gathered at the end of the tube and climbed inside with Edgar.

"From the desk of Professor Cedric Hawthorne," he read. "Well, that's helpful, isn't it? New York to Heathrow. Flight 603. These must be Professor Hawthorne's travel arrangements! Excellent!"

Sam peered through the tube opening.

"Heathrow? That's London, England, isn't it?" asked Sam "*England*! I thought he'd have gone somewhere mysterious like Africa or Antarctica, or something." Disappointed, Sam spoke out again. "What else does it say?"

"Train times to Wiltshire it would appear and, if I can make out this last bit, a final destination of...Chipping-on-Bradbury," called Mr. Goodfellow.

"What's Chipping-on-Bradbury?" asked Sam.

There was silence for a few seconds, followed by a sudden whoop of excitement from Mr. Goodfellow.

"Of course! Crop circles, my boy! Crop circles!" he cried. "You know, those symmetrical patterns of circles and lines that pop up every now and then in crop fields all over the globe? It just so happens that the highest incidence of crop circles has occurred in that very part of the world that our professor has fled to! I should have made the connection right away!"

"What connection, Uncle Jolly?" asked Edgar.

"The symbols on the scroll, Edgar! Remember I told you

288

that I'd seen them somewhere before, but I couldn't quite recall? They're exact replicas of the pictograms that turn up repeatedly in crop circles. The ringed circle! The ringed star! The laddergram! The dumbbell and the dolphin formations! Professor Hawthorne has made the connection, boys, and he has gone directly to the source!"

"I've heard about those crop circle things on the news," said Sam. "I thought they were just tricks—that they weren't real."

"Not exactly, Sam. Some of them have been deceptions, but a large number of them remain a mystery. They have been around for hundreds of years after all. There have been many theories about their origin and purpose: alien landings, military maneuvers, even the bizarre nighttime behavior of local animal populations. Some more popular explanations involve unusual weather patterns, whirlwinds, electrostatic fields, magnetism."

Mr. Goodfellow rambled on as he rolled out of the tube, clutching the yellow sticky note in his arms. "Professor Hawthorne is hot on the trail to discovering the true source of the crop circles! Anything can happen when a great scientist tackles a great mystery."

Waving his paws about, Mr. Goodfellow shouted instructions to the contingent of mice that had already started to push the scroll in at one end of the tube. Edgar stood at the opposite end and guided the scroll through.

"I predict that the professor is about to make an amazing discovery!" Mr. Goodfellow continued. "He's brilliant, you know, absolutely brilliant! But his thoughts do tend to wander at times. He needs focus. I must be off immediately!"

With the scroll now in place, Rollo and the old gray-whiskered mouse rushed forward with the silver discs, which were actually stoppers for each end of the tube, and pushed them into place. It came as a great relief to Mr. Goodfellow, Edgar, and Rollo that the scroll's noisy emissions had finally been contained. Edgar pulled the pink putty balls out of his ears.

The discovery of Professor Hawthorne's scribbled note breathed new life into Mr. Goodfellow. He dashed behind the bookcase to his trunk. Between off-key strains of "Back in the Saddle Again," a flurry of activity was taking place.

"Let me see... England this time of year, what to wear, the dormouse perhaps?" he murmured absently.

He peered out from behind his trunk. Sam was reading Professor Hawthorne's note. Edgar, sitting quietly beside him, was gazing at the floor.

"I must try to get on the earliest flight possible, lads! Although an ocean crossing would be more relaxing... but wait, what *am* I thinking? I've got to make up for lost time!" He paused and looked intently at his nephew. "Besides, a sea voyage wouldn't suit you at all, would it Edgar?"

"Me, Uncle Jolly?" said Edgar looking up.

"Well, of course, my boy! We're a team, aren't we? You don't think I'd leave you behind after all the time it's taken to find you? Come on! Get moving Edgar—we're going home! I can hardly wait to see your dear mother's face when she lays her eyes upon you again!"

"Is there anything I can do to help?" Sam offered.

Mr. Goodfellow called out from behind the bookcase. "No, no, my boy. You have already been a great help to us!"

"I guess now that you're going home for awhile, you'll be able to visit all your old friends, like Beatrice," Sam said.

There was a sudden silence from the other end of the room.

"Mr. Goodfellow? Mr. Goodfellow?"

The little man shuffled out from behind the bookcase, looking troubled.

"What's wrong, Mr. Goodfellow?" asked Sam.

"Nothing, my boy."

"A trouble shared is a trouble halved, remember?"

Mr. Goodfellow smiled. "Well, Sam, the truth of the matter is, Beatrice and I have not seen or spoken to each other since our final farewell at summer's end all those years ago."

"Not ever, Uncle Jolly?" Edgar asked in disbelief.

"No, I'm afraid not. And, truly, it has been my greatest regret."

"But why not?" asked Sam.

"It was a time of great turmoil back then. Events were happening quickly. Beatrice returned home and was instantly caught up in her work. And so was I. I was also preoccupied with Edgar's disappearance. The years passed and the world changed and it suddenly seemed too late. Many years later Edwina Sparrow told me that Beatrice had found her peace in a little cottage by the seaside. Some time ago, Edwina forwarded her address to me."

"Well if you know where she is, why don't you go and see her?" cried Edgar.

"It's really not that simple, my boy. It's been decades since we've spoken. She may have moved, she may not even want to see me. What if..."

Sam interrupted.

"But what about knowing your heart and following your dream?"

Mr. Goodfellow's dark eyes twinkled.

"It is nice to see that you've been paying attention to me, my boy. But not one amongst us is perfect, Sam. Sometimes it's easier to counsel others than to face our own limitations—even the wisest and the bravest among us, I'm afraid."

"But Uncle Jolly," pleaded Edgar, "promise that you will try. I have a feeling. I heard you say once that 'a faint heart never won fair lady.'"

Mr. Goodfellow sighed and returned to his packing. An awkward silence followed. Sam stared absently into space and Edgar fiddled with the fur of his suit. Mr. Goodfellow, anxious to change the subject, began to chatter on about his plans.

"Once home, I will attempt to locate the professor and provide guidance. I will also contact the Governing Council and ask them about you, Sam, and the Sacred Seal. You will hear from me again. And..." he raised his eyebrows.

"You always keep your promises," finished Sam.

"That's right, my boy, I do."

There was a bit more clattering from the direction of the trunk and then the sound of a door slamming shut. Mr. Goodfellow emerged with a long coil of rope over his shoulder, pulling the trunk behind him. He was wearing a newly brushed dormouse suit. If a mouse could look dapper, this one certainly did. Edgar walked over to join his uncle, wearing the black and brown spotted mouse suit again. He was sure that when Mr. Goodfellow had more time he would be able to repair the rips and tears that Bogg's nails had inflicted on it. They stopped in front of Sam.

"Well, I'm afraid this is goodbye, lad," said Mr. Goodfellow sadly. "It's time for us to go."

Sam nodded and knelt down. "I wish you didn't have to leave. I'll miss you."

"And we'll miss you, Sam. You're the first of your kind that we've come to know on more than a professional level and, I must say, I consider it a great privilege to call you my friend.

You're a fine young man, Sam. You must always try to stay that way."

Sam stared at Mr. Goodfellow then at Edgar. He struggled to swallow despite the sudden presence of a large and uncomfortable lump in his throat. "Will I ever see you again?"

The little man in the dormouse suit hesitated.

"Good heavens, my boy, I certainly hope so! I have every faith that we will. The Sage are swept along by the same fates as you and your kind, Sam. I believe that the fact that you, Edgar, and I all met here was no accident. Perhaps we will be fated to meet again?"

"Maybe moving to this creepy, old house was a good thing, after all, right?" asked Sam.

"Indeed, my boy! Funny, isn't it? If it hadn't been for our mutually sad predicaments, we might never have met each other, and I might never have found Edgar again!" Mr. Goodfellow patted Sam affectionately on the toe. "Take care of yourself, dear boy. We often find our dearest friends where we least expect to and friendship and love are two things that can sustain us through many trials. Always remember that."

With those words, he held out a tiny dormouse paw, which Sam gently shook. Edgar stepped forward placing both of his paws on Sam's other hand.

"I don't want to say goodbye, Sam," he said with a whisper. "But I do want to go home again."

"I know," Sam replied. He wiped his eyes with the back of his sleeve.

Mr. Goodfellow took hold of his trunk handle. "The welfare of the scroll is in your hands now, Sam," he announced solemnly as he made his way toward the window. "I know that you will take good care of it until we return. There is a cosmic convergence happening here, my boy, and I believe that the scroll is behind it. Even though we have contained its power again, I can't help but feel that it is still at work. It has succeeded in drawing us here: man, Sage, and Fen alike. Whatever for is beyond my comprehension—I have no idea where our journeys may lead us or what our searching will uncover. Not yet anyway."

Mr. Goodfellow suddenly looked over Edgar's shoulder towards the crowd of teary-eyed mice that were rushing across the floor.

"Quickly, Sam! Give us a hand! The mice are coming! I don't think I could face one of their emotional farewells just now!"

Sam lifted Mr. Goodfellow, Edgar and the trunk onto the ledge beside his open window. Edgar quickly tied one end of the rope to the corner of the windowsill and the other end around the middle of the trunk. Then he and Mr. Goodfellow lowered the trunk over the sill and down into the bushes below. They waved goodbye to the mice, thanking them for all their help, then Mr. Goodfellow stood on the edge of the windowsill and stared straight into Sam's eyes. Then, holding onto the rope, he jumped into the air and, with a wink, he disappeared. Edgar grabbed the rope and hurled himself out of the window after his uncle, landing in the bushes with a muffled thud. Sam untied the rope from the windowsill and tossed it down into the bushes after his friends. When he peered over the sill, Mr. Goodfellow and Edgar had already vanished into the night.

The following day, a few thousand miles away, a little gray dormouse was pulling a large tan trunk, and a smaller black and brown spotted mouse was drinking in the sights and sounds of the English countryside. They stopped briefly to rest and take a breath of the sweet country air. Lifting their whiskered noses towards the setting sun, they let its soothing warmth soak into their tired bodies.

The gray mouse sniffed deeply and a rush of memories filled his mind. What was that wonderful fragrance? Surely it was lavender. A proverb came to him. "An old man loved is winter with flowers." His furry hand searched under his suit until it found a crumpled piece of paper. It was Beatrice Elderberry's address. Turning it over in his fingers, he took a deep breath of the cleansing air. Then he called to the smaller mouse and they were on their way again. There was still a long way to go and a great deal of work to do. As they walked across the green, rolling hills, dotted with woolly sheep and wildflowers, the elder mouse made a solemn promise that he would take time out later for a long holiday in a cottage by the sea.

20

TRUE FRIENDSHIP IS

IMPERISHABLE

After the dinner party, it took a few days before life in the Middleton household began to return to normal. Sam's mother, refreshed after spending an entire day in bed, had decided to put the whole unfortunate affair behind her. It would be a while though, she suspected, before she would even begin to think of tackling another social occasion. Besides, she and Sam's father would soon have their hands full with the gallery renovations.

The dry cleaning charges for the bed linens and Professor Mandrake's clothes and shoes (the bill for the last two items having been sent in the mail a few days after the dinner party) were astronomical. Since expenses were tight at the Middleton home, the wildlife removal people were put on hold until further notice. Sam's father suspected, with a great deal of reassurance by Sam, that Leonora's mouse had been nothing more than an isolated incident. This came as a great relief to the twenty or so mice living behind Sam's bedroom wall.

Leonora Jaffrey's operatic career was suddenly in full swing. Opening in a local production just the day after her close encounter with Rollo, the critics had been particularly generous. The range of her voice, particularly when she reached for those high notes, was quite impressive, they reported. There was even some talk that she might be cast as the lead in a brand new international production of "Madame Butterfly." Leonora was thrilled.

At the Jaffrey home, under the watchful eyes of Sam and Fletcher, Brunhilda's brood was thriving. The runt of the litter, the puppy that Mr. Goodfellow had rescued had attached himself to Sam, and Sam was busy trying to convince his father to sign up for an experimental allergy treatment that the university medical department was offering. But even the mention of dogs these days seemed to send Trevor Middleton into fits of sneezing.

Professor Mandrake appeared to be maintaining a low profile. He spent most days locked in his office at the university, pouring over a mountain of research papers. Basil (to Fletcher's relief) seemed to have grown uncharacteristically quiet too. Perhaps he had learned his lesson after all. Sam was convinced, however, that this was simply the calm before the storm. It would just be a matter of time before the Mandrakes were on the prowl once again.

It was three weeks or so after Mr. Goodfellow's and Edgar's departure that Sam received a most unusual piece of correspondence. Measuring only one inch by one inch square, the miniature letter was addressed to Sam. It had been delivered into the care of the Hawthorne mice by express mouse courier. Members of this elite corps were chosen for their speed and bravery, and were afforded special status in the mouse world.

After enjoying an invigorating "rub down" and a special meal, the mouse courier was soon scampering off on his next delivery, leaving, as was often the case, a group of star-struck mouselings behind. After much discussion amongst the house mice, Rollo (who had been invited to make the Hawthorne house his new home) was granted the personal honor of delivering the express letter to Sam. He approached him at night, climbing into his bed and tapping him solemnly on the shoulder. Sam recognized the handwriting immediately. Pulling the magnifying glass from around his neck, he carefully tore open the side of the envelope and, lifting it to his lips, blew a short gust of air inside. He then gently pulled a minuscule piece of paper out with his fingernails. He was having a great deal of trouble steadying his hand. Mr. Goodfellow had promised to approach the council about the Scared Seal, and Sam had been patiently waiting for that promise to be fulfilled. He held the magnifying glass over the paper and began to read.

Dear Sam,

Well, here I am, lad, as promised. I am pleased to report that my computer problems have been attended to, but I thought this more traditional method would be a safer route.

I am fine, but in another "pickle" again on this blasted Hawthorne case. If only I had Filbert's complete files in my possession, I warrant I could solve this in no time! I have been on Professor Hawthorne's trail since delivering Edgar to his mother a little over two weeks ago. (The dear lady fainted on her doorstep.) I have insisted that Edgar spend some time at home before joining me later. I have not yet managed to track the professor down and I am studying the latest rash of crop circle formations for clues. The visions of Filbert are occurring with great frequency these days. I am convinced his disappearance may have something to do with Elijah Hawthorne, rather than The Fen. I am more determined than ever to uncover the truth.

However, I am not writing to let you know about my problems, my boy. I have presented the case of your Sacred Seal to The Sage Governing Council. At first, they were reluctant to even consider that such a monumental error could have occurred. However, they could not dismiss the evidence before them. They retired to review the facts. I received their decision just this morning and have been asked to pass it along to you.

Sam put the magnifying glass down and breathed deeply. His heart was beating wildly. He had waited a long time for this. At one time, he was to have been guided by a Goodfellow. What fantastic discoveries was he to have made? He picked up his magnifying glass again and continued.

The Governing Council has declared that you, Sam, are to remain assigned to Edgar as was originally intended. However, since Edgar never finished his training, the council has also decided that you will be the first and only person to ever have two inspirers. They have decreed that I am to assist Edgar in his work.

"Wow!" Sam whispered. "This is better than anything! Edgar *and* Mr. Goodfellow! I'm going to be an amazing scientist! I can't wait!"

The letter continued.

> The Council has acknowledged that you
> have a great gift, Sam. Your destiny may hold
> many successes. They will not stand in the way
> of that. There is, however, a price to pay for
> this.

"A price?" Sam whispered. "What kind of price?" His eyes
raced across the page and he struggled to hold his magnifying
glass steady.

> The inspirational process must be as it was
> destined to be. You cannot be aware of those
> who have been assigned to guide you. The Sage
> must be left to work in secret. You will not
> remember Edgar or me. We must be erased from
> your memory so that you can reach your poten-
> tial alone, as it was meant to be.
>   You do have a choice, Sam. If you decide to
> forgo your path as a "gifted one," your memory
> will not be erased. But then Edgar and I cannot
> act as your guides and inspirers. The act of
> inspiration must remain a sacred and secret
> undertaking. You must understand, Sam, that if
> you decide to forgo your inspiration, you will be
> making a great sacrifice. You do not know what
> your future has in store for you, or what you
> may have been able to offer the world. This will
> be a difficult choice for you, Sam. I cannot
> advise you on your decision. It is hard for me to
> be objective. Edgar knows nothing of the coun-

cil's ruling. It must be your decision alone, Sam.
Just remember, you must consider both sides
very carefully. Let me know when you have
made your choice and I will advise The Sage
Council. Write it down and give it to the mice.
They will know what to do with it.

Yours in friendship,
J. Goodfellow

Sam had wanted to become a great scientist for as long as
he could remember. When he had first learned from Mr.
Goodfellow that he was in fact destined to become one, it
had been a dream come true. But the thought of having to
forsake the friendship of Edgar and Mr. Goodfellow and of
forgetting all of the wonderful and fantastic things that had
happened these past few weeks was torture. The Goodfellows
were the best friends he had ever had. They had taught him
how to believe in himself, how to have courage in the face of
evil and how to be strong. He couldn't imagine life without
them. He couldn't imagine going back to the way things had
been before.

Using his magnifying glass and an extra-fine tipped pen,
Sam wrote to Mr. Goodfellow that very night. He called out to
Rollo and handed him the letter. A mouse courier was quickly
ordered and the letter was on its way the following morning.

Once the letter was gone, Sam realized there was no going
back. He remembered Mr. Goodfellow's words about fate and
destiny. For some reason, he had been chosen to guard the
ancient and powerful Hawthorne scroll, and when fate
stepped in with such an important assignment, it was best not
to argue.